DISCARDED
From Nashville Public Library

WALTERLANE

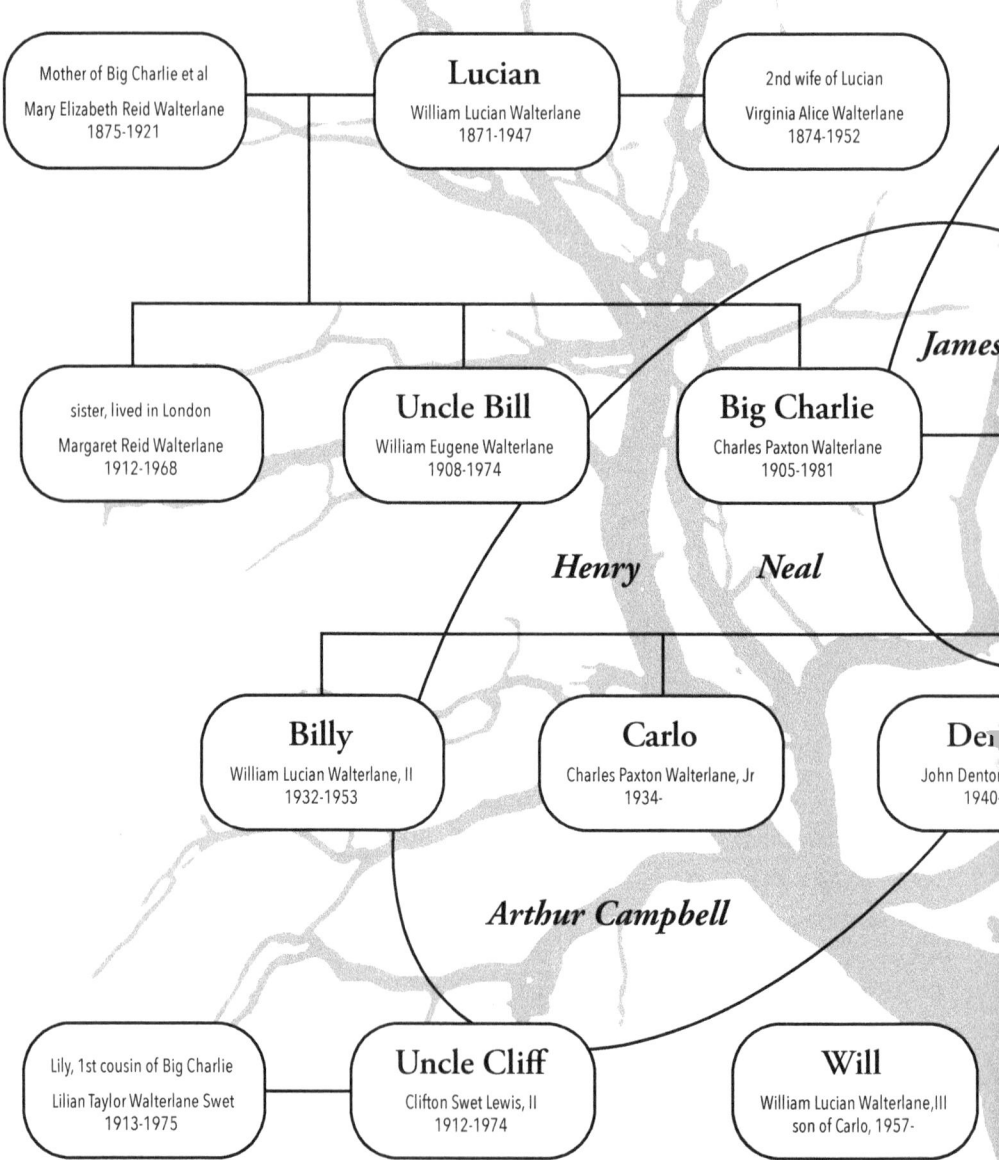

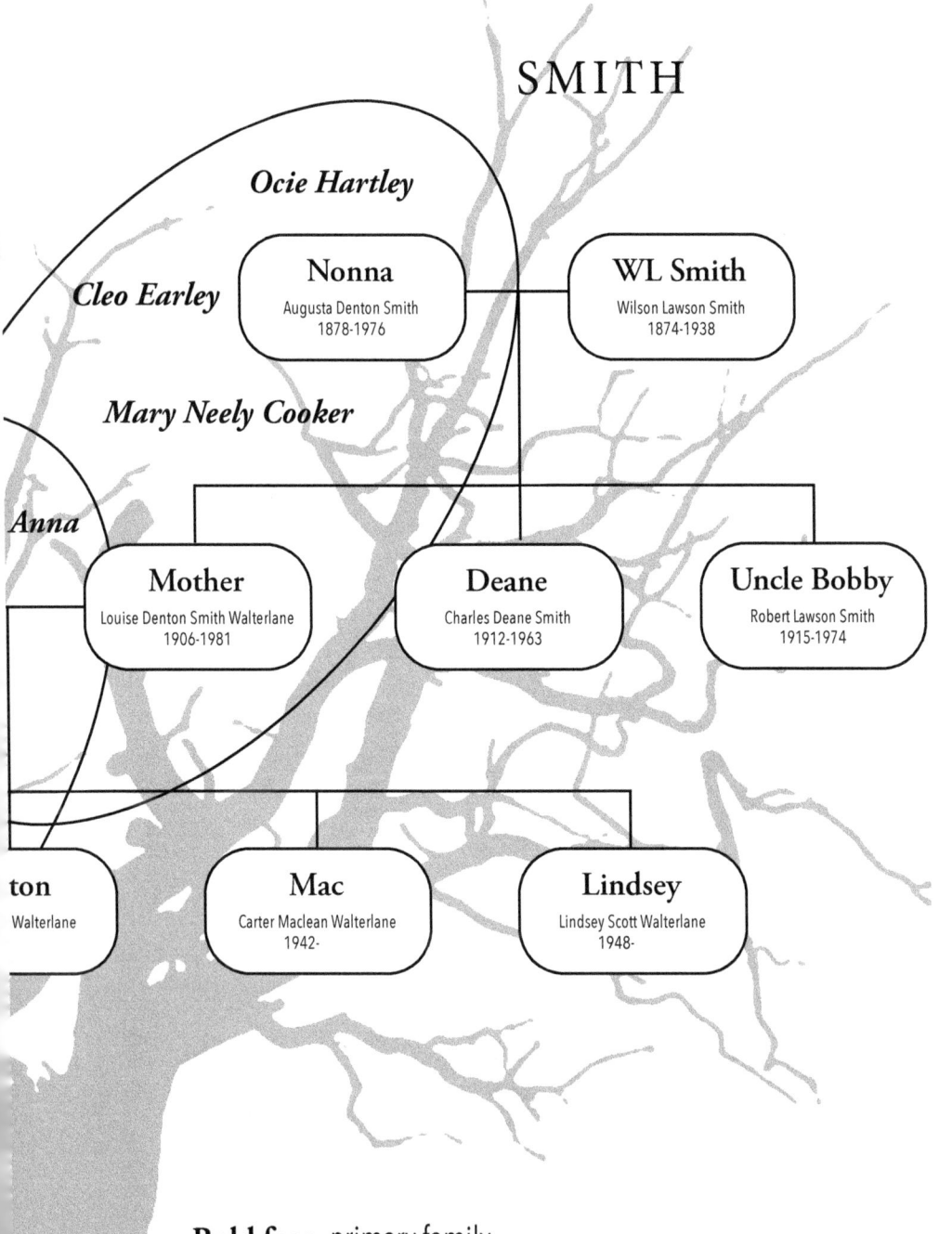

DUCK HUNTING IN QUICKSAND

a novel

Will Sonnet

Nashville

DUCK HUNTING IN QUICKSAND

a novel

Will Sonnet

A colored guide at a hunting club in north Mississippi in the 1930s, prescient, expert in the ways of the woods though barely literate, Arthur Campbell enters the employ of a prominent Memphis family until the 1960s, profoundly impacting their lives even across the Pacific, becoming a second father to the narrator (in the absence of his father) through the War years and after.

This book is a work of fiction.
Names, characters, organizations, places, events and incidents are used fictitiously, or are products of the author's imagination.

Copyright © 2019 by Will Sonnet.

All rights reserved. Printed in the United States of America by ASLAN TAYLOR

FIRST EDITION 2023

LIBRARY OF CONGRESS LCCN

Sonnet, Will

Duck Hunting in Quicksand / Will Sonnet / 1st ed.

Identifiers:

LCCN 2023905870

ISBN 979-8-9878475-0-3

1. World War II—Family History: 1920s – Present— Fiction

BOOK DESIGN BY OATES DESIGN

for
Jane, Brier, Donovan, Day
and
Carlo

Prologue

0025

March 1, 1942

Ensign Charles Deane ("CD") Smith injected two morphine vials into his dying captain from the emergency first aid pack on his belt, and dove into the Java Sea, beginning the greatest challenge of his life.

Intelligence reports just hours old indicated that the Sunda Strait was free of Japanese warships, yet one of the largest Japanese task forces assembled during World War II was found steaming to invade Java by way of the northeast entrance to the Sunda Strait and Banten Bay, on the northwest tip of Java (north of Australia).

Here, the heavy cruisers HMAS PERTH (Australian) and the USS HOUSTON met their destinies, in the waning minutes of February, and the early morning of March 1, 1942.

Twenty minutes after the PERTH was cut in half by torpedoes, the HOUSTON took a shell in the aft engine room, bursting steam lines, and killing all contained there. Another salvo which did not explode pierced the control room in Turret 2, and started a powder fire, requiring all local hands. As it was being controlled, two torpedoes tore into starboard and one to port, and she took on a ten-degree list.

Captain Albert Rooks, down from the bridge to see the damage to Turret 2, gave Seaman William Stafford the order to sound the alarm for Abandon Ship, a moment before another blast struck the communications deck passageway, and shrapnel made Swiss cheese of them both from behind.

As the firing from the HOUSTON decreased and the ship began to list, emboldened Jap destroyers closed to inside 200 yards, and illuminated the HOUSTON with searchlights, machine-gunning the decks from both sides at a great cost of life. But those with operable guns aboard the ship under siege tried to take out the lights, staying at their positions until all ammunition was expended, and firing at last star shells, which would only illuminate the carnage and the ship's last gasps.

The water was warm. Despite a thumbnail-sized shrapnel wound between his shoulder blades, Deane swam furiously, pausing only to catch his breath, for 500 yards off her starboard quarter. He knew the ship would create a huge vortex when it finally waterlogged, indiscriminately sucking the living and inanimate down to the depths to share in its fate.

He could hear nothing in his left ear, and the right felt and sounded like it was full of water. He thought probably both ears were waterlogged, and was surprised to hear anything after the nonstop violence of clashing metals and firepower of the last days.

Fires burned across all decks. Midships to port she was struck by another torpedo while Deane was watching; he braced for the concussion. It whooshed past, and the HOUSTON rolled onto her side. By the light of the brilliant full moon, Deane could see her hulk on his horizon whenever he glanced back, over half an hour, until finally, the ship disappeared under the surface.

0130

A peak to the south was visible in the moonlight… it must be the northern tip of Java, as the ship's position squarely in the strait had been noted before the last battle. Deane adopted a stroke that he thought he could maintain and began to distance himself from the carnage and the murderous patrol boats, still circling, spraying lead into the black waters and the men played on by the lights. Seventy-five yards back toward the HOUSTON's carcass, a sailor held his arms as high as he could hold them, waiting for the wandering light from the approaching boat to fall on him.

"NO! NO! DIVE" Deane shouted uselessly. The surrendering sailor was finished almost the instant he was found. Dozens of rounds of automatic fire boiled the spot well after the first .50 round to reach him completed its job.

With no life jacket and little profile, Deane was very still, slipping below the surface when lights played his way. The closest boat drew once to 30 yards, but the lights were concentrated on floating trash on the other side. Deane turned to the coast and worried more about sharks.

He came across men floating among debris, their conditions good to desperate, to lifeless. Swimmers he knew from the HOUSTON in life jackets: Corporal First Class Ryan, Chief Fire Controlman Gary, Seaman First Class Bubnis, Seaman First Class Roberts, and First Class Quartermaster Stewart, treaded water surrounding a plank which supported Radio Electrician Gillett, whose arm was broken below his shoulder. They spoke of an organized effort to get to safety, to land. Fifteen minutes passed with no steps toward this goal; no one took the lead. The men's strength faded a little more while they discussed it. None considered that the strong current in the strait would sweep them out to oblivion while they studied and discussed their problem.

Marine Captain Batt Russell appeared alongside, swimming unassisted, like Deane. Bartholomew Russell could hit a baseball out of the park, and gave further evidence he was aptly nicknamed every time he played.

"Deane."

"Yessir."

They breathed and paddled.

Russell whispered, "These men are looking after Gillett. They'll hold us back in life jackets. We've got to get out of here, to land. Current's strong–can you do it?"

"10-4. S'go." They swam.

1
Menashay Lake

May 1944

THE TOPS OF MY FINGERS were splayed over the gunnel, dragging little trails in thick duckweed so dense at the surface that there was hardly a stir. Gliding along, I imagine a golf ball would roll over it endlessly. We made a trail but it's a momentary tear in the color, quickly healed by the duckweed. My fingers were spotted with tiny seed-like leaves. Every surface of the water was carpeted bright green, interrupted only by hundred-year-old cypress trees and deadfall all the way out to the open lake, and I wondered how many leaves that was or if it's even a number you can count.

"Getcho' hands inside d'boat," commanded Arthur.

He guided us around dead logs and the stumps of immature trees rising everywhere throughout the swamp. The motor hammered into an unseen object, and he had to tilt it up by the back. The propeller over-revved, spewing muck in all directions with a hollow 'burrop' sound that echoed just like the bullfrogs we stalked when the cypress trees were too dense to cast a fly. They competed for female attention without interruption. We stopped when Arthur saw another big one. I looked where he looked, but the shadow of his fedora obscured his eyes, so I always had to ask, "Where?"

Arthur said, "Other side 'o dat stob dat looks like a owl's head. Look—his eyes is stickin' up left 'o that turtle on the log..."

Impossibly far away, I rarely saw them first, and sometimes not at all. I've not shot one yet today. One from the pile of Arthur's dispatch eyed me deadpan from under a tangle of limbs.

We aimed for the polished knees of two cypresses that seemed too close for us to pass, into an open channel to the main lake, which had enough motion to keep it free of duckweed. Contacting the knees on both sides, the boat stuck fast, and for a moment we sat there as Arthur looked back to see if that last frog had skedaddled. Close as my gun barrel, up the fluted slope of the massive cypress on my right, a thick gray snake rose slowly, endlessly out of the water, already halfway to the wood duck house nailed to the trunk five feet above the surface.

"Cottonmouth… doantouchit," Arthur said unnecessarily. He gunned the motor and we shot through the slip and out into the open channel.

"Put down nat rod, and pickup at fo'-hunderd-an-ten."

I haven't had time to be frightened and reached for the shotgun as soon as we were clear.

"Hang on."

Arthur turned the boat around. The snake's head was gone but its body continued to disappear into a trough in the bark between the back of the house and the tree. The moment its tail cleared the water, the head appeared at the top of the roof. It glided out and down over in an arc like a question mark. Its tongue stabbed the air.

I reached again for the gun.

"Doanshoot til he stops," says Arthur, "Wait til he stops, away from the house. Try not to hit the house."

With a paddle in the crook of one arm, Arthur maneuvered us sideways so we looked back the way we came, and the duck house was in profile against the woods.

The snake's head went into the hole in the front until about a foot of him seemed to be in there. Its entire body heaved with a jerk, and it started to back out for a second, then stopped suddenly.

"More'n he could swalluh… Shoot 'im."

I lifted the single-shot, Savage shotgun off my lap, and with both thumbs, pulled back on the hammer until it clicked. (Arthur can do this with just one thumb.)

"Git that gun off'n me! Watch yer aim!"

I swung around easy and calm, and drew a bead on the body of the snake outside the hole, over the angled roof of the wood duck house, not 10 feet away, and eased pressure on the trigger. The blast rocked the swamp and the boat. Two thick pieces of snake flailed wildly for a second. Its back half was jammed behind the house, quivering, and then it was limp, hanging straight down. Held in place by the head, still in the hole, the front half loosed something out its bloody end which plopped into the water. It floated. Arthur reached over with the paddle to stir it toward us. As soon as we were close enough to see that it was an egg, the snake's head-end landed on the paddle with a meaty *thunk*. A second later the other half splashed down.

"Damn!"

"Damn good shot." High praise coming from Arthur.

Arthur took out a pouch of Bull Durham and some papers and rolled a smoke. This he could do in moments, and in the shadows, only his eyes and the smoking cigarette contrasted against his black face.

"Lemmehave one, Arthur."

"Stuntyer growth."

"C'mon."

It was a game we played. He'd taught me how to roll with one hand. I liked rolling them better than smoking them... back then anyway.

Soon, we were out in the open, at the edge of Menashay in the long shadows of the cypress, casting back into the duckweed with big popping bugs Arthur had made from corks, dabbed with wild colors in impossible ocular and thorax arrangements, to which he glued too-large hooks. They were supposed to be bumble bees and cicadas, I think. Maybe one was a grasshopper. But now, the bass and the bream were great patrons of Arthur's art, and we were catching them about every other cast. I would tangle my reel, or hang one of his ungodly creations in a low hanging branch, or knot my fly line because I couldn't time it to straighten out behind me, so Arthur's stringer grew heavier, and he had to lean over toward the other side of the boat for balance.

2

Delta Cotton

2012

My son Will has been on me to tell his camera about his grandparents, and my grandparents, and their grandparents, and what I know about our family, which is a lot of stories I really can't remember the beginning or end of— mostly I can bring to mind just being there and a bit of detail.

My 56-year-old son comes in the back door and gives me a hug and a kiss. We've done that his whole life. I think he must have started it because I remember no such a display from my father, Big Charlie. It's always been natural for us, though.

He fixes his camera on me and says "Anytime," and I start talking. I'm remembering, trying to start at the beginning, but not sure which beginning. I decide on my granddad, Lucian.

"Your great grandfather, Big Charlie's father, William Lucian, lived in Vicksburg. He made his living moving Delta cotton up the river to Memphis and Chicago, and downriver to New Orleans. In those days, they didn't have the levee system that the Corps of Engineers would build later, and in the twenties, the Mississippi River flooded for thousands of square miles up and down the river into Arkansas to the west, and into Mississippi, where the bluffs weren't high enough naturally to prevent it. The flood silted in the port of Vicksburg and barges couldn't get in there to deliver the cotton. The George H. McHale Cotton Company of Memphis was called McHale and Paxton in Vicksburg, and McHale and West in New Orleans, and Lucian was offered the opportunity to move his operations to Memphis or New Orleans.

He said "Too many mosquitoes in New Orleans," but honestly he just loved the Delta, his friends and family, and hunting ducks. He was a member of a great old hunting club a good bit closer to Memphis at Robinsonville, Mississippi. But, I digress. The company became McHale and Paxton of Memphis and that has everything to do with why we all ended up here. Before that, the family was in Houston. I don't know if any of that matters, probably too much explanation, but maybe it's interesting. Lucian was a veteran of the First World War and he's buried in the cemetery there... in Vicksburg.

On Mother's side, I never really knew my grandfather, Wilson Smith."

Will presses a button on his machine. "Dad, let's talk about you a little. That's great background, and I want to get that kind of detail, but tell me... I don't know much at all about your growing up. I heard stories all my life about you growing up in the '30s and '40s learning to love the outdoors. You can still out-shoot and out-call your friends, and even the younger guys in your club can't keep up with you. You can tell what kind of ducks are coming in before I can even see them, and you'll be shooting crows or squirrels or fly fishing, or building something to assist in those efforts when there's nothing in season or you just can't get there because of the weather. Tell me about growing that... passion. What do you remember most, that kind of stuff... learning to hunt and fish with Arthur? Tell me about Arthur."

"Well, I don't know about that," I say. But he's right. I've slowed down a little, but not a whole lot, and I'm in the woods most days since I retired... if the season's out, preparing for the next one, or on the water, fishing.

"Well OK," I say, "Arthur Campbell." And I think about a box of damn ugly homemade lures I've got somewhere in the attic, I hope... haven't seen them in years.

And I start sifting through pictures in my mind, which get sharper with the telling: it's a bright, sweltering August day, and Arthur and I are sliding around Menashay amid the cypress, shooting frogs and catching the hell out of the crappie. I'm counting down the weeks until the fall season opens up at Robinsonville, because... not a man in the county can bring ducks and geese out of the sky like the call of Arthur Campbell.

March 1942

Our house on Central Avenue was a place of potent memories. This was before there was a median or street lights, and the houses were set back from the street for what seemed to us a city block. The yard was terraced, five levels of concrete steps bisected it from the street to the porch— did you ever see Laurel and Hardy pushing the piano up interminable flights of steps in *The Music Box*? On either side were great trapezoidal columns of stone— a common feature of homes built around the turn of the century. No window was the same and many had heavy, rolling casework. It seemed cavernous to us, a behemoth with four stories, a basement, and attic sandwiching a floor for entertaining and one for sleeping. So many places to hide, to play. Billy and I were explorers, kings, fighters, soldiers. Our imaginations carried us, and I do not ever remember being challenged for something to do.

The backyard was like the front in area but was contained on the left side with a mature holly that ran away from the house a hundred yards and seemed ten feet high. It was kept trimmed into a box shape by Henry and Neal, ever-present somewhere, but visible only often enough to maintain the pretense of keeping the rest of the yard in similar repair.

On the right, shrubs and trees, dogwoods, and two huge pin oaks separated from the yard the old servants' quarters, a barracks-like structure that was opposed to the house perpendicularly. This structure was not occupied as it was in a run-down condition. The floor of the rooms closest to the driveway was rotted through, and we were warned to keep out, which we ignored. Dad— Big Charlie, had opened up the right side of the house like a garage, for easy access to the operation supporting the quail he raised there in the summers to release at the farm, Skytop.

Neal and Henry had kept the grounds for a generation, alternating between our house and Aunt Eunice and Uncle Bill's, and Nonna's. When only one or neither, surfaced on a weekend, it was assumed they were in the service of others until Aunt Eunice's silver began to disappear. Evidence of their guilt was never confirmed, but Big Charlie and Uncle Bill each were called to bail them from jail after nights and fights on Beale Street, and Dad said he did not want them in our house anymore. He referred to them as Abbott and Costello, though if either had more brains, it was the short round one, Neal.

Neal was shorter by almost a foot, and thick as a barrel. He had a wheezing laugh that Billy and I were always trying to set in motion because it would devolve into a phlegm-laden cough. Sometimes the payoff was a thick loogie he would expel to swing hanging from nearby bushes, which we thought was very funny. He wore an unkempt mustache, and whiskers trimmed into a caterpillar where his neck met his jaw, some vestige of his service in World War I, of which he was quite proud.

A clearer picture of Henry will probably occur to me, but presently I see a lanky man with a perpetual grin, a crooked hat, and crooked teeth (of the six or eight that remained). He smelled of sardines. Dad said all Henry ever required for sustenance was his "box of fish" and a Coke. Like Neal, Henry bragged of marksmanship and conquest in battle, which would set them to arguing. Neither saw combat, they were a driver and a mechanic. Big Charlie's discarded clothes were on their backs, coats in the winter, dress slacks and white shirts in summer.

Nonna's home was also on Central Avenue just a block away, the same sort of imposing four-story turn-of-the-century home as ours, set way back from the street with a sloping lawn. Granddaddy Smith died when I was four, and so to us, the natural order at this place was my grandmother, Nonna, Ocie, her chauffeur, and her maids Cooker and Cleo.

Mary Neely Cooker went by Cooker which we always thought was kind of disrespectful until we learned it was her real name as if Nonna's chauffeur Ocie Hartley was called "Chauffeur." Ocie drove her about in a 1932 Ninth Series Deluxe Eight Packard sedan limo. Heavy and sculptured, long as a trolley car, Ocie kept it immaculate. Driving it was one of my brother's great ambitions.

Cooker was smart and funny (if a bit quick-tempered), and broad-shouldered, so somewhat on the heavy side, very dark black, with a nose big and flat as an eclair, which she talked through, ending her consonants and her i's and th's biting her tongue so the last syllable was nasal. She called Billy "Bent-ths." She was always sweet to us when we were at Nonna's, but Cooker was the enforcer— until we got to be teenagers. If you didn't mind my grandmother, Cooker would pull out a switch.

She and Cleo were the kitchen help and housekeepers. Cooker was Hardy to Cleo's Laurel. They were Laurel and Hardy because Cooker fussed at Cleo, and Cleo would just look hurt, and say hardly anything.

Cleo Earley was not too smart, not too talkative, so I don't remember much else about her, except she was tall and thin, a good bit younger than Cooker we thought.

Big Charlie said Cleo was "high yellow." I heard him say "high yellow" meant she was half-negro or more. When I was about four or five, I asked Cleo which one of her parents was a darkie, and got a whipping. I got no answer, but since she had the raised black pimples all over her face like a lot of colored people had, we guessed there was more colored in her than white.

Cooker had been with Mother's mother for more than thirty years. She was about Nonna's age, she came into her service before Uncle Deane was born, and raised him from a baby. Pregnant herself at the time, she likely even suckled him; such a primitive function still seems contrary to our grandmother's innate elegance.

On the day we got word that the HOUSTON had been sunk by the Japs, Billy and I were over at Nonna's. Cooker met the Navy officers at the front door. She listened to them for a second, and with trembling hands clasped, bade them into the foyer while she went to inform her mistress.

One of them set a crumpled sheet of paper on the small table at the foot of the stairs. The other looked up and saw us staring down from behind the second-floor stair railing. Nonna entered the foyer.

Cooker would normally have shown herself back to the hall at least, respectfully out of earshot, but she missed her cue and stood there, clutching herself tightly. We could hear only snippets in a grave tone. In a moment, Cooker collapsed where she stood, crying to Jesus in a loud wail.

Taking little notice, my grandmother murmured a "thank you", then said loudly to her quivering servant, "Cooker will show you out." She ascended the staircase and walked past us without a word or a glance, to her room at the far end of the hall. We learned in later years she was not seen for almost a week.

The impersonal block capitals of the telegram on the table imparted the dreadful news in typically void language, perhaps why the Navy sent officers to the homes of officers lost.

MARCH 2, 1942 STOP

USS HOUSTON torpedoed IN THE JAVA SEA STOP...

The HOUSTON was at the bottom of the sea. Ensign Charles Deane Smith was listed among the hundreds Missing In Action; there were no other details of survivors.

Within weeks of the news, all able-bodied Walterlane and Smith men set aside their lives to *go get CD*. They enlisted, went for emergency training, and were deployed overseas in 90 days: my father, Big Charlie, re-enlisted in the Navy, Uncle Bill in the Marines, and Mother's brother Uncle Maclean in the Naval intelligence services. For most of the three and a half years America and the Allies were engaged, the only male adult relation of youth and vigor stateside was "Uncle" Cliff, married to Lily, Big Charlie's first cousin once removed. Cliff claimed IVD Deferment, which means clergy, but the most he did was a semester in seminary at Sewanee, and was thereafter a drunk and troublemaker. I don't know why everyone put up with him except he was "family."

Spring of 1942, the neighborhood was painted white and pink with bursting azaleas and blooming dogwoods, displacing chilly mornings and remnants of winter. In this setting, we were joined by Arthur Campbell. Of course, to us at first, Arthur seemed just another slightly aloof, always-suspicious-of-us servant. But by the time our father came back in 1945, Arthur was my best friend. Big Charlie got busy trying to get re-established in the cotton business in Memphis, traveling and building his business, and he didn't have time for Billy or me. Lindsay was five, Denton was four, and Mac hadn't come along yet. For my years growing into a man, we had Arthur.

3

Providence

A coin thrown down could come to rest on its edge at its whim, rather than that of its owner, who, witnessing the thing, snatching it up excitedly... might not duplicate the feat in a thousand tries. Is the tea of time and space truly such a random brew?

Big Charlie, my Dad, my namesake, told me of his grandfather, a steamboat captain on the Mississippi. He was at the helm when the river was well over flood stage one spring, and its waters overflowed their banks for twenty miles in each direction. Landmarks gone, he steamed upstream on skill and intuition *for days*. Suddenly, he decided to pull into "port" guided much the same way. He spied a willowy woman with flowing hair and scarf, and with the first step on dry land he strode directly to her. She became his wife. Would we have been... were there no flood? Mostly our paths cross randomly to little consequence.

The Robinsonville Dam Hunting Club clubhouse burned in 1925. Don't they always seem to do that, eventually... resort clubhouses, for one reason or another? "Resort" is probably generous, it wasn't much more than a barn, a chicken coop of sorts, though legendary, and it housed the most affluent of avid Delta waterfowlers from New Orleans, Shreveport, Memphis, Tupelo, and Jackson, sometimes Little Rock, since its establishment in 1878, especially when the Arkansas Rice fields froze, or a dry winter pushed the flyway east of the Mississippi.

Generations of duck hunters since the late 19th century were introduced to, and (those lucky enough to belong) nurtured their sport at the Club, on a snatch of an oxbow lake in north Mississippi spectacularly attractive to waterfowl from September through January, plus a month on either side when you weren't supposed to shoot them.

The members, such as they were— three wealthy Memphis families, two Tunica cotton farming families, and all senior partners of a prominent Memphis law firm (totaling some 35 individuals with full hunting rights) quickly drew up plans to rebuild, and by the next spring, the new clubhouse was being framed, with a living room, den, dining, and poker rooms fore and aft of a large stone fireplace, and four bedrooms left, and four to the right. Out front, a gravel bed was being laid for the rail tracks that would bring members right to the porch over thick, Model A-burying mud, in a panel truck fitted with steel wheels.

Almost as if the Lord drew a line regarding new plans for the obliteration of more of his creation, the framed sprawl was ripped to pieces by a tornado just as the roof was completed in the summer of 1926. With that storm began the rains that would become the Great Mississippi Flood of 1927. By May the river was 60 miles wide below Memphis. The members, when next they met, were undeterred but found they were of the consensus that their plans had perhaps been a tad ambitious (in the days before property insurance was a common thing), and so the clubhouse finally took its present "shape" in the summer and fall of 1928, better than original only by its having running water and electricity. Of the new plan, only the mile-long rail line was preserved.

What is meant to endure though, will endure, and so the seasons, which in the natural cycle attracted clouds of every kind of magnificent waterfowl, also attracted legions of hunters.

Arthur Campbell came to work at the Robinsonville Dam Hunting Club in the early fall of 1925, at the ripe age of twenty-seven. It was an ideal transition for him for several reasons, not the least of which was he needed to disappear from Jones, Louisiana.

He grew up in Jones, in Morehead Parish, which is to say that it was about a half mile up Hwy 165 from Bonita, and more or less where Hwy 83 hits 165. That is, in the middle of nowhere, on a rice farm in the heart of the Mississippi flyway, working the berms to control flooding and hold water in the growing season, and guide the white men who came to shoot geese and ducks in winter. His mother had died in December of the year before, and therefore Arthur had accepted "Mistuh" Slidell's offer to take up residence on the place in the colored barracks, help look after the equipment, and also head up Slidell's Guide Service. He was good with machinery, but already legendary in his ability to call in ducks. They stayed busier in the winter generally than they did in the planting season, except when it was time for the harvest.

It was a pretty good job, considering Arthur wasn't so good at reading or writing, to be somewhat in charge, and have a little change in his pocket, and he thought himself quite lucky.

Mrs. Slidell was a mystery. Few of the farm hands had ever seen her outside, but her pallid face could sometimes be seen through an upstairs window. Shortly after New Year's, the Bonita undertaker showed up and they took her away— "pneumonia," he told one. After the waterfowl season ended, Mr. Slidell disappeared to New Orleans for three months, returning in May with a beautiful Creole woman he introduced as Mrs. Slidell.

Thus entered the catalyst to repel Arthur northward. He had a reputation for catching the eye of a woman, which he did little to dispel in his own circle in Bonita. The new Mrs. Slidell was fond of being outside and around the workers. Arthur found Mrs. Slidell staring at him on a couple of occasions. Just when he thought he may have imagined it, she appeared behind him in the barn.

"*Appelez-moi Mlle Amélie, Arthur,*" she said, smiling sweetly.

Understanding only her name, then his, he managed "Yessum."

"Emily... EMILY!" came the voice of his employer, approaching. Slidell pushed open the door. "There you are." He saw his wife drop her gaze and looked to where she had. His eyes found and stayed on Arthur uncomfortably. "Don't you have something to do?"

A white man in Slidell's employ was jealous of Arthur's position, and he lusted after Amélie Slidell. Arthur knew this, but it took another incident before he admitted it was too dangerous to stay. Slidell went into town one humid afternoon. Before the cloud of dust kicked up by the truck fell away to the rice horizon, Amélie jumped on his back, giggling. Rumors in the barracks coalesced. By dawn the next morning, Arthur's absence evolved into kidnapping in the night by local Klan members on horseback, but by then Arthur was well underway to north Mississippi, where his patrons had spoken of clouds of ducks in the Delta.

Perhaps Arthur looked suspicious, his face was a perpetual half shadow under his fedora, which would accompany him across the waters in 20-degree weather or indoors in summer. He was photographed only three times in his life, twice at the Robinsonville Dam Hunting Club in member photos celebrating great hunts, and at Billy's funeral 28 years later, and each time the camera recorded only his mouth's stern expression. He displayed proper manners for a negro at the time, and he was not without humor, nor was he an angry man. But his constitution was as difficult to unseat in the service of a laugh, as was Arthur himself immovable physically. The combination imparted a sense of wisdom, but also— fearlessness. Whether this was overly generous would be argued, but there was no debate that he was unusually capable and strong, and could call ducks from the sky like few others. Late nights into their cups beside the fire, members sometimes confided in him, and Arthur often came to know more about them than their wives. By the end of his first season, at 28, he ran the club. War years were tough on the club and it shut down after the 1942 season. Spring of that year he came to Granddad in Memphis and said, "Mr. Walterlane, I need a job."

"Well, Arthur," Lucian said, "I haven't got anything for you to do, but my son has three boys, and he could probably use you." Arthur came to work for us at 1510 Central Avenue. He was respectful as they all were in those days, and never used bad language. He drove us to school and stuff like that. I was eleven, so Billy was thirteen let's say.

I have always thought this was divine providence.

4

Arthur Campbell

April 1942

Like anything worth building, friendship takes time to forge. The first lesson I learned from Arthur, I didn't think much of at the time. In the corner of our backyard, through the gnarly stalks of a mature holly that had opened up below, we wore a path to Andy Troutmann's yard on the other side of the chain link fence marking the edge of our backyard. Billy was in love with Andy's eighteen-year-old sister, Teresa, and of course, hearing his schemes of how to woo such a beautiful creature all hours, so was I. We were more or less invisible to her, but her fat kid brother Andy was a constant in our backyard, which was little wonder. His mother hung the sheet from the bed he wet each night out the window each morning, the vivid yellow target in the center a scarlet letter she hoped would dissuade his urinary incontinence. His father beat him.

Almost six feet tall at 12 years old, Andy was the troll under the bridge. He was a bully. I was completely intimidated by him, but I think my brother put up with his crap because he saw a link to his sister. Andy pushed around every kid but Billy, whose cool confidence confused him.

We got up a baseball game with other kids from the neighborhood that day. I caught a fly Andy hit, and he walked up to me and pushed me down. Later I got a hit, and he tripped me going around second. I bit the dust and my lip, and got up spitting blood.

It was Sunday. Big Charlie walked out of the den to the back patio in time to hear me call Andy Troutmann "YOU STUPID NAZI PIG," before I rammed my head into his fat. Unfazed, Andy simply twisted my hair with a beefy fist and punched me in the ear. He picked up the brick that was second base, but Arthur stepped between us and grabbed his arm, and shook the brick to the ground, narrowly missing Andy's foot.

By then Big Charlie was there. "You want to fight?" I have always thought he must have seen some misguided teachable moment, looking at the obvious mismatch and the circle of kids looking for leadership. I did not help my case. Though I could hardly see through tears of anger, I snarled "YES!"

"OK... Fight. But you will do it like men. Fight fair."

Arthur stood just behind my father and stared at me. He brought his fists up to his face like a boxer. I missed the implication and lit into Andy Troutmann with everything I had, flailing, landing maybe one glancing blow on his stupid face, but then seeing only stars as I got punch after punch, and took one to the guts that left me on the ground gasping for air.

"That's enough." I heard Big Charlie say. "Game's over. Go home."

James Anna held ice on my lip, and raw steak against my eye, and I remember Arthur's first advice: "You listen to me. Listen heah. You know you gone hafta fight. You know you gone have ta git into it, OK? You reach down. Look heah. Look! Now, you reach down, like you gone tie yo shoe or somethin', and you ball up yo fist like a rock. You watchin'? An you come up with every single thang you got behind that hard fist, and you punch him right through the face. You try to come out the back uh his head. You got that? You try to come out the back uh his head. You do that..." He paused, and looked me right in the eye. "You do that, an he ain' goin getup. I'm tellin yeh. He ain't goin to get up."

With a shiner under both eyes for two weeks, I practiced it on Mother's couch, imagining I was pounding Andy's stupid face. I was still mad at my father for throwing me to the wolf, but Arthur reminded me that if they hadn't both been there who knew what he would have done with that brick? Besides, I said I *wanted* to fight.

It was a valuable lesson. Years later, at Pat O'Brien's in New Orleans, a table of us from UVA had been getting shit from a drunken Tulane football player and his mates, who zeroed in on me. We took it outside. Before his friends and mine even began to surround us in a circle, I reached to the ground, and came up into and through his face like I was trying to crush a drive... and flattened him, to everyone's complete astonishment, especially my own, that it was so immediately over. I wore the cast from the resulting boxer's fracture to my hand with great pride. My buddy, Sid Wilroy, stenciled on it "Seven In One Blow" an homage to the little tailor in the *Grimm's Fairy Tale*, who wore a belt adorned with that text, which instilled fear in other's hearts, though it simply recorded seven flies he slew in one swipe.

5

Sea Wasp

March 1, 1942

0330

Ensign Smith and Captain Russell maintained a consistent stroke, but Deane, the more formidable and athletic of the two, pulled ahead, and the distance between them multiplied over the hours. They rested every few dozen yards, each holding his breath in a tuck position, face down. Deane thought he would pass out, his shoulders ached so terribly. He feared the loss of consciousness, feeling he could easily nap during one of the pseudo-restful embryonic breaks. Saltwater sloshed deep within his ears.

The swimmers would have made the mainland sighted at midnight by now but for a two-knot current, which fought their approach. As they drew closer, the peak dropped onto an island, probably a half mile off the northeastern tip of Java. Russell was no longer visible but could be heard when Deane rested, and he resumed swimming.

0500

Deane thought of Katherine. The picture he carried in his wallet of his best friend, folded in her latest letter for protection, would be ruined. But the picture he carried in his heart was clear. Images of her beautiful face lifted him, the girl from Nashville he chased as a child summers in Linville, the teenager who hopped aboard the train to Memphis without telling her parents, the woman who would one day be his wife. He was finding an improved stroke. The island grew larger.

Suddenly, Russell began to scream. The splashing and flailing sounds brought to mind the sailor Deane had seen being machine-gunned in the water. His screams got more intense, broken only by gasps for breath.

Spent, Deane could only drag himself backward at a fractionally faster pace, thinking sharks certainly, and— what could he do if he got there, sooner?

The screaming and flailing lessened, then ceased after a few moments, Maybe Russell wasn't being attacked or eaten by anything so ferocious as a shark. Deane closed to 15 yards. The man stiffened with a jerk and was still. Almost alongside, Deane saw Batt's head was thrown back and his jaws were working rapidly. He began to hack and spew.

His eyes were growing accustomed to the brightening dawn. A low ceiling of heavy clouds blocked the sunrise, diffusing all shadows so that some detail in every reach was apparent.

Russell vomited a fountain of foam. Miraculously, he still floated, for his arms seemed frozen along his body, which was now clearly in shock. Something the size of a basketball was in his lap, his legs punctured by the glistening ropes of nematocysts wrapping his thighs— the sea wasp, Australia's deadly box jellyfish.

Deane remembered the lessons of his training. One of the most lethal creatures on earth, the thing was not even a real jellyfish, it could propel itself and had eyes, though with no brain biologists were not sure what it saw.

When Deane reached him Russell started to sink, as if the paralyzing beast was intent on pulling him to the depths. His head went under. Deane bolted out of his stupor, and swam a wide swath to behind Batt, grabbing a fistful of hair. Trying to see the length of the jellyfish's tentacles, he gave a tug. The muscles in the back of his neck screamed in agony, and he released. Russell spewed bubbles under the surface and began again to sink. In an instant, Deane saw that the sea wasp floated now just at Russell's feet; he had felt only the pain of tortured muscles, not the attack of tentacles. Grabbing desperately below the water he found the man's collar and lifted his head above the surface. With an arm around Batt's neck he kicked backward toward the island until he could move no more, then his feet found the bottom. They were fifty yards offshore.

Russell was frozen and convulsed like he was being shaken. His eyes blinked rapidly showing only the whites. Thick snot ran in and out of his nose, as the jowl muscles worked and bulged. Gnashing of teeth. Deane tried to pry open his mouth to see if he had swallowed his tongue.

"Batt! Batt! C'mon, BATT!" It began to rain.

After standing there awhile, Deane noticed the delicate waves would sweep over them in a pattern, a tugging, insistent claim on the sputtering man at his fingertips. With the next roll came over him a consuming exhaustion, and a morbid calm, like the creeping death of falling to sleep in subzero temperatures. Captain Russell's eyes were closed, but he was breathing. Deane tightened his hold.

He was thankful for the calm of the sea and the tropical temperatures and said aloud a prayer of thanks for their survival through the night.

He heard splashes, another refugee from the experience, approaching from the west, out to sea. Any technique long gone, the swimmer's arms slapped the surface, forcing himself forward while it was calm. Deane called, "YOU CAN STAND UP THERE!"

Boilermaker First Class Bertrand "Birdie" Cox must have followed the same course by fixing on the peak. Drawn by the sound of Deane's voice, he came to arm's length before he realized he no longer had to struggle to keep himself afloat. Cox recovered enough in a few minutes to help pull Russell to the shore. In shock, he cooperated involuntarily, shivering with eyes closed.

0600

The shallows seemed never to end, but finally, barefoot, they dragged themselves and the injured man onto dry sand.

Completely spent, Cox collapsed. Deane peeled up the pant leg of one of Captain Russell's legs. They were crisscrossed with thick lines of bright red, varying in width up to an inch, and the skin was hard, and sunken into the muscle of the leg. Skin turned to jerky at the touch of the Medusa of the Sea. A sandy, torn pant leg brushed into the crevice of one and Russell jolted like he had been electrocuted, almost sitting up, but the wounds were hard, like binds. So unchanged was his face that Deane was sure he felt nothing, his body continued its involuntary fight to free itself.

"Batt! I'm sorry! Batt! Can you hear me? BATT!" He said 'You're going to be OK' or some such sentiment, knowing better. Batt gagged, a little fleck of foam flailed from his lips, but his body could spare no moisture, and he began to choke. His neck muscles and eyes bulged and he stopped breathing, jerking ever more slowly. In a minute more he was still, eyes open but caked with salt and snot. Deane lay cheek down on the hard beach beside him and looked out to sea. Before closing his eyes, he again gave thanks for the calm, relief, and safety, however temporary.

0700

Splashing in the surf 100 yards out… another had come this far into the shallows, yet did not realize he was safe. Numb from exhaustion, Deane slowly sat upright, feeling the anvil on his back. He watched himself enter the water again and slide forward into a stroke toward the flailing man. Seaman Bailey Douglass would tell his grandchildren how Ensign Smith saved him from drowning that day.

Deane dragged the young sailor onto the beach next to the dead man and lay down on the beach alongside him. He dreamt the scene was repeated: each time he entered the water, men were screaming, drowning in the distance, and then he collapsed next to a different man on the beach. When the war finally ended, four more men returned home who would not have, and each told the story of the broad-shouldered swimmer Smith who dragged them to the shore.

Far into the distance, the lights they had seen behind and to the side, which he had hoped were some civilized village, were by the light of dawn now clearly enemy ships, shifting backward and forward, unloading, loading, patrolling. The Japs had control of the coast road. Beyond, in the distance, a mountain chain stepped down all along the peninsula into the sea. Deane's last conscious thought was getting to those mountains, where they might be able to make their way to the rapidly disappearing Dutch lines.

They slept.

0815

Heavy, pelting drops awakened the men. The force had picked up from the drizzle that met them ashore. Deane thought it was hail. Twenty yards south another group from the ship was getting to their feet: Marine Sergeant Clayton Percy, First Class Quartermaster Larkin Edmonson, Chief Fire Controlman Les Wilson, Seaman Elliott Jonasson, Coxswain David Huffman, and Private Gary Pogue. The drops multiplied into a downpour, which became a drench, and then an absolute squall— walls of water with even less definition in the darkening morning overcast. Weary but alert, they all filed back into the ocean, sharing the unspoken thought, relief from the pelting, but also... no time better than now to make their way to the mainland.

In the hour swim against the strong currents of the straits, the weather slackened into a steady hum, of which they were hardly conscious. Heavy enemy water and air traffic could be seen more clearly, miles to the southwest, where the coast road led into the harbor. The sound of an engine cut through the rain, a patrol boat, which Deane guessed to be about the size of a PT boat, was pushing up the coast at about 25 knots, on a collision course with the swimmers. He dove. In seconds the boat cut through the group, and Deane saw their frightened faces underwater, just before the propeller churned up the water between them. When finally he surfaced, the shrinking vessel could still be heard crashing down through the whitecaps, but he had seen no enemy sailors searching or even exposed to the elements. The craft did not alter its course, or speed, and disappeared into the rain. He counted the men, looking for nine heads. Someone was missing. Exhausted, 100 yards from shore, still fighting a strong seaward current, and an overhead torrent, they must continue with no wasted effort to get land to survive.

Two men were close. "PERCY! DOUGLASS! Who is missing?"

"Cox," coughed Douglass.

Percy added, "he was just in front. I don't think the patrol boat hit anyone, but he was—" The tropical storm turned violent then again, and especially so where they were, and what he said was lost.

The sea picked up its heaving. With a herculean effort, the men concentrated on land until they dragged themselves almost to the mainland shoreline. Rocky, unforgiving in the squall, great geysers of foam were kicked up against huge stones, both submerged and craggy, threatening. The Marine was leading them to a likely spot, with smaller rocks and less violent wave crashes. Approaching from the left toward the survivors, along the coast road— lights, a convoy of trucks. He motioned for them to get back, down in the water. The men lay down and were lashed by the exploding surf, fighting to breathe. Salt water filled all eardrums.

So too did fourteen heavy trucks pass without additional incident, laden with all manner of containers and earthmoving equipment, trailing guns and cannons. The enemy concentrated on his larger mission.

The rain stopped. The men crossed the coast road, which Deane noticed had recently been graded, and started up the embankment to come to rest on a natural terrace at about 20 meters elevation, where they could look out over the road, and the sea which they had just crossed, to the island which had been their resting place since they escaped the doomed ship. It seemed a stone's throw's distance, and days ago.

"COX!" Douglass pointed down. A man floated face down, almost at the spot where they had hidden under the swirling sea, but his body was held off the rocks by the backwash. Douglass leaped to his feet and started down the hill.

"STOP, STOP!"

Another pair of lights could be seen coming, from the same direction as the convoy, below and to their right now. This truck was slowing, and appeared it would stop lateral of BR1 Cox. The men scrambled further up the hill, behind scrub and heavy-leaved flowering bushes, a safer distance from the peripheral vision of a casual glance.

The truck stopped. "*HEI! HEI!*" Six troops scampered out of the back through canvas flaps, rifles in hand. They stepped down over the rocks toward the body, which one tried to reach with his rifle. Unsuccessful, he barked something back toward the truck. In a moment a soldier emerged with a rope tied to a grappling hook.

A wave blasted the rocks closest to Cox, sending a backwash that rolled him over, and he coughed and began flailing. Two soldiers fired their weapons at him at point-blank range. They caught him in the hook and dragged him to within reach.

"We need to get out of here," whispered Deane, though the enemy was well clear of earshot.

"NO. Don't move," someone said. "They have no reason to think there might be more."

Deane looked behind them. The thick tropical forest was a 50-yard dash. The men below were concentrated on the unfortunate Cox and his personal effects, if any. And, their position was hidden by the bush.

...ING IN QUICKSAND

...hat they will conclude, any second. Move out, one by

6

Dutch Lines

1030

March 2, 1942

The men punched into thick reeds and rhododendron, grabbing stalks stubborn and slippery, and sometimes the sharp edges of nipa palms just taller than themselves, their faces draped with spiderwebs at every step. Without shoes, there was difficult purchase on the soggy earthen hill and giant leaves on the forest floor, and progress was made only by the lucky grasp of a stalk stout enough to still the slide. Though the rain had stopped, the downpour in the bush was continuous because as they moved forward, the massive leaves of rubbery trunks grabbed for progress poured onto the climbers, keeping them drenched. It was quickly clear that one man could not follow another because each footstep became a mudslide, each had to blaze his path. They ascended through the jungle that way for almost an hour until the grade suddenly leveled at about 3 times the height of the palms at the shore, about 40 meters above the road.

Deane reached the top first, and stood atop a porous black rock to peek above the palms and wild mango, looking back down the way they had come. He could not see a truck, but two Jap soldiers were setting up a tent where the truck had been on the side of the road closest to the water. They must be installing a lookout in case more of the enemy had made it ashore.

The others reached the top of the ridge within five minutes. Percy stepped up on the black rock and took in the view. He said what Deane was thinking, "They're gonna figure out we got out when they start looking on the other side of the road." As the soldiers secured the last tent stakes, another appeared from the bottom of the view, gesturing with his rifle back the way he had come. From the tent emerged an individual with neither helmet nor rifle, an officer in a field cap. With binoculars, he began scanning the embankment and hill about where Deane thought his men must have begun their ascent to the ridge. Two more infantrymen emerged from the tent. Their CO barked something, and all others quickly crossed the road toward the foot of the hill.

Deane stepped off the rock. "Japs're coming, time to *MOVE*! This way!"

He hurried into the woods, continuing away north, through rhododendron and snarled vines no less relentless but with some relief in slope. They picked up the pace as was possible. For another hour Deane and Percy took turns bearing the beating of being the first to blaze the trail. Suddenly the thick tropical vegetation and canopy fell away and they stepped into a wild garden, with knee-high shrubs and splashes of bright color everywhere: white jasmine, a bank of bushes bursting violet with moon orchids, snatches of yellow, daisy-like Javanese edelweiss, and bulbous red pitcher plants. Stopping surrounded by these, which he thought looked exactly like unrolled condoms hanging from the tips of branches, Bailey Douglass doubled over, hands on his knees, to catch his breath and rest his back.

"A couple of minutes rest," pronounced Deane when all 8 men reached the garden glade.

Douglass's gaze fell into one of the pitcher bulbs. It jiggled with the slow-motion flailing of a bright green tree frog inside struggling to escape. In time a bath of enzymes would dissolve it enough to be digested by the carnivorous plant. A couple of rubbers away another red pocket held a bat, which appeared to be wakening at the disturbance, a furry wing appeared along the lip... he stood up quickly.

A distant commotion from the direction they had come, which could be a falling tree or a company of soldiers, bade the group continue. Clay Percy started ahead across the half-acre glade, toward rainbow eucalyptus trees marking the resuming forest— cover that would provide the group the best chance of evading capture.

Soon after they re-entered the forest, the ridge dropped away again sharply. Percy lost his balance and slid down the embankment for almost fifty yards until finally, he slammed into a mound of volcanic pumice which shredded his pants and tore his foot and calf. Others slipped but none so severely, and Deane was first to reach the Sergeant. Percy was already wrapping a piece of his pant leg around his right foot. His calf was torn in a nasty scrape wound, which looked painful but not life-threatening. Wilson and Douglass stopped to catch their breath, then continued to pick their way slowly down the ridge. Pogue felt his knee give way and fell forward on his face, slip-sliding on his belly for twenty meters along Percy's path, slamming into the sergeant with enough force to knock the wind from him, and jamming his neck in the process.

Percy gasped, someone screamed in fear and frustration, and everyone instinctively... stopped. They held tight and just listened, to hear what their disorder had betrayed. At first, they were conscious only of the sound of the constant drip from leaves, but with restored volume came the layered cacophony: chirping bugs, birds, and the sound of running water. Deane caught Wilson's eye and nodded and he and Douglass again began to make their way forward. Pogue pulled himself together, turning his head slowly. Judging himself otherwise unhurt he started behind Huffman and Jonasson as they passed. Deane helped Sgt Percy get to his feet and they carefully negotiated the hill for safe descent.

They found the others resting, drinking from a fast-flowing stream at the very foot of the slope. "There is no time to lose," he said. "We cannot rest now. I think the Japs know we are here." Northeast, along the rising ridges of volcanoes, would be the closest way they might get to and across the strait somehow, into Sumatra, perhaps to safe territories. None of them knew that by now, the Japanese controlled almost the entire Dutch East Indies... the Dutch had virtually given up without a struggle.

Northeast was a gentle climb upstream.

"The stream will hide us." The water was cool, the streambed kinder to tortured feet, and there were fewer flies, but the walk was no easier than navigating the steep ridge. For two hours or more, they trekked sometimes chest deep around dense, silted sediment of rocks and sticks, stepping over bamboo stalks as big around as cannon muzzles. Wilson stepped into a hole that swallowed him almost completely, but he bobbed right back to the surface, inches from a large green python wrapped around an overhanging branch, which started to uncoil itself as he floated past, quickening briefly the group's exhausted pace.

When Deane thought they might have traveled one mile, the stream and the forest opened into a beach of uniformly smooth gravel. Ahead was a great open space, a *sawah*, an irrigated rice field with giant palms at the far side, and beyond that a mountain range.

They walked shin-deep. A great silhouette stood between the crew and the open field, along the gravel bank. Deane stopped suddenly enough to communicate alarm, and they all froze. A rhinoceros, larger than a jeep, turned to face them. Eight haggard men stood facing an impossibly strange creature 30 yards ahead in their path, in an impossibly strange and dangerous place, though this was so beyond expectation they were simply without direction, or for a moment, a constructive thought. Perhaps the beast was repelled by their collective astonishment. After a long quarter of a minute, it crashed noisily into the thick growth at an angle well opposed to their course.

After another long moment, Deane and Wilson, who was the tallest, slipped to one of the last large palms at the edge of the forest and looked out over the field. The organized open landscape was spotted throughout with figures occupied in every task of managing the crop. The stream that had been their path advanced into the field and split into a pattern of troughs at right angles. Mud berms held water in some and workers were bent over to the ground with hands in the water, moving almost in unison, snatching up rice plants. Closer and beyond, pairs of ox drew plows guided by others. More attacked the ground with long poles. All were protected from the peeping sun by conical straw hats.

More or less in the center, two figures sat under a roofed hut without walls and the refugees assumed at first they were soldiers on the lookout. Just beyond, a levee that appeared to be a road dividing the *sawah* was piled with bicycles. Deane saw that the bent-over figures were women, the men drove the plows and beat and troweled the ground with hoes. The two under the hut rejoined their coworkers, clad as they were in bright colors like the others, presumably taking a moment's rest from the heat. 20 yards to the left, approached a plowman. Though his attention was on his beasts, they were only seconds from being discovered.

The men were starving and would not fare further without food. Deane motioned to stand firm and they waited for the ploughman to come alongside rather than startle him by stepping out. The ox looked their way and then to its master, who then shouted, and they had the attention of the entire field. The men held up their arms and motioned that they were hungry. Deane stepped back to reveal Percy's bloody leg.

Two other natives close by dropped their sticks and one immediately took off running, splashing across the field toward the mountains. Some of the women stood and stared, but quickly dropped back to their work, and the plowman recovered his composure and continued on behind his oxen. The one that had not run off motioned for them to follow and led them to the open hut shelter, where they found a table laden with the remains of lunch: bananas, coconuts, fish heads, and rice.

Hunger and exhaustion outweighed the fear of being captured and the men ate lustily, and for the first time in 36 hours, they inventoried the group's condition. The farmer who had led them to the hut saw the bloody feet and Sergeant Percy's legs, and said something to the woman who had brought more food. In a few minutes, she brought jugs of water and a basket of sandals with clever slips made of straw.

"*Tuh-REE-mah KAH-see*" said Deane in Malay. "Thank you" and "Hello" were souvenirs of the language he recalled from the HOUSTON's emergency repairs at Tjilatjap just a week before.

"*Ja*", said their host, just a boy of about eighteen. He looked beyond them for a moment then motioned for all to get up and follow. "*Hah-ti hah-ti!*"

His alarm was clear, and the haggard group followed as quickly as they could stand. He led them, running, to the levee road pointing to the north where the road led again into the forest. No one looked back but Deane, who saw a truck enter at the far edge of the fields to the south.

7

Java Sandals

1345

March 2, 1942

The boy on the levee anxiously pushed the Americans, perhaps frustrated they failed to see the danger in remaining. Percy and Douglass had stuffed their swollen, bleeding, blistered feet into the tiny sandals but there was no running in them even if they had not been so exhausted; no one was in condition to expedite.

Finally, they reached the north end of the open space into the visual protection of the forest. Could there be the slightest chance they had not been observed? The first truck, same as those they had seen loaded with troops, the two-and-a-half ton vehicles with tarps of oiled canvas, stopped only seconds at the hut and the bicycles but continued in their direction, so Deane was sure they were in pursuit. The men scattered, scrambling away from the road up into the thick bush, and on both sides, they made a wide swing eventually back to the north edge, at field level. When the Jap trucks reached their position they did not slow but kept on down the road; the Americans had not been seen. To be sure, the men were only too happy to maintain their positions and rest for an hour. Douglass made makeshift shoes from a downed bamboo shoot padded with giant leaves and bound them to his feet with vines. They were better than walking barefoot, but only just. Others made less successful attempts; those that could wear the sandals they had been given found them tortuously small and discarded them at the base of the mountain.

When they regrouped, Deane again suggested ascending the mountain range would be safest, and the best chance of reaching the northwest edge of the island, perhaps getting to Sumatra, towards Dutch-held territory.

Under Dutch colonial rule for the last two centuries, the local inhabitants embraced the invading, occupying army of the Japanese. Captain Rooks had briefed his officers this was one of many snippets of intelligence. Though not supported by the men's experience, the officers were to likewise instruct survivors— those exposed to capture, to avoid contact with local inhabitants as was possible.

"We were lucky," said Deane. "Most natives are anti-Dutch, so anti-Anglo. They think the Japs are their liberators. I'm afraid we hadn't the choice but to trust those farmers. We are the enemy. That kid or others could still send troops right after us."

He noticed his shirt was almost dry, but saw that all were covered in mud and blood from the knees down. "We must keep moving, find some food."

They followed the road into the bush for half a mile until it turned serpentine— zig-zagging up the mountainside in a gentler switch-back ascent, and it was decided to enter the thick again rather than be surprised by an oncoming vehicle. This jungle was kinder to the step, except for the injured Sergeant Percy, being helped by Wilson. They made decent progress. By late afternoon all the men reached a landing where there was an outcropping of rock, and thus an opening in the canopy.

Pogue removed his shirt and raised his arms. "How bad is it?" His sides were bright red from his armpits to almost his waist, where the straps of his life vest had rubbed his skin off muscle and tendon in a six-hour swim to the island. He had not complained. Then an intense itch drew his fingers to a lump right below his left hip, and he peeled a cigarette-sized leech off his side, just under his belt line, doubtless a souvenir of their walking the stream. A trickle of blood flowed freely from the site and would not be suppressed.

Suddenly every itch was suspect. Huffman and Edmonson pulled leeches from aside their testicles, and Wilson from the underside of his penis.

Percy extracted a six-inch worm a quarter of the way into his anus. Their utter revulsion pushed back exhaustion for a long, disgusting moment... and simultaneously each man noticed his own aghast expression frozen on another face... and they laughed. And oozed.

Shortly survival came back to focus. For all, thirst was the great tormentor. Jonasson, the smallest man, was helped to ascend a coconut tree and managed to secure two. Chewing the sweet meat provided enough moisture that they were able to rest for a short while. Until the rains came again.

Deane's eyes jerked open. A headache fog of total exhaustion, eyes open but unseeing, made for an uncertain consciousness. Thunder rumbled, and he found himself in a tropical rain, sitting up against a coconut tree. Blood at his waist ran pink with the increasing downpour. Blood?

Leeches. His mind forced recall, and the last hours drifted in until they were front and center again... what would they do?

The men were splayed about the clearing in reclining positions; at least they had found momentary comfort. The sudden increase in rain had brought everybody around. Larkin Edmonson, the youngest man, was first on his feet.

"We should stay on this ridge." Every snatch image of the coast and the sea below that could be glimpsed through the thick tropical canopy showed enemy activity: troops in trucks, convoy ships in the background, heavy equipment, and planes... suggesting the complete picture was exponentially menacing. Edmonson's observation couldn't be argued.

The men got to their feet and began to punch through the jungle again to the north while availed of level ground, Percy hopping along slowly, leaning on Wilson. Travel was more bearable than being immobile in the rain. Brightening the picture slightly there were fewer mosquitoes, and they drank water from the folds of the largest leaves. A few hundred yards along, the level ridge top began to twist around to the south, so that soon they would have to decide: continue along the top or descend the slope to continue north. The decision was to split the difference and hope their cover resumed direction... another quarter mile and the ridge played out suddenly. As it had the day before, their descent increased sharply with every step, yet with increased danger, it was getting dark. They would rest for a moment, looking uphill, their backs against trees...

The congregation was seated. Jesu, Joy of Man's Desiring *by JS Bach directed the pace of the ushers. Deane stood at the Narthex of Calvary Church and offered his arm to the groom's sister-in-law, Eunice, and they began toward the altar to her seat on the front row, groom's side. He concentrated to slow his long stride to match hers, and wore a natural smile, as he had been coached. At fifteen, his body was beginning to show the sculpting effects of competitive swimming. Every female eye in the packed church watched him kiss his mother on the cheek, and turn to retrace his steps. But he noticed only the eye of Katherine Levelle, and when he caught sight of her with her parents, in the center of the congregants on the groom's side, there were no other girls or women in the room. In a few moments, after the dozen bridesmaids and groomsmen processed to Pachelbel's* Canon in D, *big sister Louise would appear at the back of the church with their father.*

Entering from the right came Rector Atkinson, followed by groom Charlie Walterlane, and his father, Lucian. The string quartet began to play again when they found their positions. The bridal party began their measured pace, two at a time, each pair stepping forward when the pair before reached the center aisles. He and Louise's plump friend from Texas, Melody, who made him nervous, were lined up last, her gloved hand at his elbow. At the rehearsal she called him "darling" while pinching his cheek, and teased him, wanting to trim his dark eyebrows. She said, "You have the most piercing blue eyes!" This cracked up the bridal party. Deane colored. He was glad they would be on separate sides of the church during the service.

Some in the congregation turned to watch the bridal party process, and again he caught Katherine's eye. She smiled.

Finally, the couple in front reached the center and he and Melody began their procession. His face aside his nose suddenly itched. Then, another tiny stab on the other cheek. Ignoring it, he held Katherine's gaze until almost lateral of her and steeled his facade to maintain the pace forward. At almost a step away from the groom, there was an unbearable pain at his jaw on the right, then on his nose, and he threw down Melody's arm to scratch...

0530

March 3, 1942

    A cloud of mosquitoes hovered, biting at the soft parts of his face. Deane had no recall of when or where they stopped, nor when he slipped into unconsciousness, but when he jerked awake it was dawn.

    Edmonson was surest of foot, so they followed him down, down, for an hour until the steep jungle slope yielded, and he thought they must be close to the level of the valley seen from above. Unexpectedly, he emerged from the dense growth and saw that their course north meant cross a creek chest deep, possibly more leeches, if it could even be done at their current energy level. When the others arrived, Deane scouted along the bank left and right, but finding no alternative, they crossed where they had come off the ridge.

1000

    A few hours later, when they had gone but five hundred meters through thick brush, up and down across troughs, over more ridges, when no man thought he could travel another step, they reached the top of the last ridge. Rising puffs of smoke rose gray-blue against a far mountain range. The canopy looking straight ahead fell away to an open field well below. They trudged down again toward voices and children's laughter— some assurance they weren't approaching Jap soldiers. Perhaps there was food ahead. The ruddy-faced young Irishman again took the lead. Soon a rice swamp appeared, and just beyond a small village.

1045

The farmer decided suddenly he may have delayed too long in attendance of nature's call. He stood up from his work and the pressure increased in his bowels. He hopped over rows, toward the forest twenty meters away, passing others ankle deep, intently pushing seed with their hoes, but who sensed his anxiety and increasing desperation. Snickers at his back chased him a yard deeper than he would have traveled until he could wait no longer, and he evacuated in mid-squat with a dysentery-pressure blast.

The sound drew Edmonson's attention through the giant leaves to the huffing figure in a straw cone hat at the canopy's edge. Before he could signal quiet, five American soldiers on his heels in single file crashed into him, then into each other, inertia fueled by complete exhaustion.

The farmer so compromisingly engaged leaped backward in alarm, soiling himself. He stared in horror into the dense swamp forest…

Because he was lame, Percy continued to tumble past the others and burst through the bush into the open. Attempting to break his fall with a dive, he met the mud hands and face first, in full view of the villager, who shit yet again. Three seconds later he turned and fled.

Caked with mud but no worse for the experience, Percy sat up where he had come to rest. The others came alongside and took in the humorous picture of the black-faced sergeant staring after the disappearing peasant with a dark splash backside, but no one could spare the strength to laugh.

Deane suffered a wave. Suddenly conscious of the terrible ache in the muscles holding his shoulders upright, he felt them go slack and his posture sagged involuntarily. A relentless headache now lurked at the back of his head and another just behind his eyes, separating input from the thinking organ. The others would be the same or worse. Logic was as fleeting as strength; soon they would be bound by desperation, capable of focusing only on food and rest.

Clayton Percy had helped drive them with his perseverance. Though

Deane knew the status quo could not humanly continue, he also realized the value of Percy's example and got under his arm to continue their journey. Warning the others to be prepared for anything, he prayed silently for the villagers to help them, and the haggard group limped into the open rice field. The looks they got from the farmers, and villagers who slowly approached made Deane feel like wounded prey.

An elderly man came toward them, and Deane indicated with hand gestures they needed food. The man said, "*Bapak kersa dhahar?* " Deane just made the gesture again, and the old man motioned for them to follow him into the village. They were seated at a circle of stones around the remains of a smoking fire, a kind of town square, itself surrounded by huts. Shortly a woman brought rice and fish on a large piece of charred wood, then passed around a bucket of drinking water with a ladle, and for a while the situation seemed stable. Maybe they could rest here.

Deane was trying to come up with the word for 'sleep' in Malay when the sounds of approaching motorized vehicles seized him in the gut. All but Percy got to their feet and scattered away from the opening toward the closest hiding, a stand of bamboo at the edge of another road leading out of the village. Jonasson, Deane, and Wilson entered the road itself and separated into dense growth beyond. Edmonson and Douglass forced their bodies into the bamboo, which pricked at clothes and skin with icepick-like jabs.

But each man found himself shadowed by a native from the village. More or less imprisoned by their hiding place, the men in the bamboo saw a peasant farmer, the shitter, leading Japanese soldiers to the circle of stones. The villagers standing nearest shouted and pointed to the bamboo, and Edmonson and Bailey were dragged out in short order, bloody and bruised, and tossed to the circle. Soldiers were kicking Percy to get up and so he tried to stand, but not quickly enough for one, who struck him with the stock of his rifle stock hard in the temple, and he went slack, down into the mud. Blood poured from that side of his head, his jaw gaped open and his eyes were rolled back.

Deane and the other two American soldiers had dashed fast as their legs would carry them in opposite directions. But with every move mirrored by rested natives, pointing and shouting, the enemy soon found their way to each. Jonasson and Wilson were on their knees facing down, when Deane was forced to the spot by his captors. A Jap private who looked to be late teens, who had captured Wilson, bayoneted him in the side and twisted and turned the long blade trying to free it. Wilson's screaming only made him angrier when the rifle wouldn't retract, so he threw it down and pulled his pistol, but the Jap Lieutenant in charge deflected it and it fired into the ground. Deane took a step forward as if to protect the wounded man, and earned a rifle butt to the head from the soldier that had spared Wilson. Daniel Jonasson had suffered no additional injury, yet thought their time had certainly come, so he circled his arms around the writhing Les Wilson in a protective hug. At that moment another two soldiers arrived with Pogue, bleeding from a gash above his eye. The Jap Lt. in charge motioned to the ambulatory Jonasson and Pogue to carry Wilson down the hill.

At the circle, several soldiers were kicking and shouting at Sergeant Percy. He would not rise, nor would he even stir, and one of the soldiers put his rifle to his head and fired.

Wilson could not stand. The adolescent private who had attempted to kill him enlisted others, and they tossed him into the back of the covered truck. The soldier then tied the right wrists of the still ambulatory together in chain gang formation (two by two), and marched them out of the village back toward the coast. Villagers of all ages waved little Japanese flags and threw stones at the Americans as they stumbled past, and in a curious exchange, the soldiers shouted angrily, aiming their guns at them. Finally, in an hour, they came to another village that had been completely taken over by the Japanese. There were about a dozen other prisoners, American and allied, being given rice and drinking water, after which their captors left them alone for a while in a muddy, fenced yard.

2140

March 3, 1942

Groups of men were randomly marched into barracks. After two British and one Australian were added to Deane's group, eight men were then lashed together to a bed for the night, but the bed would only hold four. The Australian, who had been at the village three days, thought himself somewhat lucky to have landed a position on the bed if just for a little while, but he was tied to Edmonson, closest on the floor, and the two quickly realized they had to alternate all night holding up their wrists to maintain circulation.

In the morning, the prisoners were rousted from the hut by an older Japanese soldier who seemed to have some humanity about his face, and Deane attempted to inquire about the disposition of FCCM Wilson, last seen wounded, in a truck. But it was a difficult charade, and the man just looked at him for a moment, then snapped at him impatiently in Japanese. He had prayed during the night for the soul of his brave friend Clayton Percy, and when the men he knew were outside and authority out of earshot, he led a prayer for Wilson's safety and theirs going forward.

1445

March 4, 1942

They trudged 25 kilometers over reasonably level ground behind a convoy carrying troops, artillery, and heavy equipment on trucks, which stopped finally at a busy village market. Except for the presence of the Japanese, life here seemed to go on uninterrupted. Deane noted few locals took notice of the plight of the POWs. In about an hour, an empty truck followed from the way they had come, and 17 men were placed in the back and trucked on northward for several hours.

2300

When finally the convoy came to a stop, guards led them into a large building containing about a thousand men, survivors of the HOUSTON and the PERTH, RAF (British) radar personnel and infantry troops, Dutch Naval officers and soldiers, and other allied troops who had escaped from Singapore and Sumatra, and were rounded up in Java, and people of every description, including Caucasian or non-Asian civilians. It was learned they had arrived in Serang, at the northern tip of Java Island. Reunited (except for Percy, Huffman, and Wilson), Deane's group was somewhat encouraged by finding officers and sailors they served with, and he considered the news of how short a distance they had actually traveled as the crow flies; their odyssey from their ocean escape seemed weeks ago.

Their shelter had once been a movie theater- seats removed. On the second day, a machine gun was installed on the balcony that could train down upon the prisoners. Shortly after, an accidental burst was discharged, injuring no one, but it caused the men to scatter and compress, fall and step over the injured such that the order was given that daytime the throng was to stand, and from 8 pm to 8 am to lie down on the bare floor.

There was drinking water and each man received a small piece of bread twice a day, and on the strip of ground just outside they were allowed to dig a long pit for use as a latrine. Some of the men were in terrible shape and there were no medical facilities. LDO Murphy Mason, one of the HOUSTON's gunners from Deane's turret had somehow made it ashore, though badly burned. Several of the men had festering wounds and there was only water to dress them. Only when you could not stand it, did you move to the door to use the pit outside— a sadistic Japanese had invented a game that was taken up by soldiers across the yard, to bet on which he would randomly assault, kick, or strike with his rifle stock.

0800

March 8, 1942

All officers were collected, tied up, and marched from the theater four blocks to a jail, where there were ten native Javanese confined. These convicts became the "cooks" for the newly arrived, serving sticky rice mixed with seaweed from a concrete bin of suspect history, but the men were starving and though the dirty vessels could hold the mix upside down indefinitely, they ate and thought no more of it. Over the next few days, each officer was interrogated for an hour or more by an English-speaking Jap who did not wear a uniform.

Soon other soldiers were added to the jail. Thirty-five officers were placed into a cell designed to hold fifteen. Forty to sixty noncoms and enlisted men were stuffed into cells the same size. A system of time for sleeping and standing was adopted so all could have some rest prone. Buckets were used for latrines, dumped once a day into an open hole in the center of the rows of cells that drained into a creek that ran through the edge of town.

Only the fittest had been brought to the jail. There had been no news of the badly wounded they had seen in the theater, but regular gunfire those weeks gave the jailed reason to suspect the worst. During that time officers with any knack for the Japanese language tried to communicate, which their captors found very funny, and the tensions eased a bit. CWO Phillipe Guillaume was found to be able to make himself understood and began to try to convince the Japanese to allow them their own cooks and doctors, which was eventually granted. Two days it took to scrub the "kitchen" before it could be used.

March 31, 1942

Dutch civilians, residents of Serang who had been rounded up and imprisoned with the soldiers, were released from an adjoining cell, and allowed to bring food and vegetables, fruit and peanuts from town, which almost certainly saved their lives. Deane noted the shrinkage of his muscle tissue, and the sharp angles of his hips, and guesstimated each man had lost perhaps fifty pounds.

8

Beale Street

February 6, 1926

When Arthur's first season at Robinsonville came to an end on January 31, the duty of securing the property until the spring, when maybe a couple of the members might come back to fish, fell to Arthur and another longtime paddling guide, Manfred "Manny" Ames. Once they cleaned the place there wasn't really much else to do, and as they would not be paid anymore, the object was to locate the means to sustain yourself part-time until at least teal season in September. With money in his pocket, this sounded like freedom to Arthur Campbell. The paddlers talked all season about all the music and the women that could be had on Beale Street in Memphis.

Off they went, buoyed by anticipation and adventure, and warm temperatures. Manny said: "'fweekin'git over to Highway 61 by fo-o'clock, we oughta catch dat night train to Mephiss." He chuckled, making it sound like luxury accommodations. Of course, they would try to hop the Mississippi Central freight line that ran twice a day from Hattiesburg through Memphis. If you wanted to, you could get as far north as Kansas City.

By one o'clock they had walked the muddy road along the levee to the paved road a mile from the clubhouse. The rain of the last two days finally trickled to a drizzle, and then a mist. They walked a long while without seeing a soul before they came upon a thing writhing in the center of the road. A possum, its back side and legs crushed and pinned to the road wrestled in agony against its ghost. Arthur was immediately struck by the oddity that traffic so seldom should find this possum the moment it decided to cross. It must have been trying to die the whole day— possums only moved at night. He snuffed the unfortunate creature with a swift boot heel, just as Manny was offering suggestions as to how it might be accomplished.

It was two o'clock before a big truck approached, and at the nod of the driver, they jumped aboard, sharing the open truck bed with giant pine logs chained in place. Those chains were too light for the job, Arthur thought. A big bump could shift a ton of wood onto Manfred, but he looked happier than a swimming drake, and he was making himself comfortable scratching the ball of his foot on a big pine knot, skating up and down on the sap with his shoe sole. He was very often right about what blind would offer the best hunt, and sometimes would even accurately predict the kill, so club members said Manny had inside knowledge of the immediate future. "Naw", Arthur would say, "he's jus dumb... and lucky."

At Walls, their driver turned east to Olive Branch, and they jumped off close to the railroad track. It wasn't so far to Memphis now. If they could even catch it the train would take them almost to Beale. In ideal conditions, it might pass through at 60 miles an hour. Boarding could be a challenge.

"C'mon, boy," said Arthur, "we got to git our asses to Horn Lake."

The curve at Horn Lake was like a station. Colored and white waited together to see if the train would slow down enough at the curve to provide them their conveyance north. There was no guarantee, the engineer might need to make up time. Or, it could be management wanted to keep down stowaways. In the old days, they didn't pay much attention to people hopping the train. But accidents and people getting hurt or killed were starting to get a lot of press, and that was bad for business, so lately if they didn't have to slow down, they didn't. But after rain over several days or a heavy sustained cloudburst, conditions were favorable for hopping aboard. Trains had to go slow on a soggy track bed.

The track made a rather sudden turn east to miss Horn Lake, which the prudent engineer would slow through. It bisected 250 acres of barren field, notable only for all the hopeful travelers sitting on crates or standing, clutching worldly possessions. By mid-September, the field would look like snow on either side of the track, with cotton heavy in the bowl.

"Sky's too dahk fuh fo o'clock, " observed Manfred. "Iss gonna rain, pretty quick."

A whistle to the south, a growing cloud of billowing gray smoke, and in moments the huge engine coughed and huffed past them pulling a dozen freight cars before they saw one with the doors open, obviously what the other travelers waited on. When it slowed to probably ten miles an hour, the able-bodied jumped aboard. An old woman dabbed at her eyes, and the white-haired man beside her simply smiled and waved to someone aboard, maybe 'goodbye' for a long time.

Arthur felt the slap of a drop as big as a quail egg, and then another. He knew the track bent way around to the south around a quarter mile, so you should be able to count fifty or sixty cars in the curve. But it disappeared completely into a white sheet of water twenty cars back. The squall seemed to be attached, approaching at the same rate.

The train started to pick up speed again, but there were no more cars with doors wide open. A half-dozen folks not yet able to get aboard started to run alongside.

"You waitin' on a invitation," shouted Arthur, and he leaped to grab the ladder handle of the next car. Heavier drops started punching him. With a great heave, he parted the sliding doors enough to poke his head and arm into the black inside. The train clicked up to twenty miles per hour. He bit his tongue when his jaw caught the inside of the steel door. Twenty-five, thirty. Another jolt like that and... a second later, a dozen hands fell on his arm, shoulder, and shirt, he was yanked in, thrown onto the floor, and the massive door was clanged shut behind him, all at once.

Sensing first wet and cold... his first thought was he was soaked, but alive. Then he wondered if that was so, because next... he heard singing:

... an that po boy got away from home, an he spent a-all that he had,
That po-or boy got away from home an spent a-all that he had,
well, That po boy got away from home an he spent a-all that he had,
and that's no way for him to get along...
and that's no way for him to get along...

"Manfred!" shouted Arthur Campbell.

"No suh," said the voice making the music, "Robert Wilkins."

—and all of the others laughed. It was black as pitch inside that freight car, but there were a lot of bodies and voices... maybe twenty, and it stunk like hell, but it was getting warm.

"Where's Manny," said Arthur to no one. It didn't matter. Manny said he had jumped the train many times. He would be fine; Arthur would find him on Beale.

He thought Robert Wilkins started his song again, but it was hard to tell. Rain started to pound the car as it picked up speed, and the combination built into a roar. Sitting up, his hand brushed something soft, female... and into it came a bottle.

The car started and stopped because of the weather, but they knew they were finally in Memphis for the sound of shouting men and banging doors. The woman at Arthur's side stiffened in anticipation just before the doors to their car jerked open.

"GET OFF MY GODDAMN TRAIN! You all clear out— *quick*!"

"GET THAT COTTON LOADED!"

The lights from the loading dock fell on a pretty young woman whose head was in his lap, and a man who must be Robert Wilkins, just to Arthur's right. Robert stood long and lean and wrapped his jacket around his guitar, his shirt collar firm and white as new despite of the humidity. Before he stepped down, he plucked a wide-brim straw hat from an unseen hook and topped his bald pate. A man in the doorway, silhouetted by the outside lights jumped off the train carrying a banjo.

They got to their feet and the woman said, "I'm Lizzie McCoy." Arthur wondered if he had perhaps not survived the jump, and was instead in heaven.

Excepting that he was in special company, it was no different than the other couple of times Arthur had jumped a train. The hands at the freight yard pretended to be surprised and angry, impatient that the human cargo had to be cleared before they could load paid freight. The men pulled canvas tarps off the nearest trailers. Wagon loads of cotton bales ten long and four high were lined up behind pull trucks as far as you could see up and down the tracks.

The rain had ceased, but the ground was soaked, and holding Lizzie's hand, Arthur stepped back a few cars to see if Manny was about. If there had been many other passengers, they were gone. The cars behind them stood empty. They started to walk north. No lights lit the streets for several blocks, but far ahead the downtown Memphis night glowed, and the other party-goers could be heard laughing just a block ahead.

"I am a guitar player," said Lizzie, and squeezed his hand.

9

Pee Wee's

February 6, 1926

Saturday night on Beale Street meant ambulances at the ready, waiting to carry the injured and the dead from a normal night's business. It was the time of Prohibition, and gambling was illegal, but that meant little here, in the heart of Negro America.

The travelers melted into a throng of people in the street white and black. Lizzie seemed to know exactly where to go and led them in front of a place called Pee Wee's, where there was a line of people to get in. It was just before 10 pm, and the place was jumping, doors open. A man with a trumpet stood on stage with another, who was blowing into a glass jug. A diminutive piano player hammered the keys and sang a booming verse:

> *Here we're goin' round and round,*
> *Me an my babe is Louisiana boun'*

The way Lizzie said their names, Arthur thought he must be supposed to know who they were. Across the street, he saw Robert Wilkins and the man with the banjo go into another nightclub, called the Monarch. But Lizzie said "They will kill a country boy in there. You stay with me," and she surprised him with a kiss on his cheek.

Arthur woke in a strange room to the sound of buzzing flies. His head hurt, and for a good while, that was all he knew. The room smelled of bourbon and cigarettes. He hauled himself up to raise the window shade and found he was naked except for his shirt. Pulling aside the shade a bit instead, he looked out over the street, thinking he would relish some eggs.

His pants and shorts lay on the radiator, but there was no wallet in his pocket.

"Watch out when you're gettin' all you want," his momma would say. "Fattened hogs ain't in luck."

Damn. Arthur sat back down and tried to reconstruct the hours before. He remembered Lizzie, and Pee Wee's and the players on the stage.

"... and whiskey... much as you want," said a man named Will Shade, who Arthur recalled was the piano player. Shade stopped playing when he saw Lizzie standing outside and had them brought into the club ahead of the line. Then Lizzie got up on stage with them, and she had a guitar, and she sang and played, and Arthur had never seen a thing like it.

> *... Boy, you better watch it 'cause she's tricky*
> *Hoodoo Lady, I want you to unlock my doe*
> *so I kin get in and get all my clothes*
> *But don't put that thang on me*
> *Doan put that thing on me*
> *Doan put that thing on me*
> *'cause I'm goin' back to Tennessee...*

When the song ended, over the whooping and stomping they asked the crowd to appreciate Lizzie, but the man called her Memphis Minnie. After a moment Lizzie leaned her guitar down and came right over and sat on his lap.

But Arthur's stomach obscured his memory further, which alarmed him less than the loss of his wallet, as it was something he came to expect when he drank. His wallet contained twenty dollars.

His jacket stunk like the train, but his shirt didn't look or smell too bad, so he made himself as presentable as possible and asked the man at the desk downstairs if he had seen Lizzie... or Memphis Minnie.

"Most ever day," he said. "She plays the club 'crost de street, 'n comes in here when it's a trick."

"Where's here?" He didn't hear what the man said to that, as he was soaking in what he had just been told. Arthur walked out the door and started with the establishment across the street, the Red Onion.

Beale was still sleeping in at eleven o'clock on a Sunday morning, and no doors opened to him until he knocked at the Daisy Theater. A light-skinned, very fat negro with a grimy undershirt and derby hat stood chewing a piece of cigar. "Well... what?"

"What is the name of that hotel there? I can't see it," Arthur lied. The man came out a little into the morning light to see what Arthur was talking about. "Cain't you read? That's the Hotel Joseph. Whaddaboutit?" Arthur heard the sound of frying, and the smell of sausage wafted out the door.

"Woman I was with took my wallet, and I need to eat something."

"This ain't no restaurant."

"I can work. Wash dish—" He noticed the ticket booth. "Hand out tickets."

Oscar's head hurt and he wanted to get back to cleaning up. This loon would just scare away the patrons. "We got a good-lookin' ticket girl." Then he saw the blood on the sidewalk and recalled someone had drawn a knife across the neck of his doorman. He'd survive but dang-it, he bled like a stuck sow... that was when he realized the man had been there a month, and he did not even know his name.

"Tell you what... "

Topped with eggs and sausage, his stomach took leave of its nagging, and a few minutes later Arthur was scrubbing the sidewalk with a stiff brush on a stick that dripped ammonia suds from a bucket. He would go over and over it and finish with a mop. It smelled better than his jacket, which now additionally bore the damp stench of the hotel room. Arthur began to suspect getting bloodstained concrete clean might be more than a day's work.

Shadow maps of equal color and oddness of shape were here and there, the geography of the Daisy's violent history.

He promised to return at dark...

10

Bad Sam

February 8, 1926

Arthur stuffed rose petals from a vase at the restaurant in the pockets of his jacket which he hung over the door to air and sun all afternoon while he napped. At dusk, his yellow-collared shirt, still slightly damp from rinsing, looked more or less pressed from being steamed over the radiator. The aroma of the jacket was less offensive than it had been, but putting it on, he recalled the last place they went. At the piano sat a man with pink skin and red hair, the albino known as Speckled Red. Next song came a riveting player, Noah Lewis, who sucked, blew, and held more notes out of the harmonica than Arthur knew there were, playing two at once, one held to his nose. He was a man possessed, twisting and rocking while he played, drawing out sounds. Arthur could not think of the name of the place, but the moonshine in a communal bottle that kept coming his way was called White... White... White Mule.

A bit rumpled but with a head somewhat clear, he made his way back to the Daisy. Beale was slightly calmer on a Sunday evening, and Oscar instructed him to remove just two people before midnight, one a simple drunk who went when asked. But another was winning steadily at the craps table, which could not be tolerated. The rolling blues music drowned his protests, and so he produced a knife. Arthur wrenched his forearm one-handed with a mighty twist, and dragged him still grasping the knife, through a boisterous, indifferent crowd, throwing him to the ground outside aside the ticket booth without a word.

Back at his post near the door about an hour later, he noticed a couple emerge from the Monarch down the street and stagger across to the Daisy side. Dressed in a tux and long overcoat and wearing a top hat, carrying a cane, a very large negro appeared to drag his lady friend, who seemed to be struggling against his grasp. They were momentarily obscured by the crowd on the walk, which suddenly parted. The woman was on the ground and he was bent over slapping her face, then grabbed her arm and like a rag doll snatched her to her feet and continued to drag her forward, stopping at the ticket window. The lights shined on the woman's tears.

Arthur blocked their entrance, looking up at the big man. "She can come in. You cain't."

The big man was momentarily surprised, but stepped forward and brought his huge face down to Arthur's and grinned a huge grin with bright yellow teeth. He threw his head back and laughed deeply "HAR, HAR, you and what other niggers going to STOP ME?" He brought the cane hard aside Arthur's neck, knocking him out of the way, and stepped toward the theater door. The commotion spread the handful of people loitering outside. Recovering quickly, Arthur stepped again into his path and came up with his right fist onto the underside of the man's jaw hard enough to break teeth. The cane fell to the ground and as the man's huge black face showed disbelief, his lips curled into a rage, Arthur brought his left fist into his nose with all his might, and the big man dropped to his knees, clutching his face. Arthur picked up the cane, removed the top hat, and struck him square in the middle of his head. Bad Sam's eyes rolled back and he fell over backward, still kneeling. Witnesses would end their tale by telling of the popping sound of his knees.

Though open-eyed, the assailant was still. Blood flowed freely from his nose and his mouth. Still clutching the cane, Arthur stood over him just to make sure, and he felt a hand on his shoulder. He turned quickly. The crying woman was Lizzie.

"You're bleeding."

Oscar was there. "WHAT HAVE YOU DONE? DO YOU KNOW WHO THIS IS?"

Bad Sam's moniker was earned. He ran the notorious Monarch, the Castle of the Missing Men. Troublemakers and those who stirred Sam's ire for one reason or another usually went out the back way, and not always under their own power. Because his back door was directly across the alley from the Monarch's, undertaker Bo 'Peanut' Doyle made a good living off the Monarch.

Lizzie appeared again from inside with a cloth, which Arthur held to the gash in the side of his neck. He had not even felt the blow. He looked at the cane. It had a heavy silver handle shaped like a lion's head, with sharp flanges of flowing mane. Oscar was quite agitated and said he didn't need that kind of crap. As the hearse which doubled as an ambulance pulled up, he said, "Well he ain't gonna be causin' no trouble tonight, but if he survives, you're dead. You look after the door here 'til the last one leaves and then I'll pay you, and you're out."

Arthur offered him the business end of the cane. Turning to go inside as he took it, Oscar grasped the lion's head and unsheathed a long thin knife nearly its length.

Standing on the edge of the street in earshot, the albino piano player Speckled Red, who had witnessed the incident, said to Arthur "Boy, you wanna make some real money? You need to be at the Vintage, fightin'."

"Hold this," Lizzie said. Arthur felt a warmth and wetness at his shirt collar, and let her guide his hand to take over the linen she held to the wound on his neck. Then she was showing him into the ambulance, just loaded in the back with his dazed attacker. He was unconscious by the time they reached the colored hospital, though it was only five blocks. When he woke, eight stitches froze his neck from his left shoulder blade to his scalp and he could not turn his head. He could not figure out where he was and remembered only standing in the path of Bad Sam, and nothing more.

Memphis Minnie dozed in a flowery lounge chair a few feet away. Arthur began to twist and turn as he reached consciousness, and she opened her eyes.

"Doctuh sayed yo head was about to come off, hit was so much blood," said Lizzie. She chuckled. "You might be able to dye yo suit, but you is gone be needin a new shirt." She came over and touched his shoulder. "It ain't too bad really. He said you be better in a few weeks."

"My wallet...," coughed Arthur. "You—"

She put her finger to his lips and leaned her face into his. With her most sultry, teasing look, and a twinkle in her eye, she said "Pay you back... double... when you get better."

When he opened his eyes again he was alone. Morning sunrays had already scrubbed the room, it was almost noon. On his chest was his wallet, empty.

With an operating room, maternity ward, and correctional ward, Collins Chapel Home and Colored Hospital had 75 beds that stayed pretty busy in those days. While Arthur was sewn up, nurses delivered a baby five feet away, on the very same table a man who had overdosed on cocaine and bootleg liquor had convulsed away his life away only an hour before. Another man in a white coat came in and said he could stay until he could stand.

Because he thought it expected (never having been to the doctor), Arthur managed this on the second day and walked out of the Collins wearing the suit of a recent decedent, which fit him perfectly in the pants, but bound considerably in the chest and shirt, wrinkle-free on his powerful frame. Stiff stitch bristles scraped against his shirt collar. But he was only slightly sore, and thinking his movement restored enough that he might load and unload cotton bales, he walked just blocks west to the Mississippi and did just that for the day, loading a barge moored to the wharf stenciled with

The Memphis Helena & Rosedale Packet Company
US MAIL STEAMER

Kate Adams — in massive letters on its side.

The men sang blues while they worked, it was Beale on the river. At dusk, the heavily loaded barge backed out of the wharf boat they had been loading from, and a short round white man paid each worker a dollar. Arthur started toward his hotel. The barge had only just reached the open river and begun to churn upstream against the relentless current when the peal of a bell sounded the return of the *Kate Adams* herself. She brought farmers, levee workers, gamblers, drifters, pickpockets, roustabouts, pimps, and whores (many of those) from Natchez and Rosedale. The dock workers stood and watched the passengers disembark. A trick might be had for two dollars. Someone produced a bottle of moonshine and another a guitar, and the wharf boat became the party.

The east had just begun to glow, beginning to brighten the west across the river when Arthur Campbell awoke in the chilly darkness, on the cobblestones. He saw that he had a badly skinned knee and judged that he must have tried again to go "home", maybe losing his balance on the slippery, round stones. He recalled that he had taken up the company of a lady with the thought of perhaps looking into her favors, and was thus quite relieved to find his dollar in his vest pocket.

It was said the train yard had better paying and more consistent work, and so Arthur found himself walking there, to the very spot he had first come into town. He was immediately put to work driving a trailer to the Cotton Exchange classing rooms in warehouses overlooking the river, just blocks to the north. Cotton shipping by covered rail and fast trucks on improved highways was overtaking river trafficking, for the speed and quality condition the product would arrive. Fine Pima cotton came from the Delta, rerouted from Memphis out to the world on demand, and could be expected at a certain time, dry, free from river rot… barges were hauling only the inferior grades.

At dark, men with no place to go assembled a pot luck dinner of chitlins, greens, and black-eyed peas, and Arthur was offered a spot aboard a decommissioned caboose, so not quite having the funds to return to his hotel on Beale, he thought he might stay awhile. Inside at the far end, near a coal stove sat Manfred Ames, his arm in a sling.

"Boy, where is you been?"

"Broke ma ahm trying ta git on yo train. I'se lucky ta be alive. Stohm liketa froze me ta def."

Manfred fell into a ditch and was collected by the next group to attempt to hop aboard. He lived here at the charity of the rail workers since. His arm was badly swollen and his fingers were blue. A near-empty whiskey bottle was within reach of his good arm.

"Cain't feel nothing, neither."

Arthur reckoned Manfred's paddling days were probably done, and he'd be lucky to keep that arm. "Why you ain't gone to the hospital?"

"They give me a bottle and some beans, and I been gittin' along pretty good, I guess. Ain't no shortage of liquor around here." Manfred coughed and gave a drunken grin.

"Biggest shortage of all is the shortage of common sense," said Arthur. You sure ain't got none, he thought.

February 11, 1926

It took half the next day to get his friend to the Collins Chapel colored hospital on Ayers Street and get him seen by a doctor. Finally, the doctor who had sown up Arthur took a look at Manfred and said something under his breath. Then he said in a hopeful tone "Well, you can't tell too much about a chicken pie till you get through the crust." A nurse came in and washed Manfred's shoulder with Mercurochrome turning his black skin orange. She injected him with morphine and they left him happy.

Dr. Hatfield, the nurse called him, took issue with Arthur's common sense for leaving, but he put some medicine on Arthur's neck and said to come back next week to get his stitches out. When Arthur walked out in the early afternoon, he decided to detour by Beale to see if he could find Lizzie McCoy.

A handwritten sandwich board promised "Memphis Slim, featuring Furry Lewis tonite" at the Ashford's Saloon. Across the street, Memphis Minnie got top billing in the marque of the Lincoln Theater. Arthur approached to knock on the door of the Lincoln and glanced at the establishment across the street: THE VINTAGE. Something about that name was familiar... the albino saying they had big money prize fighting there. It was just after 3 o'clock, quiet as Beale was going to get, so he crossed the street to the Vintage. Because the front doors were locked, he walked around two other clubs to the back alley and twisted the handle of the door he thought might be it. The light from the end of a dark corridor illuminated lockers and open closets. He stepped out into a large room with a polished concrete floor, past pool tables and rows of chairs to the ring illuminated from above, where two fighters were sparring fiercely. One was getting the best of the other, so it seemed, as his fists and head were down, suffering staccato blows. Then suddenly he exploded with a combination that knocked the other man back to the ropes, which launched him onto his knees and then face down.

"HEY! EASY! EASY!" shouted an obese red-faced white man sitting on a tiny stool inside the ropes. "He's got to fight tonight! EVER'T! EVER'T!" Despite his size, he was quick to get into the ring carrying a soaked rag the downed fighter. His sweat-stained shirt said FAPOSI across the shoulders in large white letters. The other fighter was unscathed but for a red smear on his cheek, and threw his arms up and did a dance.

The white man seated in the front row eyed Arthur as he stepped toward the ring. He unplugged a large cigar to speak. "Who are you? What do you want?"

Arthur said, "Yas-suh. I'm Arthur Campbell. I'm a fighter."

11

The Fighter

"Yeah? And I'm Mae West." The man put back his cigar. Arthur could see his patent leather shoes matched the beige color of his suit.

"Niceta meet you, Mistuh West," said Arthur.

Out came the cigar again, and he stared. ""What the... whaddayou mean, boy? You somekinda wise guy?"

"No suh." I'm a fightuh."

Arthur was so stoic, that after a moment Jim Kinney, owner of the VINTAGE and arguably the most powerful man in the community, the unofficial Czar of Beale Street, realized the man had no idea who Mae West was, and he said, "Ah jeez. No shit... OK, I mean, what makes you a fighter? I never seen you. I ain't never seen you and this is my joint, and I know all the fighters. How many fights you won?"

"I won all of 'em," said Arthur.

The kid that had been pummeled was sitting at the edge of the ring holding an ice pack on a growing shiner. His huge coach shouted toward the other side of the gym to the other boxer, disappearing out of the ring light into the shadows: "Everett! You remembah what youse supposed to be doin' tonite, you hear?"

The man with the beige patent leather shoes stood. He was taller than Arthur by perhaps a hand but saw before him a thick black buck that might take a ton of punishment in the ring.

"... and how many would that be?"

"Three, countin' the other night," Arthur answered, truthfully. In the muddy field behind the tiny school house in Bonita when he was about 10 years old, a baseball bat was cracked over his back, breaking one of his ribs. But Arthur got up, and punched, kicked, and beat the 13-year-old batter to the ground, and held his head face down into a mud puddle for almost a minute, such that they wouldn't let him come back to the little school for a month, which was fine with his momma anyway, he could earn 25 cents a day picking cotton.

On his way north from Louisiana, he spent the night on a bench at the Illinois Central Railroad Depot in Hazelhurst, Mississippi, as he waited for the *City of New Orleans* to take him north into the Delta. He wore his only hat, suit, and white shirt. The *City of New Orleans* pulled up at about 10 am, and the station was soon bustling with passengers coming or going. A young white woman's hat was swept from her head by a gust. Arthur collected and returned it, and she smiled. He watched her appreciatively the thirty yards or so to the platform until she climbed into a car.

"What're you lookin' at, boy?"

A large figure stepped into his view and three others circled, two to the side, one in back, "Don't you know no better'n even look at a white woman?" He removed his homburg, revealing a thick bald head that poked neck-less from his shirt collar, like a turtle's. He spoke loudly to passersby: "You know what? This is your lucky day, because I see a nigger needs some learnin', and these boys jest' love to help niggers." Chuckles and snickers from the 'boys'.

Like a fungal outbreak, a gallery started to swell, enlarging by the second. Arthur reached up and swept his hat down so it dropped at his feet. He raised his fists and bowed his head.

Turtle Head said "Whoa, looky here. Here's a nigger thinks he can whoop back. Better...WATCH... OUT" and shoved Arthur toward the man behind him. Arthur jerked his head back violently into the nose of the back fellow, twisted his body to the right, and jammed his elbow into the face of the man there. His right fist shot forward into Turtle's nose, crushing it. Turtle covered his face with his hands, but blood flowed through at the knuckles. The wide-eyed man still standing to Arthur's left took three steps back into the throng, which then dissipated like smoke, fast as it had formed.

And then there was Bad Sam. None of them was much of a fight, and the boxing he had just seen, wasn't either, as it turned out one-sided. But Arthur understood that it was big money if you just got in there and did what you needed to do, and he had thought if the audience got what they were looking for too, well then that was a fine thing, and maybe it could even add to your value from the point of view of the people paying you to fight.

"...so where was you fightin? Chicago? St. Louis?"

"No Suh. I was lookin' afta de doe' of the Daisy Theater. Sunday evenin' last. Mistuh Okscar aks'd me to watch de doe,' and I woun' let a man in. I seen he wuz beatin' on a lady, crost de street, an I woun' let him in."

As had everybody on Beale, Jim Kinney of course had heard somebody cleaned Sam's clock pretty good, and now the guilty party stood before him calling himself a fighter. His scheming mind began to chew on the possibilities.

"Whuddi-jou say your name was?"

"Arthur Campbell, suh... Mistuh West. Is you de man who I needs to talk to, to fight?"

Kinney laughed. "Yes, Arthur. You've come to the right place. Hey, Tony! I want you to meet Arthur Campbell. Arthur's going to take Everett's place tonight. Everett don't look like he's going to mind that too much anyway. That's your coach Tony Faposi, but everybody calls him Fapo."

Faposi made no acknowledgment. "I call him Fat Piece of Shit, 'cause he don't hear so good" said Kinney, louder, " TONY! Get your fat ass over here."

Everett's coach stopped dabbing at his inert fighter finally and twisted himself around to see. With his big red face and long neck he looked like a bull.

"Arthur kicked Bad Sam's bad ass. Ain't that right, Arthur? See if we have some shorts, and gloves he'll fit into, and let's get him dressed out and warmed up. See what he can do... Well, don't just sit there on your fat, wop ass, get on it, man!"

So, within two hours of settling Manfred for repair at the Collins, Arthur was naked to his waist in an oversized pair of purple satin "boardies" which dropped below his knees, and boots he thought might be a little small after all, which were laced to his shins. His hands were buried in huge red padded gloves. At Fapo's weary behest, he started to work the bag. Antonio Faposi put his hands out after a few punches and said, "No, no... make it a combination, like this," and demonstrated— right one, left two, right undercut three, left roundhouse four, and so on. He got winded after doing this twice, and his arm flab slung sweat onto Arthur's face. But Arthur got it down quickly. The rhythm of the train and the blues came to mind. It was just like one of Lizzie's songs. He could speed up and slow down, keeping the rhythm, he was a player, a musician.

Kinney got back to the gym sooner than he expected— Jack McGurn's train from Chicago was right on time. His back to them, Arthur Campell stood to the side punishing the bag with rhythmic intensity, and the two men stopped for a moment to watch. He was impressive at first glance, a light heavyweight with muscled shoulders expanded from a trim waist, but something was not quite right about his timing. He lacked... *finesse*. Kinney said, "That nigger kicked the shit out of Big Bad Sam Jackson, even *after* Sam walloped him in the head with his cane."

McGurn had pulled a cigar from a case in his overcoat, and was patting himself down for his lighter, then remembered leaving it on the table where they had played cards, in the lounge car. *Damn.* "Got a light?"

"He just walked in here a little while ago..." continued Kinney, "I don't know whether he can fight or not, but I put him in a match tonight... might be interesting." Technique won bouts, but the new man at least looked like he had stamina. "We'll see."

"Who's he fightin'?"

"A wild-ass nigger from Atlanta named Tiger Flowers, who was once the Super Middleweight champ."

"C'mon!"

"Seriously. Flowers is past his prime, but he can still punch and he always fights above his class, to try and get back on top. Wins too. He'll kill this fellow. Easy money."

6 pm

February 11, 1926

Bad Sam did not recognize the name of Arthur Campbell when the first runner bounded upstairs at the Monarch with cash for the opening bout at the VINTAGE. Per the word from Kinney, starting odds on the new fighter were set at -200 for Flowers, and +400 for Campbell, meaning $200 would have to be put on Flowers to earn $100, but a $100 bet on Campbell would net $400 should he win. By the time the opening bell, no one had bet on Arthur, and his odds thus rose to +800 and Flowers' to -500. Odds of a draw ballooned to +2500.

The odds on a chalkboard at the "betting window," a framed hole in a street side door, changed every five minutes when runners were dispatched to and returned from the Monarch, until five minutes until the bell. McGurn had made good money on his friend's recommendations and watched the odds swell on the new fighter. He said, "You need to lean on Flowers to throw it."

Kinney said, "Can't my friend. You saw the new one punch. Nobody would buy it."

So McGurn put $1,000 down on Flowers, to win $500, and another $200 for the thing to finish under six rounds, which should pay him another $500. "Easy money," Kinney said.

7 pm

Sunday was a capacity crowd since some of the juke joints were closed. William Christopher Handy himself strode in followed by an entourage of the most notable local blues musicians, including Will Shade, Alberta Hunter, Lizzie McCoy, a.k.a. Memphis Minnie, and Robert Wilkins, yet all had to find seats behind the white folks that came down for Sunday Night Prize Fighting on Beale.

No noticeable appreciation from the spectators followed Faposi as he opened the ropes and Arthur stepped into the ring, but a moment later when Flowers emerged behind his coach, the crowd noise became a roar. In the ring, his coach pulled off his robe to reveal a muscular, compact fighter of 5'10", taller than Arthur by at least a couple of inches. He danced around holding his gloves high and grinning, displaying a mouthful of metal teeth. Arthur stood still, stoic and solemn, his brow and countenance hardly changed. His lighter skin from mouth line down to collarbone made him appear to have a shadow over his face. Eagle eyes focused only on his opponent, no gaze out at the spectators, and Lizzie could not guess what he thought.

At the bell, Arthur strode to the center with his gloves at his face, and the other boxer danced around him. Flowers offered test-reach taps with his right, which was his opener, hoping to surprise with his southpaw hammer. Though he had a few knockouts, Flowers won fights by decision, with points, being generally more nimble than those he fought, wearing them down. It was a minute into the round before he got aggressive with a double combination: jab, straight, hook uppercut, but each punch was met before it could reach its target; Arthur was lightning quick. Neither Arthur's position nor offense changed, he was just a pillar of stone, keeping his body to Flowers with the same protective stance. Ten seconds to the bell, Flowers scored with a left, then right to the ribs, but with little apparent effect, and except for the fixed stare the round ended without aggression from Arthur.

"Boy you ain't gonna do shit unless you start punchin'," berated Faposi, "You cain't wear out this kid or out-wait him, he's gonna do that to YOU. Your only chance is to catch him when he closes, that's his style. Use it against him."

Round two: Flowers came out punching. A wild combination: a right which was easily met glove to glove, his body behind a powerful attack from the left finding only air, then a weak right hook, but which glanced the stitches on Arthur's neck that until now, because it was healing well and located just below his hairline, not even Faposi had noticed. But Arthur contacted Tiger Flowers in the chin with his mighty left then, popping Flowers's head back so that he took a couple of steps backward to work his jaw, which was so painful he thought it might be dislocated. The crowd noise shifted to high. The referee bade them to come together. Flowers tried to shake it off and buy a moment, dancing around. By now it was clear Campbell was not a punching machine, he was reasonably safe outside, but inside, carelessness could be costly. Then he saw blood seeping from Arthur's neck on his left, and resolved to concentrate there.

Round three: Flowers went to work on Arthur's neck, raining blows and jabs to try and open up the tear. Arthur met these two out of three and only weaker jabs touched him, but blood was starting to flow. Flowers decided to end it by closing in, getting in Arthur's face, clutching his opponent until the ref pulled them apart, then striking with a right hook to the neck at the sweet spot. It was a mistake. Arthur managed to counter every move, and when the ref pulled them apart for the second time, he ducked his head and pummeled Flowers in the ribs with his powerful left, then a right to the solar plexus, two blows that dropped the lighter man to the mat gasping. Arthur stepped back for the count, his face unchanged, but blood was flowing freely from his neck, dripping onto his shorts and the mat where he stood.

At the count of nine, Flowers leaped to his feet, almost at the sound of the bell ending the round. Every person in the place was on their feet screaming. Arthur heard only Faposi, who held ice in a towel to his neck. "You can finish this. You can. You got to. You gone bleed to death if you don't. Do it THIS time. Drop him!"

McGurn glared at his friend. "What the HELL!" I thought you said this was easy money!"

Kinney said weakly, "Nobody knew this guy was a slugger. Hang in there. Flowers is the experienced one."

Round Four: Arthur had a newfangled Band-aid on his neck now, bright against his dark skin. Again Flowers danced around him, appearing to taunt him. Again Arthur turned his body to his opponent, automatically, slow as a tank turret. Fighting in close was Flowers's strength, but he had a different tact now— survival. His right dropped a bit to protect a broken rib, less painful than holding it up. He threw a half-right that pulled up short and followed with a left uppercut, but Arthur simply stepped back out of reach. Flowers tried it again: half right, left uppercut. Swing and a miss. Arthur stepped in and threw a right hook, uncharacteristically aggressive, forcing Flowers to defend with his left, then Arthur drove his left with the full force of his powerful frame into the ribs Flowers had been protecting, knocking the man spectacularly off his feet. It was over.

The room erupted.

12

Chess

2012

I thought of the chess piece. "Lemme show you something." Will followed me to the bookcase. I reached up and handed him a detailed six-inch walnut wood figure carving, a man in a heavy coat and hip waders standing on a square pedestal a half-inch tall, his right hand clutching the handle of a paddle, blade down at his feet. His other hand held a duck by the neck. The wood carver's stylized technique exaggerated angles and size in facial features, which could be a suggestion of race. Seeing it up there every day, but only now telling the tale of Arthur's wayward youth did I think of it. Now I couldn't wait to explain. "Do you know what this is?"

"It's a statue of... a hunter? I always thought it was curious that he didn't have a gun. But I've seen it up there."

I handed it to him. "Arthur made it."

"What?"

"It's part of a chess set. Arthur was a guide— a paddler, and there was another colored paddler actually named Bishop. So these were the bishops. It was amazing."

"Arthur played chess?"

"Absolutely. Arthur taught me to play chess. I think a club member, I believe it was a friend of Big Charlie's, taught him to play. The Robinsonville clubhouse was where he lived sometimes between seasons, and I think he worked on this after his Beale Street adventures... or... my god, I forgot. Arthur went down to Greenville on account of a woman and almost died during the 1927 flood. He was caught up in the crevasse when the levee gave way in Mound City. I'll have to tell you what I know of that amazing story. Anyway, he got back to Robinsonville and spent time recovering.

"What were the other pieces? Do you have any of them?"

"Aw... there's no tellin' what happened to them. The club shut down when the war started, and this was in the box of lures Arthur made, which he gave me. It's in the attic somewhere... I think. I always thought it was a 'second', a less-than-perfect one, maybe his first try, which he decided he could improve. So, maybe the set is intact somewhere, but I doubt it."

Will held it under the lamp over his shoulder. "Were the white bishops white people?"

"No. There weren't any white paddlers. They were... it's walnut, so maybe it was one of the black pieces. Walnut for the dark pieces and poplar or maple for white or something like that. Had to be something he could get in north Mississippi. I saw the whole set when I was probably about thirteen. The King and Queen were standing hunters, male, and female, like Mother and Dad, you know... holding shotguns. Queens had their guns aimed at the sky... you know, Arthur was always telling me to be a gentleman, the ladies always got the first shot. And, let's see... I remember the knights were dogs, black and white labs. Duck calls or maybe shotgun shells were the rooks, but the pawns were really amazing— all ducks, each carved on a tiny block like it was swimming, so they would stand up the same height. The blocks themselves had ripples like water where the duck disappeared into it, and some of them were diving, tail up. Each side had at least one duck flaring, leaping into the air, with the wooden splash supporting the escaping duck. I thought they were masterpieces.

"Incredible! What that would be worth... Shoot, sounds like a fun project, for another life. I love wood carving and the smell of fresh-cut wood- but my hands get blisters. I'm sure it took forever."

"Well," I said, "you know Arthur had all the time in the world then. He was convalescing."

The winter of record cold, Robinsonville Hunting Club

January 1936

Cooper Permuter was some kind of writer, Arthur recalled. Fighting temps in the teens to kill ducks all day sent most members to bed after dinner, but he would sit up late tending a scotch, studying his chess board. Permuter sat against the largest single window before a chess set, sheathed in the oiled canvas greatcoat he hunted in, with its collar of thick lambswool. The fireplace pushed back the cold in the great room, except at the window, but that's where he liked to be, pondering moves and moonset, while he marveled at the stars. Arthur freshened Mr. Permuter's drink, knowing when to top it off a finger or drop in a cube.

"You play chess, Arthur?"

"No suh."

"Ahhh. Well, we need to fix that. Chess is at once the simplest, but most complicated, the most cerebral game man has devised, because it tells us all about science, warfare, and who we are. Are you a thinking man, Arthur?"

"Yass suh."

Member-to-paddleman conversations were not as rare after hours, when liquor could limit the condescension, and some drunk needed a rhetorical sounding board, or thought he offered humanity. Late evenings, club attendants acquiesced wearily.

Want to learn?"

Before Arthur opened his mouth to respectfully decline, Permuter said, "Sit."

So began Arthur's first chess game. He rose at 3:30 am, guided and paddled white men sometimes a mile-and-a-half to hunt for four or five hours in 18-degree temperatures (when the outboards wouldn't run), calling ducks most of the time, paddled through ice hundreds of yards into the willows to recover the kill, shooting cripples when their aim was off, and paddled the same distance back to the club. Sometimes a member would have a dog to retrieve the kill, but not on the coldest days. At noon, Arthur lay down for half an hour, then at high season away they went for the afternoon hunt. Washing his face upon his return, he shed his waders for a white jacket and black tie, and served in the kitchen and later, at the bar.

But shortly... he was fascinated.

"Attack. Think ahead. Attack. Think ahead. Sacrifice."

Permuter was a good teacher. A chronic insomniac, he thought he might sculpt a sparring partner at best, a punching bag at worst, as no one kept his hours, nor shared his passion for the game. He allowed Arthur to retire after the lesson, but only with the promise of a match on the morrow.

It was sleeting at 4:30 am Keehn Thornberry was present for the morning draw, as was Snowden Barney, the youngest son of a wealthy Memphis cotton merchant— one of the founding members. Young Barney had the duty of entertaining their Indian guest, for whom the entire spectacle, including the weather, was delightful. Barney had also asked for Arthur Campbell, but the senior members got to choose their paddlers, and so Arthur paddled the humorless Thornberry to his favorite blind.

Despite the inclement weather, they had a fine hunt. Arthur played virtuously on his instrument and the waterfowl fell all over them. Dr. Thornberry shot a huge banded pintail which almost lit on the blind, such that it folded up and struck him, knocking off his hat. He thought this a story like a hole-in-one, all day it evolved in the telling. The gadwall and eight greenheads piled under their guns also evidenced a productive morning.

Barney's Indian landowner-client-guest, said to be the great, great, great, great-grandson of the Shah who built as a tomb for his Persian wife the Taj Mahal... had fallen into the water in the 20-degree north Mississippi weather reaching for a cripple. He shivered happily, holding a mug of bourbon, watching his very foreign, drab, heavy clothes raise steam by a roaring fire, trying to think how to explain the day to his father, and for the first time in his life thought... that he might not.

Mr. Permuter was there in the den when the hunting party returned. He seemed to enjoy simply the serenity of the place and of course his liquor. Arthur could not recall a day that he had actually hunted in the couple of years he had been around.

"Ahhh, Arthur," he said, "ready to try out your newfound skill?"

When brunch was set and the handful of members about was sated and began to gather themselves to leave for home or retire for a nap, Arthur found himself sitting at the chilly window where he had received his first exposure to the game just hours before.

Cooper Permuter used his first several moves to advance pawns. Arthur could not understand this when one had so much power at his command. He leaped forward with a rook, drawing an attack from the queen. Arthur took the queen in the sixth move of the game, inspiring Cooper Permuter to later document the experience thusly:

> *I created a monster. I began the game playing as a beginner would, planning to point out the error of my own moves as the game progressed. In this way, I teach, and I hoped to demonstrate to Arthur, in his first game, possibilities; force him to think ahead– the lesson I begin with my journalism students. This man, a negro of questionable literacy, a paddler at a duck club in the north Mississippi Delta, kicked my ass. He was two moves ahead of me from the moment I opened my front line; he saw my weaknesses, my exposure. I was in check three times, the first time before we were ten minutes into the game. I had to marshal my greatest skills, call up plays I knew from studying the best responses in chess, the greatest all-time moves... and just barely won the game.*
>
> *This was no accidental stumbling, but a sophisticated grasp. Have I been had? Is someone else present? I think I know the answer. Arthur wears a mask. He plays an ignorant Step-and-Fetch-It so that his greatest weapon... is surprise. In time, however, I found a man reasonably con-*

tent with who and where he is, and what the world, the white *world, wants with, and without him.*

Subsequent matches were ever more challenging. But Permuter kept up his guard, and it was not until more than a year later, in the late fall of 1937, that he gave up a game. Arthur offered to teach the other paddlers the game of chess, but no one had time or patience. Because he could only be found playing late hours with Permuter, few knew of Arthur's growing skill, until one legendary evening.

The cypress-lined oxbow cutoff hunter's paradise which was Robinsonville Hunting Club had come to be the coveted retreat of select Southern gentlemen, but manners were not among the original written prerequisites for club membership. Milford Richards's ruthless industrialist father had been a founding member in 1883. Training inherent in a lifetime of entitlement, Milford's son Jamie carried on the family tradition of assholery: control and the incessant belittling of others. The University of Mississippi freshman was a know-it-all and bully. Permuter noted fewer members when the Richards were present and wondered if the two were related.

This particular balmy 40-degree morning Warren Oates, his wife, and their paddler, Nate, glided up to the blind Oates had drawn last evening, to find Milford and his son Jamie already installed. It was a large hole, and Oates simply smiled and they occupied the other blind structure, aligned at 45,°over the whispered objections of Nate. Jamie then committed the unpardonable sins of the lowest sportsman: leaping up prematurely to get the first shot, consistently shooting before Mrs. Oates, before the ducks were on their final lowest pass. The last volley of the morning he jumped up first and shot the leading mallard in a large group falling all over them, then turned and dropped the gray duck just sailing into Mrs. Oates's line of sight the second before she fired, a double. His idiot father came in bragging about Jamie's shooting.

Richards noted the chess board on the card table and began to talk of his son's victories on the chess team at times through dinner. Permuter knew the others had had enough of the Richards, and decided to set a trap. He gulped the rest of his scotch and stood.

"I don't believe you are so hot. In fact, I will bet you the negro who runs this club could beat your dumbass, loud-mouthed son."

"I beg your pardon?"

There were only three other members at the table, two with wives, but all conversation ceased. Arthur was pouring Olivia Oates a glass of burgundy.

"You are a blowhard, and your son is a spoiled horse's ass. I am told it runs in the family. What I said was, Arthur Campbell could beat you or your son in any chess game."

Jamie stood, with balled fists. His father held up his hand.

"Mr... Permitter or something? I don't believe I was speaking to you—"

"Are you up to a little contest?"

"— but regardless, don't be ridiculous."

"Let's make it interesting. If Arthur wins, you are banned from the club for the remainder of the season."

Richards said "HA!" and started to guffaw. Seeing no one laughing and feeling all eyes, he looked up at Cooper and his eyes narrowed. "What could you have that I could possibly want when we win?"

"If you or whoever plays for the Richards wins, I will tutor your imbecile offspring in civility, or English, or enter your service in whatever way you direct for the same amount of time remaining, two weeks."

His face flushed with wine, Milford Richards also stood. "This is preposterous, I will not be spoken to this way, nor play your ridiculous game." He felt dizzy and stumbled into a stuffed chair. Pulling himself up again slowly, he said, "C'mon Jamie." and started toward the bedrooms.

"Dad, you don't think I can beat a nigger? Shit. Set up the fuckin' board, boy."

The match lasted less than an hour. Jamie Richards's tentative setup, in a rush of pawns, left his vitals open, no match for Arthur's power moves, and saying not a word, he made swift work of the Richards kid. Jamie's King was cornered, subject to attack on three sides by the only remaining white pieces on the table, Arthur's Knight, his last Bishop, and pawn. Checkmate. Jamie Richards kicked over the table and stormed out, and father and son were gone by breakfast.

13

Cold Dreams

0800

April 4, 1942

A ranking Japanese army officer, *Rikugun Shōsa Something Unpronounceable*, (Army Major) no one had seen before came into the jail and spoke to the men in English, calling out by name eight officers: Commander A. J. Maher, Lieutenant Commander W. J. Galbraith, Lieutenant T. F. Payne, Lieutenant R. B. Fulton, Lieutenant J. F. Dalton, Lieutenant H. G. Kirkpatrick, Lieutenant W. J. Winslow and First Lieutenant F. E. Gallagher, Marines Corps. They were marched out, and there was no more word of their whereabouts or condition.

April 13, 1942

HOUSTON and PERTH survivors were loaded into the back of troop-carrying vehicles and trucked to Batavia, to be housed at a Dutch Military camp that had housed the Tenth Battalion Bicycle force, in the center of the city. There was electricity and drinkable water and latrine "facilities." Pogue rejoined them and shared something he heard aboard another truck: the eight officers extracted from the jail the week before had been removed to a camp outside of Tokyo, which seemed to communicate their immediate fate at least, was intense interrogation.

0800

May 14, 1942

A National Guard unit from Texas, the Second Battalion, 131st Field

Artillery, Thirty-Sixth Division, the only other American troops, were marched through the camp gates. Their arrival was precipitous, they helped shore up the physical and moral backbone so many would survive what was to come. They came in with extra clothes, shoes, and funds to help supplement the diets of many of the prisoners, Deane and his men included.

The group solicited the somewhat relaxed Commandant to allow one American POW to go into town to buy food from the Chinese merchants at Tanjung Priok. Typically out in front, Larkin Edmonson volunteered. He went into town once a week, returning with all the tins of food he could carry, which helped the men temporarily regain some of their health. The snippet of freedom usually also enabled him to learn something of the war and their forsaken corner of the earth, however minimal. On one notable excursion, at great personal risk he returned with batteries hidden in one of the tins. Deane had commented they needed to assemble a radio, and surely one of the engineers could manage this. The batteries were buried under a wooden step inside the concrete barracks, but no additional parts were obtained before the prisoners were suddenly moved, unable to recover them.

Deane and other American officers were sent to the docks at Tanjung Priok for several weeks to unload gasoline, bombs, ammunition, guns—everything used to fight a war. From the very first day, they became saboteurs: sugar in fuel tanks, filings in a bullet lathe so it would work at first, then seize up... Other groups were sent to motor transport sections at different places around the city to label spare parts for trucks and tanks, tasks which provided opportunities for simple misrepresentation if not outright destruction of the property. Anything to impede. To say this work was enjoyable would be a great stretch, but they were somewhat on the battlefront again, and of course, the labor relieved the stifling tedium of everyday life in the camp.

The Japanese more or less let them be during these weeks, with two notable exceptions: on June 14 the HOUSTON survivors and a handful of the 131st returned to camp to find all POWs standing in the yard. The order was issued for every prisoner to sign a "no escape" oath. No officer moved forward to answer or respond, and shortly the order was refused outright. For forty-five minutes the men stood at attention in the late afternoon heat, until they were simply... dismissed. It was a small victory, yet one greatly relished... for a while.

For their insubordination, there would be no food or water for the rest of the day. The prisoners were packed into their huts. Outside at least there might be a breeze to help dry their foul clothes, but still, the men's spirits rose a bit. With barely room enough to stand most tried to rest sitting with their arms around their shins. Deane looked at the red scar on his knee and tried to remember when he got it. Alongside him was bunched one of the newest arrivals in their camp, Army Corporal Louis Hahn. Hahn had been a Golden Gloves boxer, taking the bronze in the 1936 Olympics in Berlin, losing to Italian Gavino Matta, who lost the gold to Nazi Willy Kaiser. Losing to a wop who lost to a kraut haunted him still. The last weeks had started to toll on his sturdy physique. Wracked with dysentery, he was very pale, his head on his knees. He said, "I can't remember the last time I was cool. Or cold."

Deane closed his eyes...

4:30 am

Lucian Walterlane was already in the kitchen with Arthur Campbell, learning to make Arthur's famed homemade biscuits. A huge country breakfast was assembled: grits, scrambled eggs, bacon, and chicory coffee from New Orleans's French Quarter. Still sleeping were his weekend guests, his son's new in-laws, the Smith family, and their long-time friends, the Levelles of Nashville.

Deane slept fitfully, images of Katherine Levelle and stories of duck hunting in the Delta cold followed him to bed. Rousted by the wonderful smells, he began layering his body with cold-weather gear.

He stepped outside in the darkness and bitter cold, his breath heavy in the air like auto exhaust, and peered hopefully at the craft in the boathouse. The large olive john boat with a boxlike cab that could protect its occupants from the elements, the legendary boat of many stories the night before— was uselessly embedded in several inches of ice.

"The Queen Mary," Lucian had explained, "will probably not see action until spring or this weather breaks."

John Levelle gently opened the door to his daughter's room a crack and whispered into the darkness, "Katherine, Honey, it's time to go."

On Thursday, guides Arthur, Manny, and Moses had dragged several smaller craft from their cradles, dangling by ropes in the barn, and shoved them over the right side of the levee. Crashing down on a two-inch skin of ice, one boat skated almost out of reach. Wind and waterfowl kept the lake mostly open, but the ice extended a hundred yards out to just past the last of the willows. While the others got their breakfast, the paddlers donned hip boots and broke it up for twenty yards out, thin enough for the bough to make headway under paddle power if necessary. If the Evinrudes were finicky in the cold, the paddlers would have to recover ducks by boat or in their waders; it was too cold for the dogs.

In the east, behind the woods at the far edge of the swamp, there was the barest hint of dawn. Shortly, the hunting parties loaded into the boats: Wilson Smith, his son Deane, and Arthur loaded into the first boat, John Levelle, daughter Katherine and paddler Moses into the other. The paddlers began to push the group toward the brightening glow and the duck blinds a half-mile across the water.

"Deane, get your waders on, son," his father called in a shouted whisper. "Unless you want to go swimmin'." He turned back around and continued talking to Arthur, pointing excitedly at the thousands of ducks in the air against the growing daylight to the east.

Only then did Deane see that everyone wore waders but he. Arthur had laid out a pair for him. And that's right where they were, on the ground next to the barn.

With a bitter wind at their backs, they closed quickly on the willows hiding the duck blinds named for the beloved, long-deceased retrievers Chessie and Peak. Far beyond the blinds, the sounds of hundreds of ducks jumping up in alarm replaced the sudden quiet, and just feet away the calls of a wondrous congregation and hundreds of pairs of beating wings filled the air overhead. It was getting light.

"Shootin' time in 5 minutes," said Arthur. "We can spread out and have us a dove shoot."

The wind's bite lessened and Deane unwrapped his muffler a little. The thermometer at the barn had read fifteen degrees. Ice plates on the willows, plateaus three inches above the water, marked yesterday's level. Only Arthur seemed unaffected, motoring straight ahead into the biting wind, calling out for them to brace when there were stumps.

Wilson Smith turned back around. He asked, "You got any waders, boy?"

"Uhm, no sir."

"Well, then this is where you get out. Arthur, let's get him into that blind. I'll shoot from the boat and we can pick up cripples."

Arthur paddled over to behind an outcropping of thick brush hiding an opening into a lean-to-like structure covered with willow brush and other cut foliage. To hold the boat steady against the blind, he grasped a thick willow with his right hand. Setting down the paddle in the crook of his other arm, Arthur beckoned Deane Smith forward with an outstretched glove.

"Don' fo-git yo' gun."

Deane shifted the gun case and shell case handles to one arm and stepped unsteadily across the boat. He was about to step up onto the icy gunwale, but Arthur caught his arm and steadied him.

"Wait. Take my hand," Arthur said. "Step over."

Tossing the gun and shell case to the blind floor, Deane shifted his weight to crawl in when Arthur seized his right hand, an iron vise even through the heavy leather glove. The light was minimal, but Deane saw Arthur's eyes were very bright, focused on his.

Arthur said, "It might be hard. It will *be..." The boat stopped rocking. Deane thought that was his cue to continue, but he could not move. There was power in the grip, something that said "LISTEN!" Their gaze re-locked.*

Arthur said, "You will *come home."*

After another long moment, Arthur's grip loosened, and his glance moved to the blind. Deane shook off his confusion and hefted his butt onto the wood floor. Using a sculling draw Arthur backed the boat away. As if to address the puzzled look on his son's face, Wilson added, "Good luck," before the two melted back into the dawn.

The warped plank floor had gaping spaces between boards, which were covered in an inch of ice. Deane slipped trying to stand, his knee came down hard on a nail head. For the cold, he hardly thought about it until they returned, but it healed into a scar he would have for life.

The odd exchange with the guide, Arthur Campbell, was still fresh in his mind, and Deane didn't think to remove his gloves, so he fumbled opening a box of shells, dropping a couple onto the floor, which tumbled through the spaces and into the water. He cracked the gleaming, tooled barrel and pushed in a shell. It went in deep, past the brass. Is it supposed to do that? He looked closely at a shell still in his hand. Manny gave him 16 gauge shells, too small for the 12 gauge shotgun he held.

BLAM! BOOM! BOOM! The others began to blast ducks from the sky. Over the top of the willows, he could see huge clouds of ducks raise up with each volley, only to settle immediately back down. The boat moved off after downed ducks. Fifty mallards began sailing to set down 10 feet away in the open water in front of the blind. The shooting got more intense. Every few minutes he'd hear shouting his way: "DEANE, over your head!" Followed by: "Wake up, boy!"

His growing embarrassment over their enthusiasm added to his frustration. Where'd these shells come from? Manny. *"Well, shit." What am I supposed to do? He knew his father would say... 'nothing, you are a guest.'*

He mellowed a bit watching the sailing ducks, catching the wind just right, seesawing down all around him to light with a splash amidst a handful of weatherbeaten decoys. It occurred to him that the blind was ideally positioned to take advantage of their inclination to approach facing the southeast wind. It was a shooter's dream. Wood ducks, greenheads, gadwalls, pintails—each perfectly displayed for an instant just feet away, just like the poses he saw so often on people's walls. The cacophony of shotgun blasts bothered them not at all. Twenty or thirty groups working the immediate area flared only slightly and settled back down to sacrifice themselves.

A faint shout floated over the stir: "CD!! Deane!" *blah blah...something... blah blah* "...O.K.?" *was all he could make out. He shouted he was, leaving out the part about freezing his ass off. He could only watch the continued assault. A string of hundreds, maybe thousands of geese appeared far to the north, undulating white, gray, and black specs crossing the sky in an organized V. This pattern had always struck him as almost mystical. Seeing them, he could just make out their chirps and squeals, thinking he might not have heard if he hadn't known they were there. Someone on the ground answered them. The line shuddered slightly, then a rift formed in one of the sides, and a hundred or so broke off, dropping fast. More calls came from below, and the descenders broke up into little groups of tens and twenties and began to work the area. About half of these disappeared below the tree line to the north.*

"And I don't have any goddamned shells," *he said in frustration.*

"I have shells," *came a feminine voice.*

Katherine Levelle was visible about thirty feet away through a hole in the brush covering the structure. In the water to her waist, close to the limit of her waders, she advanced slowly, leading a trail of muddy, cloudy water that wound back fifty yards through the cypress trees.

"*You came to bring me shells?*" *Deane was incredulous.*

"*Your father was wondering why you weren't shooting.*"

She wore aviator's sunglasses glasses and her hair was tucked under a camouflaged cap with flaps that reminded him of Sherlock Holmes. If she hadn't spoken he'd have thought it was one of the men.

"*I was closest so I was elected,*" *she said, hefting her gun from its traveling position on her neck into the crook of her elbow.*

"*How'd you know I needed shells?*"

"*How'd I know? What do you think?*" *She looked at him with a frowning smirk that made him regret the question.* "*Besides,*" *she said,* "*Manny told me he thought he might have handed you the wrong ones. Made me promise not to tell. Here.*" *She handed him her gun and twisted around to reach a shell case that hung from her shoulder like a handbag, (somehow he could no longer picture her carrying a handbag) and pulled out a box of 12 gauge shotgun shells.*

"*Manny? He stayed with Lucian Walterlane. Only Arthur and Moses were with us,*" *he said.*

"*Right.*"

"*So when'd he tell you this?*"

"*When your boat was pulling away.*"

"*Well, why didn't you—*"

"*Shhhh! Get down!*" *She took her gun back quickly and crouched down a little, motioning for him to do the same.* "*Load your gun, quick!*" *Her face looked skyward and he turned around to see.* "*Don't look!*"

Falling around them was a cinder block hailstorm of geese. He cracked the double-barreled side-by-side, quickly slid in two shells, and snapped it shut. Katherine had her gun at her shoulder. He picked out a gander that seemed about to land in the blind and pulled the trigger—BOOM. With great excite-

ment, he watched the huge splash as the big snow goose bit the dust thirty feet out front. Katherine shot twice, and he heard two more splashes. She reloaded. His second shell was spent shooting way behind a flaring gander. Katherine drew a bead on it, now at least 40 yards and climbing, and fired. It crumpled up like a stone and dropped straight down into the center of the decoys. She smiled at him calmly.

"Thanks for the shells," he said, grinning. It was the only thing he could think of.

Deane came to in the same position- forehead down on his knees. The story had always been a memory of Katherine to cherish, he had not thought of the strange words uttered by the guide that showed him into a duck blind for *years*.

Someone had given up space and Corporal Hahn, soaked with sweat, lay on his back, staring, vacant. Deane could not know what lay ahead, but he saw no harm in offering a few hopeful words. He said, "We WILL make it. We ARE going to go home."

As time passed, when he dreamed, his mind created images and sensory experiences of abundant food and drink: country club spreads of fruits, fish, cheese, prime rib, cakes... Dreams of family or friends fell off. After nine weeks as a POW, Deane found he could no longer consciously bring Katherine Levelle's lovely face to mind. He tried to see the athletic tomboy in her aviator glasses, who made chest waders fashionable, bringing him shells, but the image would not materialize, only snippets of their budding romance, their conversation... was it imagined? The line separating real and unreal blurred.

That night, Deane began the journal he would keep for over three years. He chronicled their struggle to evade capture, and the inexhaustible cruelty of their captors, including the bashing the men endured on long marches, when the speed of travel was insufficient for the Japanese, and men were gashed in the head with rifle butts. He wrote in tiny script, a kind of shorthand he could decipher, on rice paper made available by their captors. Paper and pencil were somewhat available, here and there. Captive men may want to please their masters and earn better treatment, and in moments of regulated despair may even be inspired to share details that would not have to be beaten out of them.

Deane wrote about examples he hoped would one day be a historical document. The details of the torture and cruelty they experienced then would not be remarkable very soon. Men were pushed for many miles in suffocating heat, with no water, and no shoes, across rocks and gravel and melting asphalt.

A small party of American and Australian stragglers who had found each other was discovered asleep on the side of a road by Java natives. As Deane's group had been, they were turned over to the enemy. The commanding officer reported that their motley party walked shoeless, herded by soldiers, until they were led into a schoolhouse to rest. The radioman, whose feet were nothing but one blister from heel to toe, had the soles of his feet ripped off by a Jap private with a pair of tweezers, who then poured iodide over them and ordered him outside, back onto the gravel path.

In the evenings, when his account made it to the present, Deane rolled the notes as tight as straw and stuck them into a stick of bamboo, and fitted it back into the space he had reamed out. Discovery of his record could not be risked.

July 4

1750

Deane wrote:

I had been out on a working party and returned. Coming in through the gate, I noticed all the prisoners of the camp lined up again. Passing the commandant's office, I marched my troops up and halted in front of the guard-

house. *The officers were called out separately.* A note was stuck in my face which said, "If you do not sign the oath, your life will not be guaranteed."

I was then taken by the guard into the rear room of the guardhouse to a room where there were several senior officers and hut commanders. We were not allowed to talk or smoke and stood there at rigid attention for 45 minutes. Other guards came in and marched us across the compound where the Japs had their quarters, into a hangar-like building where a dozen soldiers against one side trained their weapons on us as we entered. Each made a show of standing, driving home the bolt on his rifle, and aiming it at the head of the next man that passed. It was simply a bullying show of force, but at the time we thought it was a firing squad. Already assembled in the room under the aim of the guns, were all other officers in the camp.

The commandant appeared and made a speech, in Japanese, that went on for several minutes. Then a lessor officer stood and crudely translated it: if we did not sign the oath, all the officers would be shot.

The senior warrant officers conferred, and it was decided the oath was being made under duress, was thus not binding. The officers signed it, and Brigadier Blackman, VC, the camp commander for allied prisoners, told the men to sign.

Because of the initial refusal, the four camp kitchens were cut to two, and thus food was cut by a third. A new commandant, far less verbose, but far more interested in inflicting misery, replaced him, and conditions got much worse. Now, prisoners were required to bow to all Japanese soldiers, whether they were colonels or privates. The men ignored this at first, consistently resulting in a crack across the chops with a rifle butt or whatever was handy. One beating during the "learning" period resulted in the death of a prisoner, an Australian Captain. Senior men now called their prisoners to attention and bowed or saluted when any member of the Japanese forces passed.

Ironically, showing respect for the Japs got easier when it became regimented. Though the lowest-ranking teenagers had to be saluted, they had to be respected in a different way than the higher-ranking officers. The

"*Kay Ray*" was a bow of fifteen degrees from the waistline, with hands held rigidly at the sides while bowing. Enlisted required this bow, whether they passed once or a hundred times a day, or the prisoner was sure to receive a rifle butt or a fist or backhand in the face. The men got into the habit of holding their arms as required, but their hands in the one-finger salute. The "*Saka Kara*" was a bow for officers and people of importance: a forty-five-degree bend, starting and stopping at the waistline, the position which had to be held until told to come to rest. Because the men were starting to suffer dysentery and other afflictions, this was difficult at best, and more beatings were delivered over this than any other single "offense."

August 1942

Jonasson and Wilson, and men from other barracks were plucked at random, it seemed at first, from a line of Deane's men returning from the Tanjung docks, and set to work with other "recruits" building a dike on a river about a mile from camp. Over several weeks, the men dug canals to feed a ditch that led to the camp for drinking water, and a rice paddy adjacent for irrigation. Jonasson reported that building the dike, each man carried a yoke, a heavy pole across the shoulders with a bucket on each side loaded with rocks, to dam the shallow river and redirect it. Jonasson, the engineer, was struck across the face with a bamboo stick (splitting his upper lip) when he offered a harness solution that was superior to the equipment provided by the Japanese lieutenant in charge. So the men continued the work in the most inefficient, backbreaking way for three weeks, until the dike was of sufficient height and strength to direct enough water into the canal and the ditches.

It was clear then that at least the men on this detail were chosen because they appeared strong, and were not senior officers. The water was supposedly boiled, but it was distributed to the men after only a simmering, and many, including Wilson, were stricken with amoebic dysentery. This would especially heighten the misery of all very soon.

14

Hell Ships

0545

October 1, 1942

The guards appeared in the barracks at dawn, rousting POWs with hollow bamboo poles cracked across sleeping men's shins or bare feet, while another beat on the concrete walls in a rhythm. In short order, the camp was at attention in the courtyard and the majority of the Americans were separated, sent on a march the five kilometers to the port of Tanjung Priok. Deane found Edmonson, Jonasson, and Pogue in the haggard line. Though reasonably strong, Edmonson was showing severe wear. All were suffering from bowel cramps. Deane was afraid he also had dysentery, confirmed when he risked stepping out of line for a particularly explosive crap on the side of the road.

With rations down to a third, sticky rice with some kind of liquid in it, not quite a soup, there wasn't much in a man's system to account for the volume being ejected. It was mostly liquid, dehydrating sufferers to levels more dangerous than they had been conditioned to endure the last months. Some relief came from the tea the men made from banana peels discarded by the Japs.

Deane hoped there would be rest for the men of the HOUSTON when they returned, but what must be the mission of so many… on foot? Would they be coming back? His fears were realized when their march continued up to and aboard the long plank onto the rusty freighter DAI NICHI MARU, and then down into the holds. One man per ton, the DAI NICHI MARU was a two-thousand-ton ship. Into these miserable giant metal toilets were already stuffed with so many there was no room to lie down or sit. Buckets of rice and putrid water were lowered into the holds once a day and once a day men were allowed topside to evacuate their bodies and breathe for a few precious moments, then it was back into the stench of more than a thousand men with dysentery, or be beaten if one lingered topside for too long.

After three days it was difficult to know whether it was day or night, unless you were close to someone who had recently been up, or the ship dropped anchor. This occurred at sunset because apparently, the captain had no charts of those waters. On the fifth day, the DAI NICHI MARU put to port in Singapore. Deane slipped on excrement and banged his temple on the hatch unloading, but by the time they were trucked to the military barracks at Changi on the southern end of the island, he could not remember what was the source of his bruise. His eye was swollen, but the pain was not enough to distract from the constant gnawing in his stomach, and there was palpable relief in the group, being in the fresh air. So stuffed were they in the open trucks, there was no danger of falling. Exhausted men slept standing up.

Changi was a large military installation before the war and the Japanese had divided it into five sections set apart by barbed wire. British prisoners were sent here after the fall of Singapore and occupied the permanent barracks and encampments. When necessary to get from one section to another, groups of prisoners had to be "ferried" across a no man's land, open areas of several acres, where prisoners were not allowed and must be accompanied by traitorous Indian Sikh soldiers, or sometimes a British officer, always bearing a Japanese flag.

Though bowing and saluting were also required here, and the food was worse than in Batavia, their existence was relatively peaceful for the next three months. Japanese were sparse in the areas where most of the HOUSTON survivors lived. But, rare was the man free of dysentery or malaria or beriberi, one or more, and their prayers took on a more urgent entreaty, for liberation, greater rations, news, and sustained rest.

0600

January 7, 1943

The American troops were herded and stuffed and trucked for a half day to a rail station, loaded onto rail cars like cattle. The smokestack belched ember-laden smoke into their cars for two days, choking them and layering upon them oily filth.

January 9

When they were unloaded from the car, and Deane's eyes adjusted to the dim of dawn, he saw they were being marched toward a ship with MOJI MARU stenciled on the side. It was a ship like the rusty freighter that had been their last vessel. Moored aft was the NITTA MEI MARU, another ship of about the same size, but each had a three-inch gun both on the bow and the stern. The prisoners were speechless, every man aghast, thinking of the ordeal of just months before. A smaller escort vessel resembling a tug, with a .50-caliber machine gun mounted on the bow, could be seen between the two large re-purposed ships, moving around them.

Confirming their fears, down into the hell holds of the MOJI MARU went 500 or more men. Out of the holds rose the familiar stench, and in the dim were hundreds more sufferers, already present— Dutch troops. For four days they all rotted, moored at the Penang Roads docks, without ventilation inside a giant oven, as the noonday sun cooked. Meager rations were distributed once per day at about midday. Someone said their tormentors must have selected the most unbearable time.

Many of the weakest died of the exposure and the heat, their corpses cooking, bloating, and finally bursting, compounding the misery below decks. Only because the dead would further deteriorate into by-products toxic even for the Japanese, were bodies extracted and tossed over the side once per day. Some hour on the fifth day, when the ships finally left the port, masses of swelling, putrid flesh were left in their wakes, attacked indiscriminately by the more spectacular agents of decay: sharks, barracuda, and finally the elements.

January 15

Lt. Bennie Harrison and three other B-24 Liberator pilots from the 461st Bombardment Group were enjoying pleasant, if warmer than ideal flying conditions as they pounded into oblivion a convoy of Japanese supply ships they found in the Andaman Sea, off the coast of Burma, which were unprotected by heavy escort. Out of reach of their guns, the B24s scored hits across each with impunity– leaving them doomed– in flames and sinking, their surviving crews abandoning ship. Turning back to the south, they spotted more freighters flying the Empire of the Sun, the two freighters NITTA MEI MARU and MOJI MARU, and their escort tug.

The first thing the men heard from the hold of the MOJI MARU was the report of the three-inch gun on the fore deck. There were distant explosions as the NITTA MEI MARU took two bombs in the after hold, the Japanese quarters, killing much of the ship's crew. Out of a thousand Dutch in the forward hold, only 32 lost their lives, before the ship was cut in half, spilling the still living into the sea before it sank.

An attack on the MOJI MARU followed immediately. As Harrison's B24 dropped in for a starboard run, the MOJI MARU aft gun misfired and set the ammunition box on fire, which exploded, killing the gun crew. The forward gun fired wildly, shooting off the wireless aerial. Before the little Japanese escort tug could close on him to within range of its guns, Harrison dropped a load of five bombs and he pulled up to avoid the fire. Three landed starboard, two to port, the nearest one landing twenty feet from the ship. When that bomb detonated, the percussion against the hold killed a few prisoners below decks who were not lying flat and wiped out a dozen Jap crew members on that side of the ship.

Bombs expended, the B24s climbed back into the clouds and disappeared. Their bonus mission would have no details of POWs killed, and would not be documented for history until the end of hostilities in 1945, when survivors of the day added their accounts to the record.

The Japanese Merchant Captain of the MOJI MARU stayed in the vicinity until 968 mostly Dutch, American, and Australian troops and 200 Japanese were recovered, greatly overloading the ship until they limped into the port of Moulmein (Mawlamyine) in the Gulf of Martaban.

When Deane learned where they were, memory stirred somehow and the opening lines of Kipling's *Mandalay*, memorized in high school, were formed by his parched lips, expressed but with a whisper:

"*By the old Moulmein pagoda*

Lookin' lazy at the sea

There's a Burma girl a-settin'

and I know she thinks o' me".

Deane realized he had not seen Larkin Edmonson or Elliott Jonasson in weeks and tried to inspect the shuffling lines as they were shoved along to debark. Men were covered in such filth none would be recognized by their mothers. By the day's end, almost a thousand prisoners were evacuated to jail. The worst wounded were sent to a Catholic convent resembling conditions at Serang: overcrowded, terrible facilities. Many died of their wounds. Dysentery ravaged prisoners of all nations indiscriminately.

15

Burma-Thailand Railroad

January 27, 1943

The straightest line from Moulmein to Bangkok was along an extremely hilly jungle ridge that crossed many rivers. The idea of a railway enabling land traffic to cut directly across the Malaysian Peninsula from the Gulf of Thailand to the Gulf of Martaban had been considered by the British, who surveyed the route early in the century, ultimately abandoning it as far too difficult an enterprise. When the Japanese seized Burma from British control in 1942 (through Thailand), Charlie had to supply his troops and protect them from attack by the Allied submarines that lurked in the Malacca Straight and the coast of the Andaman Sea and undertook the notorious Death Railway in June. 12,400 Allied prisoners and more than 90,000 Asian civilians perished during its fifteen-month construction, from disease, starvation, or murder.

From the port of Moulmein, the "healthy" prisoners were moved 40 kilometers to the south in groups to Thanbyuzayat to join the work on the Burma end of the Burma-Thailand railroad. From Thanbyuzayat to the south, smaller base camps were established for groups of prisoners to work on different sections simultaneously, named for their distance from Thanbyuzayat.

Before the construction of the railway section could begin, dense rainforest had to be cleared. Trees were felled, and embankments were made. Deane's group was trucked to the 18 Kilo Camp and immediately began work digging through a "cut" (leveling rock and earth to minimize the grade). At first, each man was required to remove a cubic meter of earth a day. The work was carried out with no tools and the prisoners removed the waste rock by hand using cane baskets and rice sacks slung on two poles.

Against the advice of their officers, the Australian and American troops completed their work quickly so they might have more time to rest, but the Japanese simply doubled their quota. Thanbyuzayat natives supplemented the diet for a time, and the men settled into the 12-hour days with a ten-minute rest per hour, a day off every ten for rest, and the occasional "concert." In a few weeks, the men even began to find hope.

February 14, 1943

Deane's "pencil" of pounded charcoal dust and spit, wrapped in eucalyptus bark around a scrap of rice paper, had worn to a tiny nub. The last entry of the month was written with a rock, a quartz crystal "pencil" that had flecks of graphite:

> 2-14-43 *The men feasted on a dog caught using a looped rope holding rotted meat we were given to eat. The dog had a collar that was entangled in the loop, the British Corporal who fashioned the trap pulled to dog to the door and we beat it to death. It was said to have belonged to one of the Japanese officers in the camp.*

March 15, 1943

The able-bodied were shifted to 85 Kilo Camp. Group Commander Captain Midsutoni consulted with the POW doctors, agreeing to send the sickest men to the 30 Kilo Camp, the jungle hospital. He selected which would get there by foot, and which would have to be trucked, by striking each afflicted man with his sword. Those that got to their feet, walked.

April 4

The schedule called for the work to be completed by August 1943. The men Deane was with were shifted back to the 80 Kilo Camp and the Americans started building bridges. The Austrians and Dutch continued to dig.

The hurry-up order came down from Tokyo: finish the railroad as soon as possible. So they started night work, and all "fit" men worked 24-hour shifts. Within weeks, 33-hour shifts. Men sick with tropical disease were worked as hard as healthy men. At a shift change, guards beat any prone man on the soles of his feet or poked at obvious wounds, until he stood and was pronounced fit to work. The death rate skyrocketed. Prisoners falling behind, or collapsing were often beaten to death. Slight scrapes became infected wounds, which would not heal in the humid clime, becoming gangrenous, rotting away to expose bone. Dysentery, malaria, tropical ulcers, beriberi, and cholera added to the misery and impacted the workforce in all camps. Allied doctors had no supplies, no drugs, and could not keep up. Barely did they manage to ease the suffering, often falling victim themselves. About this time they lost a marvelous American doctor, Captain Lumpkin, to cerebral malaria. Graves could not be dug fast enough, and he was buried as was the growing practice: multiple bodies to a grave.

Deane recognized Australian and British prisoners he knew from camps months earlier, and at every camp sought faces familiar from the origin of their hellish journey, those who had survived in his witness. He lost track of most of the HOUSTON survivors and could get no knowledge of their fates. The food was far worse, and an explosive case of bloody dysentery began to manifest. He lost ten pounds per week.

May 26

Deane's group moved up to the 100 Kilo Camp, the worst yet. Under a mountain, on marshy ground where springs bubbled up, huts had to be built on stilts. The minor positive was you could fish for minnows through the bamboo poles making up the floor. The men there held a Dutch doctor named Hekking in particularly high regard, and Deane quickly learned why. Hekking had many years of experience with tropical diseases working in the Dutch Army in the large islands surrounding Indonesia. If the disease originated in a particular area, said he, so too did the plant that could cure it. Under the noses of their captors, Hekking foraged and provided makeshift medication to his fellow prisoners at a time when the Japanese were unwilling or unable to supply regular medicines, undoubtedly saving lives.

Small bits of charcoal mixed with rice eased the excruciating discomfort but did nothing to address the disease. Delirious, Deane lost consciousness under the weight of the rock buckets and collapsed where he stood. A short Allied bombing raid nearby, which coincided almost exactly with Deane's collapse, distracted the guards and probably saved his life. When he returned to consciousness, he was sipping saffron-smelling tea made from the perennial flower Montbretia (*Crocosmia Aurea*) and was instructed to also chew the leaves. Dr. Hekking knew that the bright red flower growing wild in the jungle would ease the misery of dysentery, and often cure it. He knew which plants might be eaten to replace vitamin B and thus reduce the incidence of the bloating condition of the feet, sometimes the entire body, that beriberi wrought. Deane wondered why his path intersected Dr. Hekking's when those of so many other brave and selfless men did not. When he recovered somewhat, he found space to add a tribute to the man in his journal, the last space on the scrap, before returning it to the tube. It was the last word he would transcribe as a Prisoner of War.

16

Throw It

Little Italy, Chicago

May 1920

Hamish Patrick was surprised that he was surprised. Taylor Street Gym's proprietor and boxing coach thought he had probably been witness to just about every kind of feisty wannabe. Nothing unusual about a scrawny neighborhood teen that looks like he will fall over for the weight of the giant gloves on him. But this one flashes you a grin that still has baby teeth missing and then steps into the ring and proceeds to beat the living shit out of kids that outweigh him by fifty pounds.

"Your name should be Jack... Jack McCullo... Jack McGurn," said Hamish finally. "You got talent, and a wop name ain't gonna get you nowhere." Sixteen-year-old Vincenzo Antonio Gibaldi needed about two seconds to consider the suggestion before he adopted it. An Irish-sounding name would certainly distance you from being pigeon-holed as just another scrappy black-haired kid from Chicago's Little Italy. No use in sharing that with Angelo, he could just be Jack McGurn at the gym.

Tenacity like McGurn's was such a rare gift that for the next weeks and months Patrick decided it would be interesting to see what he might make of the young fellow. The kid was so incredibly intense in the ring, so mean, he seemed to will himself into victory. Jack matured, put on some meat, got meaner still, and won. In four years at age 21, he was a prizefighter. Low-level Chicago mobster muscle bet on the amateur matches and the youngest pros, because there was still so much sport in it, and the name of Jack McGurn got around. Bet on McGurn, and you might turn a neat profit, especially if he was fighting outside of his weight class, as he often did when odds were therefore higher.

1925

But, prize fighting would not be Jack's destiny. His stepfather, Angelo, a grocer, had developed a fine industry selling sugar to all of the neighborhood distillers, in prohibition-era Little Italy. Anywhere there was money, there was the mob, and another distributor soon wanted a piece of Angelo's business but was gruffly put off. Within 24 hours, Angelo was assassinated, mob-style.

Young McGurn put his ear to the pavement and leaned on his shadier friends who were regular patrons at the ring, for a weapon and information. He learned the names of the perpetrators, and even heard that they spoke of his mother's husband as "nickel and dime." Was that a comment on the value of Angelo's life or his frugal business style?

Lugging a heavy bag, he rode the train out of town to a nearby quarry and practiced handling his new "Chicago Typewriter," a Thompson model 1921 automatic rifle, the Tommy Gun "that made the twenties roar". Methodically, one by one, he found and killed the men who took his stepfather's life.

Emilio Schiavone probably died after the first or second .45 caliber rounds struck his face. But, so intoxicating was the complete power in the distribution of death that McGurn held down the trigger, spraying the entire 50-round magazine into the remains of the man's head and neck, half of these before the body was completely prone, until the weapon halted abruptly, smoking. There seemed a continued ringing in the sudden silence once the machinery starved, hanging in the air like the final notes of a thrilling concerto. He closed the corpse's fingers over a nickel and a dime.

It took some control not to slaughter the others as spectacularly, because he was not afforded as secluded an opportunity, and thus noted the value of precision if not discretion. The second assassin, Domenico "the agent" Fattore, met his end with but a simple burst in a crowded market. McGurn left two nickels in his palm, honoring his name, the Italian form of Domenicus, meaning, "belonging to the Lord".

Vito "Curly" Crespo, was stapled across his torso in the alley behind the Green Mill, ironically a night club McGurn himself would have an interest in one day.

The spectacular efficiency with which this business was conducted, and the brevity of it (three days), attracted the attention of the highest order of Chicago criminals of the day, Al Capone. Capone had already followed McGurn in the ring and was especially impressed. McGurn soon found himself in Capone's employ, as one of his meanest bodyguards, and most effective, though temperamental killers.

February 1926

The near-termination of singer Joe E. Lewis, the star attraction at the Green Mill, whom McGurn was simply assigned to convince not to move his act to a competing nightclub, led McGurn to Memphis while his neighborhood cooled. McGurn had lost a wager on a prize fight that afternoon and when Lewis surprised him with insubordination, he slit the man's throat. Lewis survived but was never the same.

McGurn won his bet for the fight to finish under six rounds, but Arthur's victory over Tiger Flowers, and its considerable effect on McGurn's wallet put him in as murderous a state. Still, he was convinced that his host, who was out similarly, had advised him in good faith. Kinney suggested a plan to use the new man to their advantage and recoup their loss quickly.

The house "doctor" working on Arthur, using a curved suture needle and a pair of pliers, seemed to be putting laces in his neck. Kinney found him in the locker room surrounded by Beale Street performers he recognized: Memphis Minnie, Robert Wilkins, and Pee Wees' piano player, Speckled Red.

"Congratulations." He peeled ten $20 bills off a fat roll and put them on the table. Arthur looked at the bills, then at Kinney. Lizzie leaned down and whispered in his ear.

"Mistuh West, you said the winnuh got five hunderd dollahs."

Kinney looked at Faposi, who stared at the floor. "That's after three bouts," he lied. "You're an employee now, and we have to encourage you to stay... some big money coming your way, my boy."

Arthur had never seen so many bills in his life. He said, "Yassuh."

When he opened his eyes, Arthur could not make out where he was, and at first, he thought he was dreaming. He found himself on a couch. Bright lines of the afternoon sun through the window shade angled onto busy blue floral wallpaper. The sunbeams zigzagged down onto a guitar leaning against the wall with a sunburst paint job, which somehow looked familiar. Then he felt the headache, and intense pain in his neck on the left side. He reached up and touched his neck, behind his ear, below his hair— crusty, more bristles there, stiffer than before. Night scenes returned: the fight Sunday night, the money in the bright room after. Arthur concentrated, but even after a couple of minutes, there was just... nothing.

Then, high-pitched voices from outside, and children laughing. The room led to a short hall with more intense wallpaper, then to a living room/parlor. He opened the front door and saw a tranquil, domestic scene: small houses up and down and across the street left, children on bicycles, automobiles, dogs barking... neighborhood sounds. It looked like the neighborhoods he walked to get away from Beale the last time he had been injured, and those between the train yard and the Collins Colored Hospital.

A taxicab pulled to the curb and a neatly dressed man in a suit emerged, smiling at Arthur as he approached. "You feels better, looks like. C'mon." It was the preacher, the bluesman, Robert Timothy Wilkins.

Arthur opened his mouth to speak, thinking of the pile of money after the fight, but there was pain in his jaw too. Wilkins went on:

"These people ain't no good, boy. They ain't got no interest in you 'ceptin' to take you. Mistuh Kinney is a criminal and his fren kills people, and it ain't nuthin' for you to stay here. You got to go find Jesus."

"What time is it" Arthur managed, looking at the floor. "Where is Lizzie?"

"You bought the house a round, then another and another, an we carried you here when you passed out. D'evil one has a grip on you, cause you cainhandle yo' liquor." Arthur's expression went unchanged and so Wilkins said, "It's Tuesday, boy. You slepp a day-and-a-half."

He looked up at the man. "I had some money."

Wilkins' head and body leaned back and he laughed heartily. "You sho' did! Heh, heh! *Did* bein' the, uhm, poi-tinent wo'id. Boy, you spen' ever dime you had and went looking to borry some mo'. That's par-ti-cully what you is doin' here. You din' have no money fo' no hotel."

It was about 8 pm before Arthur started to feel like himself again, except it was painful to hold his head straight. Looking in the mirror, he had to reassure himself that his neck wasn't sewn to his collarbone. Seized by the smells of frying chicken livers, he realized he was ravenously hungry. Emily, who Arthur assumed to be Mrs. Robert Wilkins, fussed at him and helped him wash and dabbed at his neck. The men sat at a card table, and Wilkins clutched Arthur's hands in both of his, shook them and shut his eyes, and said "Lawd, Lawd, send yo good grace down he-ah upon dis mayne, yo' servant Ah-thah Campbell, an' show him what yo' plan is fuh him and hi he goin' assist you in yo' great werks. Bless dis food. Ah-men."

That night, Arthur had a dream he would remember always. The picture he described, dialect removed, is compelling:

The figure stood looking out over the river bluffs just south of Beale, in a punishing nighttime storm but was neither moved by the violent winds nor dampened by the downpour. The heavy corners of his oiled canvas dust coat buzzed below the lowest button, and huge pieces of debris were frozen in the air when a great lash of lightning momentarily ruled. He heard the bell of the Katy Adams *and the sound of screaming, and there she was, on fire, being tossed like a toy on white caps. Somehow he was alongside her crowded decks, and witness to the overboard of just one, a young woman of about eighteen or twenty, terror clear on her face even through the whipping blackness. He was sure she saw him. The paddle-wheeler continued to be hurled across the waves leaving the girl behind, flailing, and she disappeared into the fury of the depths in a roar of attacking hail.*

A warlike cannonade far out to the west illuminated spectacular cloud shapes, silhouetting distant knolls, but the far west horizon and that to the south was otherwise without distinction, Where was Arkansas, where was the edge of this furious black sea? A giant hole appeared in the river, rimmed with white water on the course the boat was moving, with water rushing downstream. On the far side, a mighty force upstream against the current, so that the hole became a swirling, open drain. Suddenly the Katy Adams *was engulfed in a great fireball and rode the walls of the maelstrom, disappearing impossibly fast, still flaming.*

The dock-like wharf boat where Arthur had loaded a barge a lifetime ago twisted and distended in a boiling, double-speed current, disintegrating before the eyes, with pieces flaking off like old snake skin. Half submerged, the big block letters on its side, MEMPHIS HELENA & ROSEDALE PACKET COMPANY, tilted and bobbed over and under the waterline. Arthur remembered then that chains with links as big as a man's wrist tethered it to the cobblestones. Soon there would be no evidence of it but the mooring cleats that clung to the most stubborn pieces of deck.

Arthur awoke shadowed by unfamiliar anxiety— about the uncontrollable passage of time, and a curious empty longing for some pretty, innocent girl who did not exist. He had only been a witness to her certain drowning, unable to act to save her.

The dream was so vivid he described it to his host, leaving out the girl. Those were images he wanted to keep for himself, and they were already foggy around the edges. Not to mention... feelings for a ghost in a dream? When he had heard a man speak of things like a woman would, the people of Jones, back home, said the man was 'touched'.

Wilkins said, "Thass de Lawd talkin' to yeh. I knowed it when you's on that train in Horn Lake. I knowed it 'cause de Lawd Hisself set you down in my rail car."

Arthur's sustained blank stare was Wilkins's license to continue: "You need to git away fo'm aroun' hyunh. Drankin' an whorin' ain't de Lawd's work. Not on yo account n'way." His brow narrowed. "You a strong man, boy. Peoples looks up to you. The day is comin'! The Lawd, he has plans fuh you. The Lawd is gone bring another flood!"

Preacher blues man Wilkins just talked of Noah, like other preachers, and Arthur did not think of the dream again until fall, months into torrential rains that would continue through the winter and become a hundred-year flood, the Great Mississippi Flood of 1927.

He walked a couple of blocks toward the hospital where Manny was. The driver of an open-bed truck slowed in passing, offering a lift. Arthur nodded his thanks and climbed aboard.

He found Manfred Ames dozing. His arm returned to normal size, so they cast it in plaster.

"I cain't feel nothin', but they say I's gone be alright, an say I gots to go soon."

A fat nurse with a pretty face came in, and Manny wiggled the fingers of his casted hand at her. Arthur had the sense that his friend was doing better than he let on.

Manny said, "Hit was two mens come lookin' fuh you."

"What men? When?"

"I heard one of them tell de doctuh you was supposed to fight. Dat was lass week. He say tell you c'mon back to de gym cause they's got money for you."

"How'd you know him. Why'd he tell you?"

"Wud'n me. Doctuh was stand'n right in nat doe. I did'n say nuthin'."

Arthur could hear the words of Robert Wilkins, and he could hear his Mamma's words. But maybe West owed him. Sure did. Arthur wanted to walk away from this table with money in his pocket. Winning felt pretty danged good. Two hundred dollars was more money than Arthur had ever seen. He held it in his hand. Yet it found its way back onto the street in hours if not minutes. Arthur recalled his mama saying something about the love of money and evil, but Arthur had never had any love of it, because he had never had any, and aside from fools like he had known in Louisiana, Beale Street was Arthur's first real association with masses of murderous and mean people. That must be what evil is. He still felt a strong pull to get out, but it could wait one more day.

Doctor Hatfield walked in and saw Arthur. He grunted in recognition as if to say 'Well look who is here', but said "You still turning my work into mincemeat?" His head cocked back so he could look down his nose and see close under his glasses. He gently lifted Arthur's chin to the left. "Hmm. This is a mess. Who did this? Looks like shoe laces. Why don't you leave it alone? You're going to have a knot like jerky... if it ever even really heals. What does it feel like?"

"Hard as a piece a wood." That didn't really do it justice. But it was too much to tell the doctor that being sewn up three times right at the same place was worse than the original injury. It reminded him of the time when he was seven, trying to keep up with older boys in the woods near the creek, he fell into an oily bog, and when they pulled him out, his neck and shoulders were covered in thick black tar. His momma scrubbed him with lye until the skin bled, but the stuff stuck to him like glue, and contracted and hardened over a large sensitive area into a solid, heavy, cement-like patch. It took skin when they peeled it off.

Doctor Hatfield said he was going to leave it be, it would heal, and then he turned his attention to Manny and confirmed that Manny's time at the hospital was about over, and could he please show himself out that night, or no later than early the next morning.

When he left, Arthur said, "It's time to getaway f'om hyunh, anyway. What is we doin?"

"I still ain't been to Beale Street," said Manny.

"Well, I been there enough fo' boaf of us, an I'll tell you all about it."

Manny was more interested in the pudgy nurse and continuing his nap than pressing concerns, so Arthur went. Within the hour, he found himself on Beale Street, having promised to return and collect his friend.

Inside The Vintage, Mr. West was in his chair watching a sparring contest, but as he got close Arthur could see it was not he, but the man who had been with him in the locker room, smoking, sweating, sleeves rolled to the elbows, without a hat. Faposi, the coach with the flabby arms, stood inside the ring, holding to the ropes, panting.

"No, no!" McGurn leaped agilely into the ring, past the huffing, sweat-drenched Italian, and fell upon the wide-eyed student, seized his overstuffed paws, and led them in a slow-motion combination. It made Arthur think of the coupling rods on a locomotive wheel.

"Make a combination starts with your left if he is a righty, and right if he's a lefty. Look, c'mon. Mix it up." A piece of a cigarette still at his lips, in his white shirt, and loose tie, he stepped back, dancing, fists up, defending with gloveless hands.

"C'mon. S'go."

Tony Faposi saw Arthur and his face showed relief. He heaved himself down. "Where you been? Mr. Kinney's been lookin' for you."

Arthur was warming up on the bag, getting up to a nice rhythm, he thought. Still, he overheard Mr. West and Faposi and the other man talking: "— throw it. That nigger owes me quite a bit of money."

A few minutes later, when the boss man and his friend had gone, Mr. Tony said "Arthur, they have you fightin' another boxer who is an unknown around here, and they got a lot of money on the fight. And what they… we, need you to do is… lose. You might anyway, but I want you to drop the fight no later than the fourth round. It'd be better if you did it takin' a spill. For that, you'll get three hundred dollars. That sound OK?"

Arthur looked at him without expression, saying nothing.

"Do you understand? You are going to throw the fight."

"You want me to lose on purpose? I don't never lose anything on purpose."

"That's right. It's just business. Make it look good."

7 pm

The Vintage was packed when word got out that Arthur, the fighter who had K/O'd Flowers, and knocked down Bad Sam was back. The match featured Arthur Campbell and Henry Armstrong, known as Hurricane Hank. A welterweight and middleweight champ from Columbus Mississippi, Hank had lost only 10 of 100 bouts with 5 draws. Like Flowers, he was lighter than Arthur by 10 pounds and often fought in upper and lower weight classes.

At the bell, Arthur stepped forward but bent down like he had a problem with the laces on his shoe. The other fighter rained blows on his head and back until the ref stepped in to separate them. The instant he stepped away

Arthur shot up with a right into Hurricane Hank's face, following it with a left that connected with his ear. Hank staggered, and Arthur dove into him again and drove staccato punches into his ribs. Trying to protect himself, Hank left open his face, a mistake which earned him a second mighty blow to the chin, and he fell backward for the entire count.

17

McGurn

Jake McGurn had murder in his eye. Arthur not only didn't get his money, he barely escaped with his life.

AS SOON AS his arm was held high at the win, Arthur was mobbed. People whose names would be blues legends were witnesses, Memphis Minnie and Furry Lewis, were suddenly inside those ropes. Lewis Handy was said to be among the spectators, as was legendary Memphis mayor, and white power broker, Boss Crump. Tony Faposi knew he better have a good explanation why the message did not get delivered, and he tried to sweep Arthur down from the ring, swaddling him in a satin robe, pushing him back toward the lockers so he could explain himself (and pay with his own blood if that was what the bosses needed). Faposi knew the smidgen of confidence Kinney and McGurn had in him anyway was probably evaporated, but it was better to appear to take charge...

Whether he sensed that wasn't a good idea, or he just wanted the adoration, Arthur twisted away easily and fell into a group of fans that moved out into the street in a uniform motion like choreographed dancers.

Faposi trailed along helplessly five, then ten steps, then ten people behind, the eyes on his back fueling increasing desperation.

Jake McGurn was screaming at the top of his lungs at Kinney, who was screaming at the top of his lungs at FAT PIECE OF SHIT, now out the door with the spectators to who-knows-the-hell-where, out of whose ass would come the two thousand the fight cost him, plus whatever it cost his associate.

People grabbed at Arthur and stroked him. Their words ran into each other so he heard only a sort of roar. Then, he was looking into the face of

Lizzie McCoy— Memphis Minnie. Her face looked big and aged to him at that moment; she was hardly the girl in his dream, not even remotely. He saw big-boned versus petite, loose and trashy versus innocent. The girl he dreamed of would have an angel's voice.

"No," Arthur said, he didn't want no drink. But, Lizzie said in his ear, "Les go back to my place," which she knew was her secret weapon, and Arthur said, "OK." They slipped away.

Forgetting what had pulled them out into the street, the circular crowd began to disintegrate. When they were inside her apartment Lizzie tugged at his robe, as she had before, but he grabbed her wrist and said, "Where is my twenty dollahs?"

Squeezing harder when she protested, crying: "Arthur! Whaddayou mean?"

Arthur Campbell held her like that, looking into her face. If just a smidgen too large, her face had a symmetrical beauty and perfect auburn skin. Flecks of white powder crusted around her nostrils. The dark wooden table in front of the couch was dusty with cocaine. With his left hand, he grasped also her right wrist, and slowly began increasing pressure with his thumb.

"Arthur, you hurtin' me! Let me go," Lizzie said, suddenly all business. "I'll get it for you."

He did, and she left the tiny parlor and entered her bedroom, closing the door. From beyond the open window came the sounds of Beale: autos chugging up the street, the whir of tires on the cobblestones, and music. Through notes mixed from a half dozen juke joints, Arthur recognized the voice of Alberta Hunter wafting over from Pee Wee's:

I may be as brown as a berry
But that's only secondary
And you can't tell the difference

After dark
I may not be so appealing
But I've got that certain feeling
And you can't tell the difference
After dark

He noticed 'Fessor Green's bucket being lowered from a window on the second story, to receive the money, or deliver a half-pint "slab" or 12-ounce "Austin" of bootleg whiskey to a thirsty customer, in full view of the policeman who walked the beat, Grantham Heckle. Colored and white called him Granny, and you better have Granny on your side if you were a bootlegger. Coke had some role in the death of his sister so he would bust you fast if you were a doper. Prohibition created opportunity. Arthur had even heard of a Memphis policeman who had a butler. Plenty of money for everybody. Except an honest nigger.

The fight sealed a decision. Arthur decided he had enough of Beale, tonight. Manfred could come or not. Maybe he'd find a job in Memphis. Call on some of the rich white folks that he took hunting at the club every weekend, like Dr. Thornberry. Or he might go back to be the caretaker in Robinsonville for the summer, but there wasn't any money to be made much. Loading cotton on riverboats maybe, except that Beale Street and all its temptations would be too close. He no longer recognized himself, here. These people fed on each other.

Robert Wilkin's words slipped into his mind: "There ain't no future in it." But I'll be damned, he thought, if I leave without the money I brought. Weeks ago, before teasing whores, drunks and cocaine addicts, street people, and evil, the party seemed his for the taking. Everything was new and exciting.

But Beale Street is a lie, a hellish place where every soul is a predator or a carrion feeder that lives off dead scraps. Lizzie or Memphis Minnie or whoever she is… is surely one of these. Education complete.

"Damn," he said like white men do when they hit a golf ball way off the fairway or miss a mallard about to light on their gun barrel. He got more irritated and felt an energy that did not get expended in the fight that should have taken place if Arthur Campbell had behaved like most predicted, and many bet he would.

Always respectful to women, Arthur was embarrassed at himself for squeezing Lizzie's wrists (though he wanted to snap them). He had thought it outside his capability to introduce pain or force to a woman. The $20 he had in his pocket just two weeks ago seemed the principle to argue. Arthur wanted at least that to head back down to Mississippi...

His eyes fixed on a framed picture on the fake mantle above the radiator, which though he had been to her tiny apartment several times, he had not noticed, because it disappeared into the busy floral wallpaper. It was of Lizzie in the lap of Jake McGurn, the white man from Chicago, who was friends with Mr. West.

CRAACK! Lizzie McCoy's front door caved in and through the space came McGurn himself, wearing an overcoat over one shoulder, just as Lizzie entered the room. The door swung wide, concealing Arthur where he stood. The barrel of McGurn's Tommy gun protruded, phallic and ready, wrapped in the other sleeve.

"WHERE IS HE? I know he is here. WHERE is Arthur Campbell?"

Without saying a word she pointed to the open window and McGurn rushed to look down. The fire escape was right there and could be climbed down to a landing with a half staircase just high enough off the ground to drop with minimal injury, but be difficult to use to go up. The walk was crowded and boisterous. McGurn studied it up and down. Arthur slipped into the hall and down the stairs two at a time, and out the back door into the alley.

18

Lillibelle

July 1926, Greenville, Mississippi

Lillibelle Tatum was the reason Arthur did not get back on the barge that had carried him to Greenville. As it disappeared around the last river bend south of Greenville, bound for Vicksburg, he realized hers was the face he saw in his dreams.

Her light coloring and willowy figure were salt and pepper standing between her black-as-coal father and light-skinned mother, the Reverend and Mrs. Tatum of Leland, Mississippi. Arthur was busy fixing the axle of the man's wagon with a shovel handle, when here came the mother and daughter, and Arthur was properly introduced.

"De Lawd's sent dis-heah Good Samaritan when we's in need."

Arthur spied a man standing aside a wagon that was askew under the weight of two heavy cotton bales. His wagon had come apart, a front wheel fell off in the street. He was struggling with his mules, trying to keep them still after a motor car honked because its path was blocked. The startled mules pulled the naked axle across the cobblestones, snapping it, and the bales slid toward the busy riverside. Seeing no reason not to be of service while he awaited his ship's departure, Arthur stepped in the path of the mules and hummed to them a meaningless "oyoyoyoyoy" a trick he learned as a farm boy. They immediately calmed and stood still.

The axle break occurred near the center, and Arthur was on his back on the ground, lashing Tatum's shovel handle to it, which he thought would surely get him home when appeared the other Tatums, and Arthur was forever smitten.

They saw him next at the tiny Baptist church for which Reverend Tatum was pastor. It was built in 1901, in a wooded setting at the foot of a bluff, about a mile before the two acres of incorporated Leland. Now, it overlooked the acre-wide path being neatly planed out of the landscape east from Greenville, for the power and telephone lines that will eventually connect all the way to Greenwood. Inside, cotton workers and catfish farmers sweltered, worshiped, and sang at a wooden cross over a picture of a slim white Jesus with His angular nose and sandy beard.

After the services, Arthur said, "Do you need help on yo farm? I have been a cotton worker and farm hand. I know how to work rice fields and I am a huntin' guide."

The preacher knew exactly what was in Arthur's mind, and he thought he knew Arthur's heart. "No Ah-thuh, I ain't got work fuh you. But it's a catfish farm on the far side of Leland toward Indianola, and you can aks them if they'll use you."

That summer of 1926, spent back and forth from Indianola through Leland to Greenville, was one of the happiest in Arthur Campbell's life. He had honest work, and someone to care about, to woo. Lillibelle was but 18 years old, and the Tatums did not allow her off of their property outside of their presence and influence. But Arthur was welcome around them that summer and Lillibelle was a picture he carried in his heart.

About mid-summer began the historic weather torrent. Tornadoes wracked Leland and tore the roof off the church. For weeks thereafter it rained at least once during the day, so that the repairs could not be completed, and standing water buckled the wood floor.

Arthur considered not returning to Robinsonville Hunting Club. For a time he began to imagine building a life here. Perhaps he would ask for Lillibelle's hand. They would live in Greenville.

He knew better. Lillibelle was not going anywhere for a few years at least. He wondered what happened to his friend, Manny. Arthur never abandoned anyone and doubted Manfred would say he had been abandoned.

The man was happy wherever he was, and dumb enough to think that if he had a drink in one hand and a fork in the other, he had life licked… for the day. And, there was no future in raising catfish unless you were the white folks with the farm.

Throughout September storms continued unabated. They spent days filling sandbags and building up the berms, but the square ponds he and 50 other workers seined once a week for the catch finally overflowed in the middle of the night. Dawn found thousands of catfish in inches of water in the surrounding fields… some flopping, some on their sides, all doomed. The clouds broke and the sun dried up the mud flats and encouraged the rising stench. Arthur decided it was time to go to Robinsonville.

He spent the next day, a Sunday, on the porch in Leland with Lillibelle. In the dream, he saw her face looking up at him desperately from churning water as if he were floating and only he could lead her to safety. But, she was still a child, and he wondered what had seized him, and if they had a future.

Arthur said goodbye, promising to return in the spring, though he wasn't certain he meant it. As he stood, Lillibelle let him hold her hands. She glanced toward the screened door. Satisfied they were alone, she looked into his eyes like a woman who has known a man and pulled his hand to her breast. The moment would plant a burning question inside Arthur Campbell that became more anxious with the passing months, sealing his return.

19

The Great Flood

October 1, 1926

Friday afternoon, Doctor Claypool was sitting in a rocker on the clubhouse porch when a figure appeared at the far end of the levee road. It grew larger and familiar: wide but compact, with a tattered homburg shadowing half of his already two-toned face. "Well I'll be damned," he said to no one, but he was glad. Arthur was his favorite guide.

Arthur Campbell was the subject of much speculation that summer among the usual handful of club members whose paths sometimes crossed summers at the club when they came to fish. There was a good chance you could fill the boat with crappie or bream in a morning or afternoon. The summer heat was usually enough to discourage overnight stays, but this year the unusually consistent rains kept the temperature down and the fishing good, even through rising water levels. The club was busier some weekends than during duck season, as more members brought family to enjoy the scene and anticipate the fall and winter seasons. By early September most of the seasonal residents: paddler guides Manny, Preacher, and Bishop had trickled in. Manny told amazing tales of his and Arthur's exploits in Memphis, filling the spaces between binges and with imaginative adventures, mostly improvising those of Arthur's, which he had some inkling of but was not witness to. When he finally made it to Beale Street, he was almost immediately picked up for public intoxication and vagrancy and spent two nights in jail, after which arresting officer Granny Heckle dropped him at the southern limit of Third Street, firmly suggesting he return from whence he came.

"Well, Arthur," said Claypool, "I'm glad you could join us. I hear you've been quite busy."

"Yas-suh... Doctuh." Arthur grinned. Under his hat white teeth reflected the bright sun.

The teal season was on starting tomorrow, so Claypool was especially delighted to see his friend. Maybe there would be a sporting day, standing in the lily pads, shooting teal like doves, and casting about for bream and crappie in the afternoon.

By the end of the month, the persistent rains turned relief from heat into depression. Dr. Thornberry reported he had just come from Vicksburg, where the river level had reached 40 feet, almost ten feet higher than it had ever been recorded. Surrounding farms' crops drowned in standing water, and the levee road into the club turned into a muddy, rutted berm. Then the torrents ceased, and there was a collective sigh of relief up and down the Mississippi River Valley. In November, members commissioned dump trucks full of gravel to shore up the road, work which club staff (except Manfred) found to be a helpful distraction from the humid weather until the season would pick up again. December's cooling temps brought few ducks, but it was still early yet.

Two weeks later water from the skies began again to overwhelm from the Smokies to the Rockies and beyond, like a persistent virus. Storms of frightening violence and intensity went on for days, obliterating records by inches per day in the central states. In the west, blizzards were recorded in feet over the average. By Christmas, creeks became streams, then rivers, in just hours. Rivers turned into oceans. The Cumberland flooded Nashville. The Tennessee flooded Chattanooga. Papers reported lives and property lost.

The Robinsonville Dam Hunting Club was a few miles east from the swollen and distended river, "protected" on the natural bluff side; the rising waters were a topic that had been discussed with some impunity, a catastrophe, but one which would have little local effect.

Not one member killed his limit of 25 ducks in one day during the season of 1926-1927. Indeed he called himself lucky to come back with three or four mallards. At New Year's the running tally of ducks taken hardly reached half of the year before: 427 total. When the Illinois Central suspended north-south railroad traffic across Mississippi, followed shortly by the Columbus & Greenville shutting down its east-west line, attendance at the club fell off further.

Then the weather dried out a little, and the trickle of members grew during the latter part of the first winter weeks. But the water was high, well into the surrounding farmland, and what waterfowl there were spread out over large areas. Arthur's magic call reached fewer, his legend was temporarily stalled. Though a late evening hunt with Goodwin Claypool yielded the prize of two banded pintails from Lima Lake, Illinois, which caused Dr. Claypool to remark during dinner several times, that that area was probably completely submerged right now.

The last weekend of the season, dinner conversation at the club spoke of levees being broken through in Arkansas, the Tennessee flooding a second time. From New Orleans to Greenville, hundreds worked on the levees to shore them up, while officials insisted the precautions were routine and pleaded for calm.

Arthur thought of Lillibelle Tatum from almost the moment he left Leland. Snippets of members' conversations, his link with the outside, brought to mind the anxiety he had felt almost a year before, near the end of the Beale Street adventure. Then, Cooper Permuter arrived from Memphis with an incredible story observed from atop the Cotton Exchange building. An undertow force sucked under a small boat, just before a whirlpool 100 feet across opened up at that spot for ten minutes.

That night Arthur was revisited by his dreams, standing on the banks of the swollen river in a torrential downpour, helpless to save the drowning. Lillibelle inhabited his mind's eye. The moment he received his money he was on the road south.

The Great Flood II

Arthur found the Reverend and Mrs. Tatum at their ragged home outside of Leland, their crop in ruins in standing water, and their home much the worse for weathering the elements of the winter. The swath being cut for the new power line now went east through Leland toward Greenwood, a lake with parallel shores as far as the eye could see. A proud-looking giant, a hundred-foot tower of steel with three sets of downward arms, stood empty-handed, straddling the center, almost lateral of the Pastor's yard, the last in a line about every quarter mile towards Greenville. All resources were diverted in December to shoring up the levee.

Lillibelle was gone. When the rains had come again, she was consigned to the safety of her aunt's house in Indianola. Tatum said "de Lawd hisself sent you. You go help save Greenville."

Floods had deluged the upper Midwest since the early fall. Northern rivers burst their banks and flooded cities every day, wiping out benchmarks that had stood for a hundred years since river levels were first measured. The rivers at the headwaters of the Ohio relieved themselves over the city of Pittsburgh in late January, finally funneling back into the already overwhelmed Ohio River to flood Cincinnati in less than a week, spilling that volume ten days later into the Mississippi at Cairo, halfway between Memphis and St. Louis as the crow flies. The Mississippi River had already gnawed at levees from Cairo to the Gulf for months, picking up speed and even more volume as Arkansas rivers sought their flood plains into its western banks. The rains continued relentlessly, and major rivers in surrounding states flooded again and again, eventually finding the Mississippi Valley.

Arthur did not have to seek work; it found him. Senator LeRoy Percy of Greenville, Governor of the Federal Reserve Bank, was preparing for war. Gathering money, government, and private resources, he redirected the workers of his own plantation and cotton gins, and impressed into service those from neighboring farms, to shore up the levee from Greenville north to one of the weakest known points in the Mississippi levee system: Scott Plantation near Mounds Landing. Negroes were picked up everywhere and trucked to work the levees and live in refugee camps and barges tethered to the levees. Many already had some sense of the collective emergency. But the reluctant were not offered much choice. They were paid 75¢ a day.

Subscribing to the idea the Reverend Tatum sold, the same as that which Robert Wilkins put in his head the year before— *destiny had selected him to protect and to preserve*, Arthur stepped aboard a truckload almost cheerfully, thinking his was a temporary commission. Lillibelle was close and safe. He would see her soon.

Arthur fell into the routine for weeks, caught up in the rising do-or-die desperation of the task. Navy planes were in the air constantly to find and address weaknesses before the river did, flying all hours despite the continuous pounding of the rain and the cold. Women filled the sandbags men carried up the saturated slope, which sucked boots from feet with almost every step. Some days he built mud boxes of planks, filling them with sandbags or mattresses of willows to be laid on the river side of the slopes to stem the mudslides. Arthur lost count of the times someone slipped and slid into the furious water forever. It hardly interrupted the work.

He worried about the Tatums. Lillibelle would not be safe unless she and her parents were taken far inland. During a particularly dark torrent, Arthur slipped out of the detail. At the foot of the hill, he was accosted by two men there to prevent desertion, who trained their pistols on him and demanded he get back to work. "WE MUST!" shouted one. There was no relief. There could be none.

Taskmasters white and black with shotguns patrolled the saturated levees searching for saboteurs from the south, bent on relieving the growing pressure downstream, with dynamite. By mid-March white National Guardsmen took over the duty. They shot anyone approaching the levee from the river in a boat.

Army tent camps all along the levee housed and fed the workers. Arthur hoped not to be selected for details too far north, for he sought a time and way to go east Indianola soon. One morning, a white man named Charlie Wilburn walked around interviewing the laborers for specific skills. Once he learned Arthur could drive a tractor and had been a fireman aboard a locomotive, Arthur found himself at Levee Camp Six, 15 miles north, feeding coal into the firebox of a Ruston No. 300 Steam Dragline.

Workers stood atop the levee, losing the battle of sandbags as the constant power of the river three miles wide pushed through deep under their levee, sending up muddy spouts 200 feet behind them. Around the clock, under lights powered by generators, the excavators were engaged in building a stronger wall behind it. The operator, Wilburn, dug into the soggy earth, swung around and dumped the load, and packed it around creosote pilings with the Ruston's giant steel bucket. It was better than pulling 100-pound sandbags uphill in shin-deep mud, but nights Arthur returned to the tent camp after his twelve hours, smelling of grease, smoke, and sweat.

The camps were lawless places. The task was the job, and no one cared how it got done, no questions asked. April 1st was gray like most days, though with only a drizzle. Charlie Wilburn and Arthur worked thirty yards from another smaller steam shovel. Between the two machines, a man struggled to push a wheelbarrow stacked with paper bags of lime up the slight grade at the foot of the levee before they could be soaked, which was part of a concrete operation to secure new pilings. Two others could not see over their burdens and were on a collision course, striking the man with the wheelbarrow and tilting his entire cargo onto the deep mud. He got up swinging. Nearby laborers quickly joined in, and it became a brawl of ten.

A patrolling Guardsman standing above them on the levee fired his weapon twice into the air. The violence continued, so he fired his rifle over their heads, striking the boiler of the smaller steam shovel. It instantly burst and shot superheated vapor onto the nearest combatants, obliterating skin and muscle to the bone. The fighting stopped, and the bucket of the smaller unit dropped to the ground as the pressure in its boiler went to zero. Wilburn and Arthur stilled their unit and got out to inspect the damage to the workers. Two men lay in the mud, shaking. One was dead–nothing left of his head, yet his body did not know it and convulsed. The other was badly burned along the torso side most exposed and was going into shock. Wilburn sized the situation and pronounced both workers a loss, ordering them tossed into the river.

"BACK TO WORK."

"That man is alive," said Arthur.

"DID YOU HEAR ME, BOY? Get your black ass back to that firebox! No time to lose."

"Nossuh."

Arthur brought the small coal shovel still in his hands, hard across Wilburn's head at the temple. He fell face-first into the mud.

There were almost 200 negroes in that camp, and soon Arthur would have the attention of all of them. The Guardsman was already running down the levee, shoving his way through the growing group, trying to figure out what happened. The men packed tighter, and he could not get through.

Arthur threw down the shovel and dragged bags of lime under the injured man's legs to elevate them. He shouted: "HE'S ALIVE. GET HIM TO THE DOCTUH." Then he ran.

One-quarter mile to the east was the supply road jammed with truckloads of workers constantly moving to points of weakness wherever they were found, which was everywhere. For days now, seepage and leaks were apparent all along. Arthur jumped aboard one going south and made it back to another camp on the levee, just another in the army of 30,000.

April 18

The water crashed into itself illogically, boiling and swirling, bearing down on the workers' slim refuge with incredible pressure. The men were on the east side in several lines down to the base, conveying sandbags up, desperately throwing them on top in six inches of water. The massive hill on which Arthur stood in mud to his shins started to shake like jelly. A foot of water pushed a dozen bags back onto the line, then a hundred. Suddenly before anyone could even shout, the river blasted through a crevasse 100 feet wide, taking as many workers. Just like that, it gouged out another 100 feet open on either side. The spot attracted the entire force of the rushing ocean, forming a massive eddy that assaulted the levee for 100 yards downstream in reverse, a maelstrom sucked back upstream to blast against anything man-made.

The river turned its entire attention to bringing crushing death. In seconds it was the intensity of Niagara Falls, then double that. One million cubic feet of water per second began a journey of destruction. Arthur was yanked from his boots and sucked deep down into the fury of rushing water.

The roar could be heard up and down the river for miles inland. A Navy seaplane raced to Greenville to sound the alarm, and every church bell was set pealing. A 50-foot wall of water a mile across collected absolutely everything in its path: trees, houses, machines, cattle, people... hissing, spitting foam, and mud. Witnesses said it was rolling dirt, barely reflective, so instantly did it snatch up dry ground.

Bodies were shot into the air and back into the mass. Arthur never lost consciousness and somehow managed to get to the surface of the muck to breathe, only to be sucked down again and again. When he rose, he was rushing along at 20 miles an hour directly into huge trees, but the water before him flattened them, and again, he was submerged, contacting things hard and soft, branches and the clutches of the drowning. He slammed into something hard and flat underwater and grabbed hold. His head came into the air, and though his eyes were caked, he saw it was a roof, slowly turning over. The rooms under it filled, and the small house stabilized upright. In a few moments, he was able to get a step aboard and maintain a foothold, but his right foot would not work. He held on like that for perhaps five minutes, the mud boiling all around for a mile, until the rolling waves began to settle a bit and he could haul himself further up. The long toe on his right foot was gone and the toe next to it was broken, but he could feel nothing below tortured ankles. He rode the small house deep into the countryside. Back to the west, there was only rushing water and nothing else but the most massive trees held up in the churning violence, collecting pieces of civilization and dead livestock.

The air was dark with geese, turkeys, egrets, innumerable smaller birds, and high above them, buzzards circling lazily. He thought that the buzzards would simply glide to the place where land remained, wherever that was… however far away that might be. There, bodies would pile and rot. Then, they would feast.

20

"I am fine."

April 1943

Mother and Aunt Jane had a birthday party for Lindsay in the backyard, with an aged "magician" whose act consisted mainly of his jumping from one barrel into another and back, and a pony, which bit the birthday girl, then began to buck. With one arm, Arthur scooped the screaming Lindsay from the back of the pony, and with the other held its bridle to the ground with such force that the pony knelt.

The mothers distracted the children with a game in a futile effort to prevent the event from devolving into a disastrous memory. As she clung to Arthur, Lindsay ran her finger over long scars just below his left ear and said, "Do you have a bo-bo, Ottie?" He smiled and dried her tears. Arthur and Lindsay had a different kind of bond. He called her 'little sister', and listened intently to the adventures of her imaginary friend, Mary Jane. Lindsay seemed the only one who could elicit a laugh from Arthur when she would twirl around the kitchen, bumping into James Anna, to prove wrong his assertion that Mary Jane was the better dancer. Mother's cook, James Anna, was impatient with small children. Driven and clinical, she would put six of her own through college on a cook's wage.

Last year, before Big Charlie and my uncles disappeared into training and the war, he came in one night after a road trip of a few days and was met out the back stairs by his excited baby girl. "DADDY!" she shouted. He squatted down and held his arms wide. Arthur was helping to unload as Dad was relishing his reunion, covering her with kisses. He asked, "Who is your best boyfriend?"

"You are Daddy! And I won't kiss Arthur anymore!"

The pony man was loading the misbehaving Shetland into its trailer when up the long driveway came their postal carrier, Mary Stanton, laying on the horn. She looked bursting to share, waving a piece of mail excitedly. She leaped from the car, which bucked to a stall. Arthur met her at the back of a porch that entered the kitchen. "LOOK! LOOK!" Miss Stanton gushed, hardly able to keep from reading aloud the postcard on top of the stack.

The postcard featured a golden eagle standing on top of the earth defiantly, wings outstretched, its talons sunk into a red European continent, the Rising Sun Flag of Japan in the sky behind. At the top, the words "IMPERIAL JAPANESE NAVY" in red across the top over Japanese hieroglyphic characters floating vertically. Appreciating the excitement of the messenger, Arthur hurried the stack around to the backyard, where the mothers who had not yet fled the scene sipped vodka and their children played in the pretty spring day.

Mother accepted the pile and looked at the postcard for a moment. She turned it over. Addressed to Mrs. W. L. Smith, it said up the left side from bottom to top "IMPERIAL JAPANESE NAVY POSTCARD" and simple left to right:

22nd MAY 1942

At the bottom of a pre-printed paragraph that began "I am in a P.O.W. Camp near Moulmein, Burma..." she recognized her son's labored handwriting at the bottom:

I am FINE,

CD

Deane's mother, Nonna, disappeared into her room for three days. The postcard, blatant propaganda imparting the Imperial Empire's "respect" for the humane rules of war (1864 and subsequent Geneva Convention protocols), would reach thousands of mothers worldwide:

IMPERIAL JAPANESE ARMY

I am in a P.O.W. Camp near Moulmein, Burma. There are 20,000 Prisoners, being Australian, Dutch, English, and American. There are several camps of 2000-3000 prisoners who work at settled labor daily.

We are quartered in very plain huts. The climate is good. Our life is now easier with regard to food, medicine, and clothes. The Japanese Commander sincerely endeavors to treat prisoners kindly.

Officers' salary is based on the salary of Japanese Officers of the same rank and every prisoner is given daily wages from 25 cents (minimum) to 45 cents, according to rank and work.

Canteens are established where we can buy some extra foods and smokes. By courtesy of the Japanese Commander, we conduct concerts in the camps, and a limited number go to a picture show about once per month.

_____

_____

21

Rationing

August 1943

The day Billy turned thirteen, Mother cried. At first, I thought it was because he was about to go off to school; she was mourning the waning childhood of her firstborn. But, she had cried a lot since Mac was born, and James Anna said it was something that happened with mothers sometimes after they had the baby, and she would get over it.

Mother had plenty to cry about, but she was always strong in our experience, and crying was not in her nature. In an era when a lady so visibly expecting was expected to keep herself out of sight until her distended body resumed womanly shape, last August, she took a solo train ride to Norfolk to see Big Charlie ship out aboard the USS CROATAN.

We had long known children were to be seen and not heard, but we had only just come to understand the same applied to Mother. Now, without Dad around, often she spoke of interests and passions such as Aunt Beth's dubious strategy at bridge, or her duties as a Daughter of The Revolution, or The Colonial Dames. My father was not at all without humor, but he had a low threshold of tolerance for things not pertinent to *his* current stream of consciousness. After a few seconds, discourse with no apparent point might earn verbal disdain, if not outright public excoriation.

When I was about eight, we all sat in the sunroom around the RCA, listening to game four of the World Series; it looked like the Yankees might be about to sweep the Reds. "King Kong" Charlie Keller stole home in the 10th inning, hammering into Reds catcher Ernie Lombardi at the same time as the ball, which hit him right in the gonads (we later learned).

Mother chose the moment to vocalize a passing thought about who had owned the oriental rug before it came into her mother's possession: "—trader found it in Bombay and picked it up for a song. But he had to buy it its own a ticket aboard the—"

Over the crowd noise, and now, Mother, we were straining to hear: Joe DiMaggio scored another run as Lombardi was writhing on the ground.

"SHUT UP, Louise! Nobody wants to hear about that! WE ARE LISTENING TO THE GAME!" This is perhaps an unfair example; Mother's judgmental lapses socially were not always so dramatic, but I remember the scene well, and it's funny. She smiled and absorbed it sweetly as if turning the other cheek. Big Charlie was unforgiving as the press, which after that game puritanically reported that Lombardi was "napping" at the plate.

The partygoers: Mother, Billy (13), Carlo (11), Lindsay (7), Denton (3), and baby Maclean, who had just come along more or less, Cleo and Arthur all sat in the breakfast room between the kitchen and large dining room. James Anna backed into the room from the kitchen through the swinging door and spun around holding a birthday cake (carrot, Billy's favorite), lit with 13 candles. Her black face was illuminated from below. Mother said something to Arthur, then led "Happy Birthday," and Arthur appeared before the song's end with a wrapped package: long and heavy, covered in rosy-faced Santas. I wondered whether it had been purposefully delayed, recalling on the back stairs rolls of Christmas gift wrap which had not yet been stored for the season.

It was the side-by-side Parker A-1 Special 20-gauge shotgun I had often admired behind glass, locked in Big Charlie's gun closet. Lavishly engraved, he had often spoken of its value, but he had let me shoot it only once. Mother was crying, and I think by then, so were we— Billy for empathy with Mother and joy quite possibly. I wept with jealousy.

But of course, we wanted immediately to go shooting. There was nothing in season yet but crows, and so we began to plan a hunt. Mother cut us off at the knees: "Your father said you are not to take this gun out into the field until he gets back."

I looked at Arthur, and he winked.

Sometime the next afternoon, Arthur took us across the Mississippi. We stood on the huge stones shoring up the river bank on the Arkansas side, north of the bridge, and shot clay targets framed in the sky over downtown Memphis until we had each shot up a box of 25 shells using the Parker. Technically, we were not "in the field."

Shells being increasingly difficult to come by then, Arthur had been teaching us to reload. They were expensive, and you could get only a box at a time. Shells then were manufactured then with a shorter brass base to save brass and longer paper hulls, but Arthur had been saving them for years and had plenty of the long casings, and he taught me to reload. It was laborious, and I imagined he spent all his free time doing it: using a roll crimper, a little machine that clamps on the edge of a workbench. There is a chamber to hold the shell case, a lever to press it in, and a crank to turn, which forces the end of the shell closed around your powder/wad/shot/seal. Until I started loading shells, even my Winchester Model 12 pump seemed like such a precision instrument. Nope. You put sufficient powder in front of that primer, and whatever was forward of it was going out the barrel when you squeezed the trigger. I screwed up a lot of shells and lived to tell about it. This is why people can load them with salt for domestic situations or mix small lead shot with buckshot for larger animals. I will say the less uniform your load, the less accurate.

The wad was pretty important. That's a sleeve made of cellulose (plant fiber) that carries the ordinance out of the barrel. You could ruin a barrel pretty quick, forgetting the wad. Not to mention your gun sort of coughs out shot with no accuracy, and it makes the most awful sound.

I learned which shells to save and which couldn't be reloaded— those swelled by water or with pinholes at the edge of the brass base, where the powder had tried to burn through. This was often the case with the shorter brass casings. During the war years, primers were the toughest to get.

While we managed the ammo shortage, fuel during the war years was also limited, and our excursions had to be considered carefully. By 1943, the Woody had a "B" sticker, which enabled Arthur to buy up to eight gallons of fuel at a time, just about what we needed to get to North Mississippi and back. You weren't supposed to drive over 35, but you couldn't travel the roads down there any faster than that anyway. B stickers were for vehicles "essential to the war effort." Not completely true, but Big Charlie pulled strings. Most cars bore the "non-essential" "A" sticker, which with your coupons, entitled you to up to four gallons a week. Manufacturers and working farms could get unlimited fuel, though, luckily. If we could get to Skytop, we would fill up at the farm's own pump.

The September day we packed Billy off on the train to Episcopal High School in Virginia, Arthur and I went to Horseshoe Lake.

Against Mother's specific instructions, I brought Billy's gun, the side-by-side Parker.

Arthur recognized the heavy brown leather gun case and said, "You ain't 'sposed to have that gun."

"*We shot it last week,*" I protested.

"That was my fault. Yo Momma say 'don't go inna the field'. She did'n say don't shoot it. But... well, I was wrong. We boaf know what she mean. Now, this heah ain't yo gun. Two wrongs don't make a right."

"I didn't bring... *my* gun."

Arthur looked out over the lake. A half-mile against the far side, clouds of small ducks zipped back and forth low, silhouetted against the clear blue sky. It would be a dove shoot.

"Well... bettuh not somethin' happen."

We flipped over the boat, and Arthur mounted and gassed up the little 5-horse Evinrude outboard as I swept out cobwebs and leaves.

Shortly we stood waist-high in water blanketed with lily pads, shooting teal. The first wave invasion of the annual assault of waterfowl in the early fall, teal fly like doves, oblivious to call, maneuvering, evasive, darting past us impossibly fast. At the movies, they played a newsreel showing Jap Mitsubishi 97s dive-bombing battleships, effecting incredible damage. I was shooting well, blasting teal out of the sky fast as I could reload, imagining I was manning the ship's giant guns in do-or-die self-defense. The third or fourth time I did this, excitedly breaking open the breech to reload, I fumbled my shell satchel, and most of my shells went into the water. A handful came to rest on lily pads, and I snatched at them with my left hand before they too could roll away. The shotgun slipped from my right hand, which frantically seized the barrel, but it was so hot I dropped the gun into the water. The next hours were spent trying to restore that gun and me to our pre-stupid condition. Arthur said I was going to have to fix what I broke all by myself. On the way home, I disassembled it as much as I dared, wiped it down top to bottom, inside and out, and returned it to gleaming display behind glass in the gun case, with no one the wiser (except Arthur). It did not come out again.

Between Christmas and New Years, we hunted at Arkabutla Lake, just Arthur and me. All afternoon, we watched and called high flights of traveling ducks and geese by the thousands and even Arthur could not pull them in. Almost at dusk, we were about to conclude the day was a complete bust when the delicious whistling hiss of wings descended suddenly, right upon us from four directions; we were engulfed by rare canvasbacks.

Git'em!" said Arthur, and we leaped up shooting. I felled one trying to land on my barrel in a blast of feathers! Instantly I turned on another flaring mallard and fired-- THOONK went my gun. Before I considered that, I pumped the third shell into the barrel and in fluid motion swung, more determined to nail the same duck before he was completely out of range, and my gun exploded. My first thought was my eyes were sprayed with burning powder. The shock of the pain and violent backlash that followed the explosion, much louder than a shot, made me drop the gun and throw my hands to my face. When I could open them finally, literally minutes later, I saw that my barrel had burst, peeled back symmetrically in slivers, like the capitals of a column. The wad from my previous shell had been in the barrel.

Arthur said, "You look [like] a 'coon."

He told me a story of a weekend a few years ago, around Christmastime, at the Robinsonville Hunting Club. Regular member Dr. Keehn Thornberry was a "stump," which was Arthur's way of saying he was somewhat humorless. He rarely hunted with the other members and preferred Manny above the other guides as his paddler.

"Mistuh Casey and Mistuh Saunders and Mistuh Ferrell was playing poker and drankin' well into the morning, an makin' noise an laughing' an hollering'. Doctuh T wuz tryin' to sleep, an they kept razzin' him sayin' they needed a fourth and why din he getup an' play poker. This went on two or three times, and the lass time he shouted at them if they din leave him be he wuz goin to getup shootin'. When they went back in the other room and commenced they game, he close de doe back, and emptied the shot out of a handful of his shells, an loaded his gun. Innafew mins, when they bus through, he come up outta his bed blastin'. Mistuh Ferrell toin'd a ankle tryin' to scoot backward and the other two fell back over they table game, one on top of another, sprayin' chips and liquor. Dr. T, he say he laugh when he tells it, but I ran in there, and I still ain't never seen him laugh."

Two years later when Dad was home from the war, and Billy was home for Thanksgiving, we went on a chilly morning hunt to Mhoon Lake. The blind we were heading to was cramped, so we put Billy out in his hip boots, at a spot where the knees of growing cypress had joined, instead of one overwhelming the others, to form a shelf in front of a massive tree, which had shaken off its surrounding parasitic twins to rise spectacularly 75 feet. He had hunted there before - it was a natural flyway through the swamp, where wood ducks passed by and often lit in the slight clearing and slough before him. We settled in at the blind 100 yards away, just at daylight, ducks falling in all over us, and Big Charlie and I had ten ducks on the water in as many minutes.

BOOM! BOOM! The blasts came through the willows from my brother's direction. A second later, he shouted, "I MADE A DOUBLE!" What a great morning!

We continued our assault for several minutes but soon noticed no more shooting from Billy. "MY GUN WON'T SHOOT!" The Parker would not shoot but one time each barrel. Days later, Big Charlie brought home the rusted trigger mechanism from the gunsmith, and I was exposed.

"I left word that you were not to shoot this gun until I got back," said he, in the low, even tone usually reserved for the dramatic act of removing his alligator belt. I opened my mouth to correct that Mother had said something about not taking it "into the field," but thought better of it and told a severely abridged version of my mishap at Horseshoe, leaving out our trap shoot on the banks of the river, which relieved Billy and Arthur of disobedience and complicity, but cost me the rest of that season.

22

Repatriation

The Burma railroad was finished in mid-September, but the death rate did not slacken when the workload did. The rate of disease was so great, and the men's resistance so impacted that between August and November, almost 500 men Deane had suffered alongside died at the 80 or 100 Kilo camps.

December 26

The sickest men were removed to Thailand on the train, and the remaining laborers were collected from various camps and sent to Kilo Camp 105, under "Colonel Ishii", to maintain the rails and cut wood for the engines. The work was easier, but the food was worse. But because the men had been educated by the Dutch doctor as to what local plants, jungle grasses, and weed herbs might be used to prevent or cure disease, this fittest group survived and fell into a routine.

April 10, 1944

Deane's group of about three hundred men was moved from Camp 105 to Thailand to Kanchanaburi, about 70 miles west of Bangkok. The Chinese and the Thais were allowed to bring in fruit, nuts, and meat, and the Japanese ration was better than Deane had seen in over a year. There were some medical supplies. Slowly, the men began to recover their health. With the improved rations were snippets of news of the war, and the POWs' spirits rose.

In two weeks began a regular once-a-month inspection by a Japanese staff doctor, Lieutenant Iguchi, who would line up and select the fittest men for shipment to Japanese factories and mills, overriding any objections from the two remaining Allied POW doctors— his qualifications: second-year dental student.

Some were sent to Saigon, and some to Singapore. The Americans who were sent to Saigon were witnesses to Admiral Halsey's highly successful Operation Gratitude, targeting Jap ships in the South China Sea to help liberate the northernmost and largest island in the Philippines, Luzon.

January 10, 1945

Japan was wholly dependent on oil, rubber, and other raw materials arriving from Singapore by way of the South China Sea shipping lanes, the importance of which was equally well understood by the Allies. Operation Gratitude's priority was to deal a blow to the Japanese naval fleet, but a secondary goal was to disrupt this vital line of supply. Scouring the Indochina coast, Allied aircraft found and attacked with impunity concentrations of merchant ships and escort vessels in Saigon harbor, on the Mekong River, off Cap-Saint-Jacques at the mouth Mekong Delta, at Cap-Padaran 150 miles up the coast, and at Cam Ranh Bay.

At the end of that single day, a total of 41 ships throughout the region were sunk, 31 others were damaged, and 112 aircraft were destroyed on the ground (or on the water). Additionally, numerous docks, oil storage tanks, and airfield facilities were heavily damaged.

Back in the camp at Kanchanaburi, Deane learned of the raid because six British officers he met there, under the command of Captain Wheaton, had a radio concealed in bamboo, which they successfully maintained for several months. Built by their radio engineer, R. G. Wells, from parts found and brought in with rations, it was an ingenious assembly of tin foil, string, tree bark, and a piece of wire rubbed with palm oil mixed with a little bit of flour, which made a fairly good insulation over the wire. It was powered by a "battery" made of a potato. Deane recalled hearing the chime of Big Ben signaling the start of a BBC newscast.

June 1945

Commandant Ishii was replaced by a fanatical sadist, Captain Moguchi, who took delight in inflicting pain and death, sharing the duty with second-in-command Sergeant Shimoso. On the second day of their arrival, the entire camp was made to stand at attention for two hours in the sun.

Finally, Shimoso and Moguchi appeared, and Captain Moguchi lectured the men in Japanese for forty-five minutes. After three-plus years of imprisonment, some prisoners spoke Japanese, and there was some general understanding among the other prisoners. The gist of the address was the superiority of the Japanese race and the luck of these men to be under his guidance at this time or something similar.

As an introductory gesture, Shimoso called out a British interpreter, Captain Greller, who had complained to Ishii just before he was replaced about some ill-treatment British officers had received on a work party. In perfect English, Shimoso politely asked Greller to restate the complaint. Greller spoke for about one minute before Sergeant Shimoso took a rifle from a private standing nearby and struck him in the face with the butt, breaking his jaw. Greller was thrown, bleeding, into a coffin-sized metal box exposed to the sun and the heat in plain view in the courtyard, where he spent one week. At the end of the sixth day, he was seen carried by two soldiers to a dugout which was the air raid shelter- to solitary confinement and was not seen again until the war ended eleven weeks later.

This was the summer of greatest despair and challenged faith, when prisoners who had held out the longest, for years, as had Ensign CD Smith, wasted away and died by the dozens each day, by the inexhaustible cruelty of their captors.

July 4, 1945

Though he was still in recovery from his Burma experience, Deane expected to be selected and shipped off to work in Japanese factories any day. The next day he was able to recall the dream that visited him in the night in vivid detail and began to wonder if his mind was rewriting its memories.

Kneeling on the deck, he cradled the Captain of the HOUSTON, barely alive. Exploding shells and 50-caliber rounds struck all around. The dazed crew and officers moved in confusion; the wounded screamed for help. Fires on deck highlighted Captain Rooks, convulsing in shock, his life streaming onto Deane and the deck near his cabin while the ship's bowels were ripped and spilling into the sea. Deane injected Rooks with both vials of morphine he carried on his belt; his Captain became still and was lain against the bulkhead so as not to roll. Deane stepped to the top of the railing and dove. Below the surface, phosphorus churned up by all the ships in the shallow channel produced an eerie green glow, a misplaced calm pierced by men diving or falling from the decks. He saw under the ship a great gash in the hull, emitting twisted rivulets of oil swirling like sashes around sailors suspended who were struggling to surface, or frozen as they died. Then, he was at the rear of the ship, in the path of the great propeller, a massive four-bladed clover that continued somehow to push the ship's carcass forward. In a moment, it was upon him, and he was turned over and over as though in a giant washing machine.

He saw himself shoot into the air and splash down into the boiling wake behind the doomed HOUSTON. Suddenly there in the water, drowning, he willed himself to swim hard laterally, clear of it. Searchlights played across the listing ship, which continued to pull away, flashes on all surfaces with exploding shells and machine gun fire...

Back home, President Harry Truman's Independence Day address was hopeful and seemed to foreshadow what would come in early August. Deane and several of the men heard the BBC rebroadcast on July 6:

"...In this year of 1945, we have pride in the combined might of this nation

which has contributed signally to the defeat of the enemy in Europe. We have confidence that, under Providence, we soon may crush the enemy in the Pacific. We have humility for the guidance that has been given us by God in serving His will as a leader of freedom for the world..."

Moguchi and Shimoso lurked everywhere. Somehow, they discovered the radio, and Captain Wheaton and another officer, who took credit for its design, were beaten to death in the courtyard as all camp prisoners who could stand were made to witness. Their arms and legs were slowly broken, their skulls fractured, and they were left in the sun. The other four were tortured behind closed doors by the Kempeitai, the Japanese Gestapo, and not seen again.

August 6, 1945

Deane had another dream more vivid than the last.

The water was calm in the early dawn. Dozens of swimmers spread out, visible only for their wakes, advancing slowly, clawing forward in the water toward bumps of land hardly visible on the horizon. Deane's view was from above, but he did not wonder about that. His mind conjured an aerial shot in Rooks's office just framed the week before of the flotilla the swimmers had just escaped. He saw himself and Batt Russell far out in front, and suddenly he was in the water again, swimming, feeling intense pain in his shoulders but nothing in his leaden arms...

The sun jumped up from the land instantly, like the rebound of a ball– it was morning. But it wasn't. The entire horizon burst in a blinding flash, then settled blue-white. There rose a donut of bright red on a flaming tree trunk of orange and black, which grew larger despite collapsing in on itself. Straight up into the clouds, it climbed, turning them to fire. In another moment, Deane saw the shockwave energy generated by the blast seeking every direction. It rolled him onto his back, and then there was nothing... neither sight nor sound and no air to breathe– his lungs, already starved by the swim, turned them-

selves inside out in the sudden vacuum... and then he felt the intense heat, superheated steam burning his face...

August 7, 1945

An increasing number of irrational events gave some inkling that the grip of the Empire of the Sun was slipping. Commandant Moguchi had all "able-bodied" assembled in the courtyard and delivered a screaming, hour-long tirade in Japanese, during which he threatened the POWs with torture and death as "retribution." No food or water was distributed on that day.

August 8, 1945

The men were not rousted at dawn, nor was there a work detail, but rice and water rations resumed.

August 9, 1945

For the second day, no prisoners were beaten or otherwise harassed, and neither the Commandant nor Sergeant Shimoso was seen. Several of the guards were trucked away early in the morning, leaving what seemed a skeleton crew. Deane's fantastic dream resumed.

Riding in the belly of a B17, Deane looked down through open bomb doors at the dark sea, at the lights of the HMAS PERTH and the USS HOUSTON, toy ships steaming northwest near Java, into the circular cup of Banten Bay. Seemingly oblivious to the Japanese cruiser pursuing from behind, they were headed into the path of two enemy cruisers bearing down on an intercepting course from the other side of Panjang Island to the north. As the plane moved closer to the flotilla, intense engagement began on the water. Sailors leaped from their ships like fleas. A great hole opened in the sea. Still under intense assault, firing back, the two Allied ships began a slow rotation.

A dark figure on the fore deck of the HOUSTON, not in naval uniform but wearing a wide-brim hat and oiled canvas dust coat, raised his arms. In that instant, a sun ripped back the darkness; all was blinding white, then yellow, then orange. A mushroom of orange-red rose far to the north, and when it formed a ring of white in its midsection, the concussive report reached them. Because it was distant, it was not as intense as before, but more like the rush of the blast from the torpedo Deane saw strike the HOUSTON from his refuge in the water, the final insult required to finish her...

Finally, freedom

August 16, 1945

Early in the morning, the prisoners learned the name of the Governor of the Chonburi Province, Colonel Kuhn *Montri*, who had supported them both with and without the supervision of the Japanese, with food and supplies (including parts for the radio). Montri had been training guerrillas, and he strode through the gates with a small detachment of soldiers, bringing news of the war's end two days before. Immediately, the POW officers organized their troops and assaulted the handful of guards remaining, easily overwhelming them.

By noon the camp was in Allied control. Captain Greller was recovered from solitary, barely alive after 11 weeks, suffering black water fever. He weighed 75 pounds. He would survive after being given five blood transfusions.

Moguchi and Shimoso were not found on the grounds. They had evacuated by the 14th, at the time of Japan's surrender, under cover of darkness.

Roaming the Japanese officers' mess hall, the men found fresh vegetables, dried beef, fruit, and cases of sake. The ample stores were distributed to all fit enough to eat after months or years on an almost all-rice diet. Soups were made to nourish the weakest. Late into the evening, Deane sat around a long table with Colonel Montri, officers, and NCOs, the men who had been leaders. Empty bottles of sake seemed to multiply.

Deane remarked, "My dreams in the last days have been more intense than at any time before as a prisoner. In fact, they were like visions, more vivid than at any time in my entire life. I have wondered about them." He told of the swim and the great blast of light and the ships in the whirlpool and the great light again.

"Ahhh," said Montri. He understood English well, though he was hard to understand. He spoke to his interpreter in Thai. The man looked around the assembled table, smiling. He said:

"You speak of the ***Ryujin,*** the great *dragons* which America loosed on Japan on August 6 and 9. They were given names by your Air Force. The *Little Boy,* and the even nastier *Fat Man,* broke the back of the Imperial Empire."

It was over. Now able to go into town at will, the POWs lived "like kings" for two weeks until the American OSS troops reached Bangkok.

September 1, 1945

Deane stepped aboard a C-47 Skytrain and flew to Rangoon. There the men were segregated by their ships or units, and Deane found Edmonson and other surviving members of the USS HOUSTON. They were sent to the 142nd US Army General Hospital in Calcutta for routine medical examination and treatment (when necessary), joining 216 sixteen surviving US Naval and Marine Corps personnel in Calcutta.

The British, Dutch, American, and Australian officers were debriefed, and each was asked to provide detailed statements of his troops' ordeals. Deane's scribbled record in the bamboo shoot, though not transcribed since a year before, provided critical names and supporting evidence for criminal trials for the earliest offenses in his experience and ultimately helped to piece together the historical record.

UNITED STATES NAVAL LIAISON OFFICE
6. CHURCH LANE
CALCUTTA, INDIA
EN3-11(CT) A8-21

SER:01139   September 9, 1945

From: The U.S. Naval Liaison Officer, Calcutta India

To: The Director of Naval Intelligence.

Via: The Senior U.S. Naval Liaison Officer, I-B Theater

Subject: USS HOUSTON

Reference: (a) Aluslo Calcutta Dispatch 05080h to DNI.

Enclosures: (a) Summary submitted by Lt (jg) Harold S. Hamlin USN, and Lt (jg) Leon W. Rogers USN, with:

1. Statement of Comdr W. Epstein (MC) USN

2. Statement of Ensign CD Smith USN

3. Statement of Harrell, J.A. Yeo/3/c USNR

4. Statement of Ensign John B. Nelson USN

5. Statement of Ensign PR Clark (PC) USN

6. Statement of Thomas, C.L., S1c, USN

23

Home

October 3, 1945

The afternoon had a chill, so we thought they would be "safer" and more comfortable under the stove.

Billy and I took the dividers out of a wooden red box once used to transport Cokes, stuffed it with grayed sawdust from the quail house (out of production since before Big Charlie went away), and placed in it six baby chicks which Arthur had given us (his rooster had got into his hen house and he said 'I cain't raise no more chickens'). My brother carried it across the porch through the kitchen door, and I followed, both of us steeled for Cooker's objections. She looked up from a big mixing bowl and turned to face us with a frown, hands on hips. Mary Neely opened her mouth to speak when the telephone rang, and she dashed off to the front hall to answer.

Billy's favorite, turnip greens, stewed in a pot on top, and my favorite, her homemade cornbread, rose in the oven. The room was a delight to the senses, warm, smelling of heaven.

The Magic Chef oven was raised up off the floor on ornate feet like a bathtub- the Coke nest just slid under it. I guess it was too hot under there because the chicks hopped out almost the moment we stepped back to admire how cozy we had made them.

In the great hall, changing light bulbs in the foyer chandelier, Arthur stood on the top step of a rickety step ladder too short for the job. Ocie leaned his weight against it, a stanchion against certain, unsecured failure. The scene was comic and absurd. Ocie was almost a foot taller than Arthur, yet some fraction of his mass. He should be on the ladder.

One's hue within the caste system helped to dictate who could get away with what. Ocie Hartley was lighter even than Cleo. He could almost pass for white. So great was his condescending demeanor; he had little time for the other (darker) help, and the feeling was mutual. It was simpler to just oblige fussy, effeminate Ocie than confront him. He introduced himself as Ocie Hartley, personal Chauffeur to Mrs. WL Smith. Self-importance was his obsession.

He secured the wobbly ladder under Arthur with growing impatience.

Mary Neely snatched up the receiver: "Miz Smith resi-deyant, Cooker speakin'."

'Miz Luvell' (Mother's Nashville friend, Virginia Levelle) was well known to Cooker after all the summers the families spent together in the Carolina Blue Ridge mountains. She was a talker, and Cooker began to think through an excuse to expedite handing the phone to her employer. She was about to say her soup was boiling but then was struck; the truth would do— her kitchen was overrun with chickens...

Unable to keep it to herself a moment longer, Virginia Levelle blurted:

"Charles Deane is coming home! To Nashville tomorrow! Did you hear? CD will be home!"

"My... baby?"

Cooker gasped, "My baby! Deane? Deane is coming home? Oh... oh... Lawd!" She burst into tears.

Instantly Ocie released the ladder and turned about-face to go and inform (and thus ingratiate himself with) his employer. With the sharp crack of splitting pine, the little wood ladder failed, crashing to the floor, but Arthur deftly landed on his feet. By then, the chauffeur was already gone from the room. Arthur found Cooker's gaze even in her semi-hysterical state, and they shook their heads.

Captain John Levelle, MD, chief of Surgery at Walter Reed Bethesda, was in the habit of noting carefully the patient traffic in his hospital throughout the war. By the time soldiers reached him, it was often the last stop before a debilitated life. Men would already have been slapped together in the actual theater of battle as best they could, bones reset, and surgeries cleaned up at the first available respite. Delivering good news to families was a rare experience. Mostly the news was otherwise. Levelle was an expert at sincere empathy.

The name Charles Deane Smith appeared on his manifest. His eye found it and moved on, yet returned and moved on... and again... Levelle took several seconds to place Smith. *Oh, my God. Deane!* CD Smith, *Katherine's beau*, Louise Walterlane's brother, son of industrialist Will Smith. Everyone thought him lost in the sinking of the HOUSTON. Then a couple of years ago... a propaganda postcard from the Japs.

Every summer, since Deane first appeared toddling about the Smiths' Blue Ridge Mountain retreat in Linville, he seemed a foot taller. Then he was a young man, smitten by Katherine, and she, him. Then he was a champion swimmer on the Annapolis swim team, about to graduate. Katherine rode the train to attend his commissioning. Levelle realized twenty-five summers had gotten by him since he first knew CD. He and Virginia had talked often, imagining the day he would give away their precious daughter in a joyous celebration— to Deane Smith.

Instead, before they learned Deane was alive, Katherine married Lieutenant JG Garrett Lee in February 1943, in front of the handful of family they could assemble, so the couple might have two weeks together in San Francisco before his destroyer, the USS HULL, sailed to help pound the Japanese in the Aleutian Islands. She saw Garrett just twice more, later that year in Oakland and for a week in 1944 while the ship was in Pearl Harbor for repairs late last October. He was just starting to get to know his baby daughter, Janie when his ship was ordered to rendezvous with fast carrier striking forces in the Philippine Sea. Then, that bastard William

Halsey ordered the flotilla into a typhoon in the Solomon Islands. The ship and two others, the USS MONAGHAN and the USS SPENCE, and almost 800 lives were lost. Dozens more ships flipped thousands of tons of planes, vehicles, and equipment into the mountainous seas of Typhoon "Cobra" and were heavily damaged. Levelle often told officers privately Halsey could not have done more to cripple the war effort if he was the Japanese Commander of the South Pacific.

Many of Dr. Levelle's patients were chewed to broken remains by their bare existence in enemy hands. Now Deane Smith, who suffered the worst the enemy could bring against him, was returning to his family, entering the civilized world through the portal of Levelle's hospital. *Three-and-a-half years a POW!* What could be left of him?

He wanted to be the first familiar face Deane saw when he arrived. He was certain to ask about Katherine, Levelle thought. *What will I say?*

But Deane did not ask at first. After a few days, when Dr. Levelle came by to see if he might be ready to embark on a physical therapy program and gradually improved diet, Deane said, "I'm sure Katherine has married."

Levelle sighed. "Yes... But—"

"Do you have a picture?"

Doctor Levelle fetched the photograph from his office, one they treasured of Katherine and her sister Christine. Summers in Linville, they were counselors at Camp Yohnanoka. Halfway up the ladder from the pool, Katherine looked into the camera wearing a beautiful smile, her soaked hair and the drops on her tanned face caught the light just right, and she sparkled. Still in the pool, Christine was grabbing her ankle, giggling. Deane looked at it for a long time.

Then, his eyes pooling, he handed it to Dr. Levelle. "After the first year, I could not see her face anymore, no matter how hard I tried. She was gone. I prayed for her and all of you for happy lives."

Levelle did not know what to say. For two days more, he struggled with whether to try to reach his daughter in San Francisco. Katherine had written she was seeing a Navy Captain. Her mother, Virginia said, "Of course we must."

"He looks pretty terrible. We will keep him for the time being. Maybe I will write her after I contact his family."

"Let me reach out to her," she said.

At 6'2," Smith was an inch shorter than his recorded height and down by almost half his mass. "You are an exceptionally strong man," Levelle observed, "you survived." After debriefing and decompression after being liberated some five weeks before, Levelle deemed Deane fit enough in three weeks at 135 pounds (down from 210 lbs when the HOUSTON went down) to convalesce at home. He would arrive tomorrow in Nashville around 3 pm.

Three autos full of Walterlanes and Smiths left Memphis for the capital city, home of the Grand Old Opry. Though inching at a snail's pace through small communities, it was faster than by train, with the interminable stops of the passenger rail. Arthur drove Dad, Mother, Billy, and me in the Woody. Lindsay and Mac were not invited, thankfully, and played blissfully in the backyard under James Anna's watchful eye. We only stopped when Mother needed a break. Uncle Bill drove his Cadillac, carrying Uncle Bobby, Aunt Maggie and their boys Donovan and Lane, and sister Dale. Ocie pulled up the rear entourage in the Packard, carrying Nonna and Cooker, and for some reason I can't recall, our twin cousins Dottie and Peggy. Ocie said later Cooker chatted nervously nonstop for five hours, recounting stories of Deane as a toddler. He said Grandmother uttered hardly a word, and I wondered if there was any regret that the hands-on of my uncle's childhood was completely entrusted to servants. So it was for her, always. Nonna had not made such as a cup of tea in her life, so she certainly had never changed a diaper.

Finally, at precisely 3 pm, all sixteen attempted an assembly in a light drizzle, huddled together behind waste-high barriers out on the tarmac at Berry Field Airport in Nashville. We were travel-weary but animated by the excitement.

3:10. A big shiny plane that said PanAm landed but taxied away from us.

3:20. Two more incoming had dropped out of the low cloud ceiling and taxied to the gates, not our plane. Loud as the engines were, we did not hear them until we could see them.

My clothes were starting to soak through. I said so and got a squeeze on my shoulder from Arthur and a nasty look from Mother and Cooker. Cooker held Billy's hand and mine and was even more soaked than we were. Her white underwear showed through her wet summer dress, contrasted against her black skin. I remember she smelled of petrolatum (her hair) with a hint of licorice. Billy was as wet but kept his gaze steadily skyward and said nothing. Uncle Bill walked Nonna and Aunt Maggie to the shelter of the terminal. Mother and Big Charlie stood under an umbrella, and Ocie held one over the twins.

Far across, where runways intersected, the clouds seemed to touch the ground, so great was their moisture burden. Right where I stared, they spat a shiny object, a DC 2, and we heard its engines. It set down smoothly and zigzagged to us, coming to a stop finally at about 25 yards.

Nonna and Aunt Maggie were out of the shelter of the terminal halfway to us, well before Uncle Bill.

The props slowed to a stop and belched a big black fart at their last revolutions. Two men positioned a staircase on wheels at the door, and seconds later, it opened.

Cooker's grasp was crushing my hand, and she began to bellow. "Whhewww! Ohhhhh! Ewww!"

People appeared and began to descend.

"John Levelle!" said Mother.

Then she gasped, "Oh, my God."

Uncle Deane still had to stoop to emerge from the aircraft fuselage, and when he was fully out on the top stair and stood, the wind pressed against his jacket, outlining his frame, a tall armature of sticks under scarecrow clothes.

Looking up, Dr. Levelle waited for him at the bottom, his hand outstretched, beckoning, and Uncle Deane started down slowly, deliberately, hands on the rails.

Mary Neely Cooker could bear it no more. She dropped our hands and burst through the narrow opening between two barriers and ran to her charge. He was only a step from the foot of the rolling staircase when she enveloped him, and he caught her. And laughing, he returned the embrace. He waved at us then, with Cooker wailing against his chest, a scene I shall always recall.

Book II

*****

24

Uncle Cliff

I always wondered what the colored servants thought of the custom of awarding a title to the overly familiar, doubtless a child of the cocktail hour. In those days, I could not say with any certainty how many uncles or aunts I really had because every damned friend or acquaintance of Mother's or Big Charlie's was "Uncle Nick" or "Aunt Beth." Last Christmas, "Aunt Beth" gave me a really sloppy smack on the kisser when turning the required cheek, I was instead pulled close. She's no relation (I learned, quizzing Lindsay), and since then, I have been doubly repulsed. Everyone smoked cigarettes, but Aunt Beth's sagging face took on the blue-gray of the cloud of smoke constantly at her head. She had ashes on her eyelashes and in her blue hair. Whenever she was in a crowd, clad in her dull hues, contrasted by the bright colors of those around her, she looked like a TV picture.

"Uncle" Cliff Lewis is married to Lily, Big Charlie's first cousin once-removed (don't get me started). An unrepentant alcoholic, he is cruel as a Gestapo chief but clever in public: streams of witticisms engage and charm people who have little knowledge of him. Not your average drunk, Uncle Cliff is always "somewhere in his cups," says Big Charlie. I imagine he tortured small animals as a teen.

He spent the war years stateside, getting a "2-D" deferment: "Registrant deferred because of study preparing for the ministry," which was such a crock, he was a drunk and skirt chaser even then and dropped out of Virginia Theological Seminary a month before the Japs surrendered. Strangely, Dad and my real uncles didn't seem to be so outraged by this, perhaps because they were occupied with the details of Uncle Deane's rescue. I'd have beaten his ass.

At the only church retreat we all went on as a family (1946, a concession made by Big Charlie to Mother, which we have regretted ever since), Cliff pushed my head into the toilet. Whatever the perceived disrespect, I cannot recall, but since he is more or less my parents' age, I had deferred to him with the same err-on-the-side-of-caution over-respect I extended to every adult (while reserving true sincerity for real relations). I have never suspected Cliff had intelligence enough to perceive any disrespect by lack of sincerity. What set him off may remain a mystery... alcohol, I'll guess.

Big Charlie discharged Cliff out into the night without much effort and no violence. I felt traumatized the next day and night, partly because I wanted to break his neck, and was thus not a little disappointed in my father's passive defense.

I have since learned Cliff was in the cotton business like Big Charlie, and there were business dealings, which somewhat explains to me our family's regular association with them and perhaps my father's discretion.

Anyway, Cliff himself isn't particularly discreet. His drunken soirées, parties in his own home, might continue into morning, long after Lily had retired. Arthur bartended at many of these, often staying past midnight.

As she did Wednesdays, Cleo (Mother's other cook) walked the two blocks from the bus stop early one very crisp spring morning, up Cliff's driveway around to the back door of the house. The paved drive gives way to gravel once you pass by the lateral of the house. As she approached the back door, her footfalls crunched gravel noisily.

Cars were where they should be, except she noticed immediately that Mr. Cliff was in the driver's seat of the massive, shiny black Buick, his head turned to the driver's side, mouth open. With something of a start, she thought that he might be dead but saw his breath fogging that half-open window slightly. A couple of steps closer and she saw that he wore no jacket, only a thin white shirt.

Cleo looked to the house and everywhere about, but no neighbors could be seen.

Not given to deep thought, she stepped forward on impulse to wake him, before he caught cold, and she reached for the handle.

Rising through skeletal, pre-bud trees, brightening the east-facing windshield, the March morning sun illuminated Mr. Cliff's nudity well below his waist: on his dingus was a neatly tied black bow tie.

Neighbor Melissa Peebles babysat the night before. Unusually tall, gangly Melissa was not, therefore so much in demand for dates on a Friday, though I always thought she was quite pretty. She sat for us once or twice when Mother and Big Chas entertained, and James Anna or Cooker couldn't look after us and serve too. Sometimes I dreamt of Melissa, wishing she was my contemporary, not an old lady of eighteen.

Arthur released Cleo at about 10:30 so she could catch the night's last bus— he would look after the dishes.

The kitchen had been clean for some time. One am rolled around. Not seeing host Cliff among the remaining guests, Arthur made fewer trips into the living and sitting rooms, hoping the lingerers, two young couples, would burn themselves out. If you picked up their glasses, they only got clean ones.

Finally, they moved out the front door, and Arthur was able to put the living areas back into order. Though Mrs. Lewis rarely stayed downstairs after 10, Cliff was not known to retire before others.

While he considered whether to just go on home, there was a laugh (or maybe it was a muffled scream) from the den.

The den was on the other side of a hall, beyond the great room where most of Cliff's parties occurred, at the edge of the house. It was his private study, paneled floor-to-ceiling in mahogany, with a coal-burning fireplace.

Arthur was glad Mr. Cliff chose not to entertain here, far as it was from the kitchen. As he approached, there was another sound, more like a gasp, and then... a distinct "NO!" in a female voice.

He knocked. "Mr. Cliff?"

After a moment, a female voice said, "Oh... come in, COME IN!

Ass up, his pants and underwear at his ankles, the host lay slumped over Melissa Peebles on a too-short loveseat couch. Splayed under him helplessly as his body heaved in noisy slumber, she said, "I think he's asleep."

Arthur lifted and threw him over his shoulder in a smooth motion, and an exhalation of relief came from Melissa. Her blouse was unbuttoned and untucked, but she seemed covered otherwise, and Arthur exited the study with his burden. Melissa stood, pulling up her stockings, and found in her hand Arthur's black bow tie.

Melissa told Lindsay that she found Cliff asleep in his car when she left, naked below the waste, and couldn't resist leaving him a message. "Uncle" Cliff would never know that Arthur Campbell, not caring to install him in his own bed, was responsible only for removing him to the car, lest Mrs. Lewis be disturbed.

Arthur never again served at the Lewis household when Cliff was present, and Cliff Lewis ever after regarded and treated Arthur Campbell with the kind of disdain handed out to the lowest, but also most dangerous, spiders or snakes.

25

Two Angels

Spring, 1946

Easter Sunday afternoon, Mother, Nonna, Aunt Margaret, Cooker, and James Anna are in each other's way, shuffling and fussing about the meal underway in the kitchen. The men in the family have gravitated to the wood-paneled den, far across the house. Uncle Bobby stood in the closet-sized bar chamber separating the great room from the den. He cracked a rock of ice in his hand with a weighted spoon slap jack and shaved the pores from a lemon rind. Twist, shake, stir. The scent of vodka tinged with twists of citrus will always remind me of this tiny passageway– each entrant brought a pungency into the den. The coal fire that was always going had just been stoked, and the glowing bituminous rock popped just slightly, releasing grain-sized air pockets trapped for millennia.

Deane has begun to settle after his ordeal. He has seen friends; he has seen extended family. After five months, he is rested but is restless and withdrawn. Upon questions about his plans, he will say only, "I made promises."

"Memphis Stone and Gravel NEEDS *LEADERSHIP*," demanded Robert D. Smith (Uncle Bobby) impatiently from the bar, with far less than the agreed-upon tact. The subject of the family business founded by Deane's father, floundering with no capital investment since his death, with virtually all income going to support Deane's mother's lifestyle, was to be broached delicately after dinner...

Dad's brother Uncle Bill said quickly, "What promises? To whom? Who could YOU possibly owe a single thing to, Deane?"

It was a pleading, though almost challenging, tone. *We understand, but shake it off, son. The family business needs you— decision time.*

Through a cloud of cigarette smoke, my lean uncle's sallow eyes fell on Dad, moved to Uncle Bobby, Uncle Bill, and even Arthur, the evening bartender standing near the bar, each for a long pause. They didn't understand... never would. He said, "To the people who got me through it. I'm going to see their families."

I had some smidgen of understanding then— why was he one of the survivors? He must visit their families and deliver messages they could not. He must make several journeys.

I have thought before that Arthur is also this type of divine agent, something that Arthur himself would find comical.

We kids, having long been instructed to be 'seen and not heard', sat silently at the card table near the patio door. We had the sense of the great reverence and esteem in which Uncle Deane was held, and we were attracted to his celebrity. But we had little understanding of the war and absolutely no imagination of what my uncle had endured. I was nearest to Uncle Deane, and I caught his eye.

He looked directly at me and said, "Want to come?"

Uncle Deane, Arthur, and I will go off on a road trip at the end of July, an adventure I could never have imagined and one for which I was completely unprepared. We would journey out into the country to the homes of men Uncle Deane was close to, shipmates on the HOUSTON, or the families of soldiers he knew from years in the camps. Billy is at the far end of our journey and is somewhat the reason for our trip: we will collect him at the summer camp in Arizona, in the dry climes prescribed for his asthma.

I wrote a school paper about the trip that fall, which Mother kept for many years. My highlights are colored by the account of my fourteen-year-old self. It's probably been 40 years since I read it, but I remember laughing at my perspective *and* lack thereof. The paper is long gone, but dusting off the memory, there are standout moments.

Before the sun came up on Sunday the 28th, we crossed the Mississippi west out of Memphis in Big Charlie's 1942 Pontiac Streamliner, headed up to Missouri, then Oklahoma, New Mexico, and Arizona.

It was a challenging day. At about one o'clock, Arthur noticed the engine temperature gauge was leaning past the H. When we pulled over, steam seeped out the seam of the hood, billowing into a cloud when it was lifted. In 100° heat, we waited an hour for the radiator to cool enough to twist off the cap. It was almost dry.

"Hose leak," Arthur quickly diagnosed. He wrapped the offending hose with a bandana and poured all our drinking water into the radiator- which, with the heater on high, was enough to get us 35 more miles to a Poplar Bluff filling station, just short of halfway to St. Louis. Uncle Deane and I had cheeseburgers at a diner across the street while Arthur, with tools and fresh coolant, and a little assistance from the attendant, got us on our way as far as Farmington, about 35 miles south of St. Louis when it happened again. We affected the same "repair" and hours later made it to the Mayfair Hotel in downtown St. Louis probably about dinnertime, walking distance from a Chevrolet dealer. Uncle Deane booked us a room, and I sneaked Arthur up the stairs. He slept on the floor on chair pillows.

The next day, the service manager at the dealer told us the thermostat had stuck because of overheating, would have to be replaced, and needed a new radiator. He estimated getting parts, and the repair would take *a week to ten days!*

Uncle Deane suggested to Big Charlie let him trade it, but Dad said to fix it. Back upstairs he thought about that, while he and Arthur blew smoke toward the open window.

He said, "Arthur, we're going to take the train from here and don't need a driver anymore, I guess..."

"Aww..." I was exasperated, and it showed, something Big Charlie would say was very disrespectful.

"Tomorrow, you can go back to Memphis on the bus."

I hung my head. Uncle Deane got up from his chair and mussed my hair before he left the room without further comment. I thought he was probably checking the bus schedule.

But the next morning, without another word about it, he picked us up in a Chevy Fleetmaster rented from the dealer for a few days. We three would continue our mission for now.

I have wondered these many years about the root cause of this change of heart. How Uncle Deane's life might have been different had Arthur not continued with us!

We made multiple visits in and around St. Louis. I never knew how my uncle knew where he was going. He directed Arthur but did not consult a map. Not far from the hotel, we stopped in an old neighborhood called Benton Park. I got up front with Arthur and talked him out of a smoke while we waited in the car. Uncle CD stepped up to a brownstone building apartment. A woman appeared and threw her arms around him like Cooker did, holding tight. They stood there like that for a long time before going inside.

In an hour, I had to take a leak, and so did Arthur, and I knocked on the door. After a couple of minutes, I was starting to back down the steps to go in the bushes when Uncle Deane opened the door. His eyes were red. Beyond him, she was in a stuffed chair with her head in her hands. I made a mental note to ask him who she was... *later*.

We drove to the house of a surviving sailor, Larkin Edmonson, who was in the group Deane led to the safety when the HOUSTON went down. Again, Arthur waited dutifully in the cab. Mr. E was white, but his rundown house was in a colored neighborhood, a great contrast to the way we lived. He seemed healthy and fit, and they drank beer in the kitchen while I strummed on his guitar in a small den just a room away. After a while, he began to cry.

We crossed the bridge east over the river toward Madison and made a quick stop in another small town to the north (the name of which I can't think of). The residents were not home, so we went back across the river going west, stopped for gas in Florissant, then drove to St. Charles. Uncle Deane directed us onto a street with a dozen identical houses. We pulled up to a little white cottage exactly like the three or four to the left and the six or so to the right. As we sat there, a very pretty woman came out of a side door with a basket and started hanging up laundry on a clothesline in the yard. Two toddlers bumped around her knees. She looked up and smiled at us, and (I was ready to go meet this woman, but) Uncle Deane said, "Wait." When the line was heavy with sheets and clothes, she was finished, and they went inside. Uncle Deane lit a cigarette and simply put a letter in her mailbox. I waited for an explanation but got none.

Uncle Deane will have moments of complete focus, animated and engaged, which I notice coincide with the restart of our journey after a stop. They do not last. Soon he looks sad and stares out the window. It was a long drive back to St. Louis. I slept.

The next day, Uncle Deane and Arthur left me at the Mayfair until mid-afternoon. They came back without the car. The lady we visited first, "Mrs. Percy," showed up at the hotel and drove us to the train station, where we caught the Missouri Pacific *Eagle* to Kansas City and got off at Columbia, about halfway. Uncle Deane made a phone call while we had dinner in a cafeteria near the train station. The next train wasn't for a while, so Arthur and I went outside and played cards at a picnic table.

The loud engine made us look up. A cop on a huge white motorcycle stopped between us and the restaurant and eyeballed us, his motorcycle idling: blub, blub, blub, blub. He rocked the bike back on a stand, cut the engine, and dismounted. Arthur stood, so I did.

Uncle Deane came out of the restaurant and walked straight toward the cop, who took off his helmet and embraced him. This was our introduction to Gary Pogue, the youngest of the group of survivors Uncle Deane led into the Java jungle before eventually being captured. They had not seen each other since mid-way through the ordeal— Pogue disappeared to another work camp. He and Uncle Deane talked for hours until the last train arrived for Kansas City.

We spent that night in a Howard Johnson's. By this time, we just walked Arthur in with us. "Ask for forgiveness, not permission," said my Uncle. Nobody said anything. In the morning, I wolfed down an omelet in the restaurant. While I ordered another one for Arthur (back at the room), Uncle Deane went in search of a telephone.

I apologized to Arthur for it being cold, and my Uncle showed up with tickets on *The Southwest Chief,* a line that would take us to Oklahoma but also through Texas, New Mexico, and into Arizona. He was smiling. "We're going to have company."

Standing in a light rain, Bailey Douglass and his wife, Anna, waited for us at the station. It started to pour as soon as we stepped aboard. Arthur and I were left to ourselves mostly that all-day leg, except for about an hour after lunch. Mr. Douglass was very drunk and plopped down next to me, across from Arthur in the dining car, knocking over chess pieces.

"So shorry. I want you to know your Uncle shaved my life." He told us about their swim from the ship when it went down, being pulled ashore by Uncle Deane, the men that made it to the island of Java, and those who didn't. Despite his breath and occasional slurred words, it was a good story. Some of it I knew.

I said, "Were you captured with Uncle Deane too?"

Mr. Douglass got quiet. He said, "Yes," and watched the landscape pass for a minute.

"The Japs kept officers together. I was shipped to Tokyo with a bunch of other enlisted men to work in the arms factories. I did not know he was alive... until this morning."

Uncle Deane and Anna were pretty sloshed too. The Douglasses caught the sleeper back to Kansas City, and Arthur and I put my Uncle to bed in Oklahoma.

That was a lot of activity for four days, and the visits eased up for a while. On the way to Amarillo, I had a window seat. Uncle Deane hardly spoke- he just dozed next to me or read a newspaper. I said, "They made you work hard. The Japs."

His mouth turned up just a little in amusement, but his eyes were so tired. "Yes." He looked past me out the window. In the distance, the land rose up into mesas, flat islands of land in the air. You might be able to ride a bike down the side.

"We got a postcard, and you said it was ok, you were well. They were even paying you."

At first, I thought he didn't hear, but gradually he moved his gaze to me. "We were dying. Starved. For years. Sick with terrible diseases. All of us. Even the strongest. What a people can do to another person is... well, we did not think of the Japs as people anymore. Everywhere, the suffering, the misery... sometimes, death was welcome."

His eyes closed for a long time, and I thought he might be sleeping. I had so little recall of "Uncle CD" — he had been gone aboard the HOUSTON since the summer of 1940 when I was six. The man I remembered was tall and strong like Tarzan– Johnny Weissmuller. When it rained yesterday, his shirt stuck to his frame. His long arms were so thin.

"If we stopped working, sat, or dropped to the ground, we were beaten. Some... to death." He told me about the Dutch doctor, Hekking, who appeared toward the end like an angel sent to sustain them long enough to survive the war.

Cooker told me a story:

"Mistuh Deane's heart belong to Miss Luvell. Thas why he cain't do nuthin', I think. Pos' Man brought dat cahd sayin' he wus alright, an me an Miz Smif cu'un hardley come outta our rooms for days. When we did, Arthur say we need to call huh. Miz Smif say hit wu'un do no good 'cause she got married. Arthur say I ought to write Mizz Luvell a lettuh, cause he cu'un write it. So I did, an he tuk hit to de Pos' Office. Din have no address but Miss Kathrine Luvell, Oakland, California.

Din hear nothin' in a few weeks so I started another one— sayin' 'Dear Miss Luvell, I want make sure you know we heard Mistuh Deane is alive, and he say he is OK.' Arthur say he hisself put that one on de mail train goin out wes.

Well ah din thank no mo' 'bout it, cause we was jes lookin' fo' mo evidence he was alive, an he was gone come home to us. But she got it, sho' did, cause ina few weeks she wrote me back. She thank me fo' thankin' of huh, and say she love Deane and pray fuh him, but she have a baby, an another life now. I shunt worry none 'bout huh and send no mo' lettuhs. Hit made me cry, dat lettuh did."

"What did you do with it?"

"I doan know. Arthur was there, an I thank he was touch too, but I doan know where Miss Luvell lettuh is. I din see no point in tellin' my baby 'bout it, so I din't."

The Southwest Chief we climbed aboard in Albuquerque looked new, a shiny red and yellow diesel with matching passenger cars. It was smoother and a far different experience than the older trains we'd been riding, better appointed than the others, especially the steam locomotives that took Billy and me to Alexandria. I still think of it every time a freight train blows past near the house today, or I catch a whiff of creosote.

Arthur and I played chess for hours in the dining car, and he beat me every time, but I told him he was winning because they ran us out at mealtimes, and I couldn't concentrate. The landscape was really astonishing, foreign, sometimes snaking through canyon passages barely wider than the train, then suddenly it was wide open, with fantastic towers near and far carved by the elements. It was straight out of the movies but in color. We traveled through The Painted Desert, a dry and dusty planet of intense red, yellow, with skies of purple and blue.

The land settled down a bit, and when we rolled into the town of Winslow, the sun was dropping behind the remaining range of mountains in the distance to the west. Otherwise draped in the purple of dusk, the shiny train reflected the few lights of the town.

Arthur would stay on the *Chief* to Flagstaff to "see about a car," Uncle Deane said. Whether that was true, I don't know. We dragged our bags to a run-down place called Bel Air Motor Lodge near the station. There was a sign in the window that said "Welcome!" right next to one that said "NO COLORED." Arthur was not going to have an easy time getting us a car.

Uncle Deane was getting out of the shower when Joe Bisahalani knocked on the door. When Sergeant Bisahalani was introduced— a Navajo Indian, the first Indian I had ever seen in person, I thought that it was weird he was dressed just like us, with short black hair. He wore a huge grin the whole night.

"*Yá'át'ééh*, Carlo," he said. "Hello."

We had a grand time. We ate burgers at the restaurant (the only patrons), and afterward, out behind the lodge, we sat for a long time drinking beer (I was allowed one beer), watching the blackest sky and more stars than I had ever seen. There wasn't but a sliver of new moon to compete with meteors crossing the night in the blink of an eye.

Some of their conversations stayed with me:

"I have been to see dozens. Some you might remember— Edmonson, Pogue... I saw Mac Percy's widow, Elizabeth... will try to catch up with several others..."

"Does it help?"

"I don't know. There will never be closure for the living or their survivors. Selfishly, it might be as much about me. But, I have had a strong feeling it is the right thing to do. I have been having... dreams."

Joe spoke slowly, softly, "You remember, and listen to your heart. You be proud of who you are... what you are, what you did. You saved many men. You are *Nizhóní*, beyond appearances, something that is good. Harmony and balance within."

When I awoke in the morning, I saw Uncle Deane standing outside through the blinds, smoking, watching Winslow wake up.

We breakfasted again in the restaurant- I had a huge Spanish omelet with chorizo which I had almost finished when my uncle told me it was sausage made from pig intestines. Seeing the look on my face, he smiled.

"Joe Bisahalani," he said, "is a Code Talker."

I waited for him to quit chewing and explain.

"Indians who fought in the war served as messengers because they developed a code based on their language. It cannot be understood by the enemy. The Navajo Code Talkers were the widest used."

Holy Smoke! I stabbed the last bite of the omelet.

"He was captured by the Japs in the Philippines. They found out about his skills, and they tortured him... to get him to translate. He would not."

Big Charlie had told me some of the kinds of torture that Uncle Deane and his men were subject to for *years*. I said nothing.

"He has a warrior spirit. They could not defeat him. He and other brave men are very much a part of the reason why I came home. Many of them didn't. Joe and I were together in the hold of a ship for many days at sea. A lot of people died because of the conditions. Later the ship was accidentally bombed by American planes because it flew the Japanese flag."

Goosebumps crawled up my back.

"I crossed paths with so many soldiers: American Marines, Air Force,

Navy, Army, and officers and troops from all over the world. We were mixed and shuffled about all the time— to different work camps. Very often, soldiers I came to know... died of their afflictions. Joe was one of the ones I knew the longest. For a year, we were in the same camps, building a railroad for the Japs. One day, he was gone."

Uncle Deane seemed a little less sad, more talkative than he had been in days. I asked, "How did you find him?"

"A letter. I knew he was from Fort Defiance on the Navajo Reservation. He wrote back he was sent to prison in Nagasaki and was in a cell there when we dropped the second A-bomb. Sitting up against the concrete blocks saved his life."

I hoped we'd see him again. Joe was maybe the neatest person I had ever met.

Billy was at Friendly Pines Summer Camp, about a two-hour drive from Flagstaff, our next stop aboard the *Chief*. The train would take us closer, but in Flagstaff, we would have the best chance of renting a car. We caught the 2:15. It was only about an hour, but I slept through more spectacular scenery. Arthur met us at the train station.

"Arthur, I don't suppose you had any luck with the car?"

"Yassuh. They called Mr. Charlie." He walked us over to a dusty black Plymouth Road King. It was pretty torn up inside. The engine ticked, cooling.

"You been driving around Flagstaff, Arthur?"

"No Suh. Had to get some gas."

"Well, if it's this hot and all you did was go to the filling station, we're going to have a problem."

My Uncle checked under the hood and studied the tires, and when he was satisfied, we were on our way— two hours southwest (finally, we had a map), on gravel roads to the camp, just south of Prescott. I sat up front with Arthur, and Uncle Deane dozed, somehow. It was a rough ride. When we got behind another vehicle, which luckily was not too often, dust would fill up the Plymouth, so we had to roll up the windows. Damn, I thought. Billy could've waited until the end of the session, one more week for the bus that brought him. I was soaked when we got there.

Friendly Pines is in the Bradshaw Range on the east side of Prescott National Forest, just south of Prescott, Arizona. The camp was really something, nestled in a small valley framed by rocky mountain cliffs and evergreens covering the hills a mile distant. We passed ten to fifteen cabins, kids riding horses, and the archery range, until we came to a big open field with a swimming pool and tennis courts before the road ended at a huge lodge (or dining hall or something). I could do this... for a summer.

Uncle Deane and Arthur *must* have to whiz like I did. Uncle Deane and I let ourselves into the big building (full of a hundred kids eating lunch) like we knew what we were doing and wandered around until we found what we needed. Arthur just stood at the car, waiting.

A burly woman with a mustache appeared and said, "Welcome to Friendly Pines. Can I help you?"

While she and Uncle Deane talked, I went back inside with Arthur.

"They're going to feed us," said my Uncle. Billy came up then, tanned and grinning, while we were working on chicken-fried steak and mashed potatoes. He hugged Arthur first.

"I'll have his bags brought around," said the burly woman.

In a few minutes, we were out at the car, thanking the woman and some other young people, counselors that had introduced themselves. Arthur and Uncle Deane were loading Billy's heavy trunk when the screened doors on the dining hall banged, and we looked up. A tall beauty with long brown hair emerged from the porch shadow and walked toward us.

"*Katherine*," breathed my Uncle.

Arthur, Billy, and I would make the return trip to Memphis by ourselves. Arthur let Billy and me drive to Flagstaff some that day, having made two trips from Flagstaff to Friendly Pines in the last twelve hours.

26

Skytop

November 1946

The end of the War and the reunification of the Walterlane and Smith families did settle my father's oscillation for a time. But, it was not his nature to remain long in one place. Mother often went along on international excursions, sometimes for weeks. I have been called "Carlo," in fact, since the day I was born because the nurses in Milan could not (or would not) say "Charlie."

Saturday after Thanksgiving, Big Charlie was off again to the Cotton Exchange in Chicago on the City of New Orleans for the auction of November cotton, then he would fly to New York for ten days or so. Mother was there already, shopping. He appeared at the top of the stairs and started down with two heavy bags. Arthur stood below, at the curl of the banister, in his white jacket and tie and driver's cap. He said, "lemme git those, Mistuh Chahlee." Dad, believing his health was maintained by challenge, often used a weights system in his bedroom with pulleys mounted to the walls. "I'll get them, Arthur. Did you fill up the car?"

Big Charlie usually carried his bags himself, and he always treated the servants with respect and humanity. Not so everyone else. Having grown up in the south, in a household of "darkie" servants, Mother fussed at me when I made sandwiches for Arthur and me, piling high the turkey from the icebox that we had just carved for Thanksgiving. She said, "Don't give him that," and pulled out the disgusting braunschweiger she kept for the servants. Nonna said that giving Cleo a raise would "spoil her." The help were second-class citizens, and this was the natural order.

Many years later, when Arthur's lifetime of servitude had begun to show signs of wear, but my father was still a vigorous man, they hunted ducks together at the lee pocket of the furthest lake at the glorious cypress swamp in Arkansas, Menashay. Hundreds of decoys were strewn in front of three permanent blinds, full that day with club members. A cloud of pintails started in a downward spiral from far overhead. Arthur's once renowned duck call fell in pitch and warbled in uncommon cadences; his hearing was failing. The ducks flared and rose over the cypress forest well out of range.

"WALTERLANE," came a shout from one of the other blinds, "if you tell that goddamn nigger to shut up, we might kill some ducks."

Dad told me that Arthur took off his call and rolled the lanyard around it, put it in his pocket, and he never heard him call again.

There is some debate about what happened that night at the clubhouse, but even the version sterilized for young ears has Big Charlie knocking the man down. The next morning, in the pitch dark before dawn, with the temperature in the teens and his boat weighed down with another hunter and bags of decoys, the man pushed out from the dock, failing to notice someone had pulled the plug out of his boat. As he sat turned around, yanking on his motor crank, the boat took on water rapidly, and in seconds it sank. The two men were pulled, shivering and hypothermic, onto the dock.

Just Arthur and me going somewhere together— my best friend driving, me in the front seat with him, black and white, normal as the sunrise. In those days, I had no inclination of the divide that seventy years would assign to our relationship, but as I became an adolescent, I was more conscious of the distance between us.

When I got on the train that next week to go back to Episcopal, three Baylor kids from Little Rock observed us through the car windows, seniors I knew from the leg to Nashville. Arthur bought me a ticket, loaded my bags, and followed me to my seat with my satchel. He returned to the car to get a book I had forgotten.

The instant Arthur left the car, one of them said, "Your nigger wipe your ass for you, Walterlane?" The others broke up laughing.

I have never forgotten my response because I am so ashamed. Before checking to make sure Arthur was out of earshot, I said, "You just wish YOU had a nigger!" No words I have spoken in my life have caused me more regret. All day I felt like I had spit on him. What if he heard?

Arthur Campbell was my teacher, my mentor, my friend, and my family. He was not at my whim but mentored me and served our family faithfully, selflessly for many years. It still hurts to think about it.

Big Charlie looked at me and said, "You and Arthur ought to go out to the farm. The dogs and the horses need to be worked, and you'll probably get some shooting."

Arthur climbed in the driver's seat of the Woody, our '39 Ford Woody station wagon. "Arthur will drop me at the station, and then you have plenty of time for a fine afternoon. Don't you think so, Arthur?"

"Yessuh."

"Kennel up," Cleo and Sweetie immediately curled up on the back seat, and I put our lunch and some water and Cokes in an ice box on the floor. In the way back was a new saddle, alongside side our guns and a satchel of shells.

"Lemme drive, Arthur. I can do it. Let me drive."

"Let's us git out a little fur-thuh."

He would, too, eventually… let me drive. That day the dogs tried to jump out when we stopped to switch places as if they knew my ride wouldn't be nearly as smooth for napping. They had that right because the car would buck, and I would grind the gear shift until I got back into the hang of it. But Arthur was stoic and not too critical, instead offering simple pointers: "You got to ease yo foot off'n the gas and ease it onna brake. An when you come to a stop, doan keep yo foot onna clutch. Yo foot on the clutch toins a flywheel, an you goan haveta replace it sooner."

It's a smooth trip. We don't have a flat, despite two hours alternating gravel roads and patched pavement. I could get to Skytop, the farm Dad bought right before he left to go to war, in my dreams, and often do.

Barbed wire nailed to the top of a creosote post makes up the gate that marks the Skytop property. Not much of a barrier except for the cows, but other than those, there isn't much to entice thieves, and we've never had a problem.

I pulled the Woody into the Jenks's driveway, scattering all manner of animals. Wilson Jenks, the caretaker, farms the place, managing the colored worker families living in a row of houses at the foot of the drive to the main house at the top of the hill, our house, maybe the highest point in the county, with its spectacular vista overlooking the lake and the valley to the north. The only thing that spoils the view is invisible during the daytime, the prison lights at the Hardeman County Penitentiary to the northwest. You can't see the stars very well in that direction.

Generations of the Jenks family have grown up in the simple farmhouse nearest the entrance gate. They simply came with the place (in 1941), recommended by the seller because his family had known them for generations (and considered them generally harmless), not to mention it was easier to sell them as an asset than explain the liability.

Wilma Jenks looked so much like Wilson that Big Charlie was suspicious of them right away. Indeed, their bony countenance, heavy brow, and matching complexion are at a glance more brother and sister than man and wife. Wilma, it turned out, is Wilson's first cousin. Six children roam the spare grounds, wandering, aimless and wide-eyed as the chickens.

Mr. Jenks is long-necked as a giraffe and as mean as a badger, and I don't like him one bit. I saw him whip one of his little girls one time in front of a lot of the colored helpers. He walks toward us, swallowed by overalls held up with a single strap. I know he recognizes the car, but he gives us a stern face walking up. Might be surprised to see me behind the wheel, though. He doesn't give Arthur even a nod. Dad said I was to pay special attention to everything Mr. Jenks says and does. I don't think he likes Mr. Jenks any more than I do.

Jenks knew cattle and farming, raising quail, and training bird dogs, all things Big Charlie lusted after, and the land was so gorgeous and laden with game that he was somewhat inclined to overlook blemishes in his new estate.

"Billy?" He calls me my brother, as most people do. Not to mention Billy has his driver's license. The dogs jumped up, panting.

"No sir... Carlo. We're gonna shoot some quail," I blurt. "Me an Arthur."

For a long moment, Jenks looked at Arthur, who didn't look up. His gaze went to the dogs, and he glanced in the way back at our guns and the saddle. He spat a brown jet.

"Better be careful 'bout who shoots Mistah Chahlee's quail." He looked at Arthur again, but Arthur hadn't budged.

"You goin do that, boy? Be extra careful?" He moved his plug to the other side of his mouth. "Round this young fellow and them dogs and my horses, I mean."

Arthur said nothing, so Jenks leaned in the car again further, with his head almost in my lap, staring.

It was hard to tell what Arthur's eyes were saying in the dark under his hat, and there was never an indication from the rest of his face.

Jenks did his best horse's ass impression, taunting, daring Arthur to do something, anything. But Arthur just wouldn't look at him or answer him, his countenance unchanged. Even if I didn't understand the one-sided hostility, it was something more than just the ordinary disdain most country people I knew had for negroes.

I wanted to say, 'Whose horses, *you backward hick?*' But instead, leaning back in the seat to escape his breath, I said: "Mr. Jenks, where are Pardner and Jigger today?"

Pardner hadn't been ridden in weeks. I walked up to him slowly. When I was about his length away, he blew an irritated snort and jumped back a few steps. This happened a couple more times, then he slipped around me as if he knew I was trying to corner him and bolted to the opposite corner of the field. Embarrassed, I moved just my eyes (that is, and not my head) to the right to see what Arthur was doing, pretending I had it under control. We both knew better. Arthur was approaching from across the rectangular field, half an acre away, outside the wood fence. Within 50 yards, he leaped over it just as Pardner picked up on the stranger's approach, lifting his head. Arthur walked toward him with a confident gait. Pardner stared back. Then, like they were old friends, Pardner closed the last of steps to go to Arthur and took the sugar out of his hand. Moments later, I cinched the new saddle on him.

"I'll walk." Arthur would hear nothing of searching the field where Jenks said the other horse was. This disappointed me, as I figured we needed to cover a lot of the open fields, close to a thousand acres, to have a decent hunt.

Arthur said, "Your dad and your brother killed six lass-yer, down in the bottom..." That was half a mile away, a long walk down a steep, eroded road to the southeast when the open area where he and Arthur had hunted most recently was right here. We'll see what the dogs do.

Arthur let them out of the car, and Cleo immediately bolted north, in front of the house, down the gentle sloping field bound on the left and right by tree lines hiding ditches, toward the lake valley. Sweetie trotted lazily behind. I followed on Pardner at a trot; Arthur hoisted his gun and began an easy pace. The dogs were crisscrossing the slope in front of us.

With so many fields in fallow to rest their soils, long overdue, Dad said the coveys would be spread out greatly. But Cleo stopped not 200 yards away at the barbed wire fence at the foot of the hill. The other dog bolted through the open gate and bounded without purpose on the other side. But Cleo stood steadfast. Arthur picked up his speed to match ours. Sweetie seemed to notice and began to trot toward our point of focus.

Arthur said, "Slow down, easy... easy." His dog, Cleo, named for the cook in Mother's kitchen, the runt of a litter that was born to a bitch owned by one of the old Robinsonville Dam club members, stood before us, still as a statue. I dismounted and eased my gun out of the holster aside from the saddle. Arthur motioned for me to go ahead. The instant I moved past Cleo, the bush ahead exploded with quail. Spastically I raised up and pulled triggers, blasting bushes and little else. The birds sped past Arthur, and he turned and dropped one that seemed about to light on him, and as the covey screamed past him in the same direction, he cut down another at a great distance in that impossible available millisecond.

Such a promising start, but it wasn't repeated in an hour of traipsing around in the north fields. Cleo had stopped to investigate at several spots, but as soon as we thought she found something again, she broke point.

From one point to another, she went until we had made it past the lake to the fence marking the north line. We turned to the east, hugging the north border, which opened up into an old road on our side of the fence, and we walked all the way east through the thick woods. Cleo ran way on ahead, disappearing over the descending road. Sweetie had always brought up the rear when she wasn't dawdling on the other side of the field behind us, but I had not seen her for over an hour. Arthur said not to worry about it, but she was Big Charlie's prized pointer.

Light diffused by a solid overcast stole all color, and there were no shadows in the deep woods. The oaks had not dropped all their leaves by this late November afternoon, so early dusk under the canopy was dense and grayscale— an underexposed black and white photograph; there were no highlights for depth.

Finally, the roadbed alongside the north line spilled out into another great field. Cleo was frozen at a thick snatch of goldenrod that grew up around a ditch, which upon my dismount, transformed into cocklebur briers, immediately snagging my bootlaces. In another step, no millimeter of bootlace was free of them. Shorthair bird dogs must have nothing for them to grab onto, for Cleo was clean and focused, her only movement a slight glance my way. Arthur was just a second behind me and nodded for us to flush the birds, if any. I took another step in, and cockleburs seized my jacket sleeves. I swore out loud, and the bush burst with birds.

Somehow, my eye caught one, and my gun jumped to my shoulder, my mind adding in that instant, the feel of a thousand tugs and the tearing sound of my sleeves' escape from grabbing sticker bushes to draw this bead. BOOM, and that one was down. I swerved the gun to another, but it was gone, and we (the gun barrel and I) were pointed at my horse, very close to where Arthur stood. I lowered the barrel.

"Good... good shot, Cahlo."

"I almost hadda double!"

"No! You almos' had yo horse Pahdner, and almos' had me, is whut you almos' had."

Back on my horse, when the wind came up, I started to feel the chill. The dogs seemed to know what direction we wanted to go— south, in a big loop that would take us back to the house at the hilltop, where our hunt began some three hours ago. I walked awhile to warm up some, letting Pardner protect me from the wind.

For a change, Sweetie was next to point. I was surprised, as it seemed to me she'd acted so distracted by her freedom this afternoon, caring little to follow that nose of such expensive pedigree. Two hundred yards ahead, a strip of road running east-west used to cut straight across our field, but it swung ever wider in a semi-circle. A giant hole that could swallow a barn claimed more and more of the road every year. Right where the road straightened back out, Sweetie stayed still as we approached, concentrating on the clumps of brush and deadfall that had been dozed (probably hopefully) into the gully. Cleo stood back as if she was saying, 'You take this one'.

Overfarming and several very wet years were causing a severe loss of topsoil, especially evident in places like this. Hidden in stands of trees at the field's edge was the flood water's repository, a great sand ditch sometimes 50 feet across. Where it escaped the thick forest, the feature divided two hundred-acre fields throughout the farm in several places. Billy and I would play in the sand, catching tiny frogs and sometimes a horned toad. It was a great place to slip through the woods soundlessly when squirrel hunting. But it could be spooky. When it had been raining awhile, you could step into a wet hole suddenly, up to your waist. Arthur said a man got buried in that sand one wet season and hasn't been found. We thought he was just trying to put a scare into us, and then early into the summer last year, after torrential spring floods, we found a pair of antlers sticking up out of the sand. They would hardly budge, and we sort of grew out of going there.

I eased out my gun and slowly moved to the edge. Arthur said, "Say when," and when I had my gun to my shoulder and nodded, he threw a big dirt clod ahead into the midst. Quail exploded. I shot, and a speeding bird fell and bounced like a rubber ball. I swung on another and fired the second barrel. I watched that bobwhite dart around, seemingly unhurt, disappearing toward the woods. Dang, I was so sure... and then it crashed into a thick canebrake south, 50 yards behind us. A double. "Arthur, I got TWO!"

"Yeahyoudid" he said, running his words together. This was as much excitement as Arthur ever generated, but to me, it was high praise. And, he would bear witness to my father.

We both noticed Cleo disappearing through a gap down into the south woods, the road to the bottom— a valley of oblong fields marking the lowest elevation of Skytop. Arthur whistled for her. I got back on Pardner, and Arthur and I wearily made our way toward my downed quail. Just over the hill to the right, the road led back to the house where we began.

27

Bamboo and Taboo

To help dispel our fear of ghosts, Dad took us one night into the thick brake of woods left of the road Cleo went down when we were boys of eleven and eight. The forest had grown up thick there around the remains of a 150-year-old homestead. About twenty yards in, hand-hewn timbers rose above the ivy, leading the eye to a great stone chimney and its shadow's distance beyond the homesteaders, a family of seven Philpotts resting under readable headstones. Curiously, two of these were more elegantly lettered and appointed with relief flourishes featuring angels. One of the simpler ones leaned against a tree at almost the south edge of the ridge, which then fell sharply downslope to the bottoms. It marked Niel Pearre Philpott, who likely died in childbirth in August 1794. I remember because we noted the date of her passing coincided with the birth of the boy next to her, who "went to be with his Lord," not quite three months later. This was very bad *juju* for the local colored workers, and they could not be convinced to set foot into those woods under any circumstances.

I still had a rusted axe head found one morning more or less right here, on the field's edge, where we watched one of them, Lucas, guiding a plow, helping disc the field for planting. If the farm's motorized tractors had not been in the service of the larger fields, the axe head would probably still be there. Metal struck metal with a loud clang, and my head turned. Lucas's horse was making time, and the thing practically jumped into his hand. Lucas was still "whoa-ing" and stumbling, but he was already examining it. Though obviously the business end of a substantial chopping tool, its surface was almost black, mottled, and pitted with rust, the only glimmer of metal being the new contact with Lucas's plow. Lucas handed it to me with a toothless grin.

This, of course, led to the summer of excavation, where we went on the unscientific recovery of other treasures, finding none, until Mr Jenks reported to Dad we were digging near the graveyard, against his explicit wishes, and both of us got the alligator belt.

The stand of bamboo my bird had crashed into, right of the old road to the bottoms, was where the farm once cut uniform stems for reinforcing concrete. Steel was too expensive in those years, and fast-growing bamboo was a decent solution. Most metals went to help defeat the Krauts and the Japs, and so every newer foundation on the place, from barns to cattle pens, had bamboo from this stand. In the couple of years since, the poles had grown so thick and tall as to be less desirable for that.

I looked into the almost impenetrable wall where I thought my kill had fallen, seeing nothing. The shoots were a hand's width apart, yet light beyond the first row or two was as blocked as physical access. To inspect more closely, I set my gun down, leaning the barrel on the X-cross of two smaller bamboo poles.

There. The quail must have bounced off the shoots, for it lay a foot short in the field; I had almost stepped on it. Picking it up, I was assaulted by a smell... at first, I thought of burned popcorn. I sniffed nearer my bird, but it was a fresh kill. Then it was gone. I got it again, taking a step toward Pardner, thinking he must've taken a particularly odiferous crap. But I saw no physical evidence of that. The smell was intense and sickeningly sweet and seemed even to knock the chill out of the afternoon. Skunks were in hibernation by November, weren't they?

"Arthur, do you smell that?"

But he was blowing his whistle for Cleo, and he ducked into the woods south, down the road to the fields in the bottom. I knew the ridge was steep, and erosion had dug into the road so many years it was impassable except by foot or horse. I suddenly felt quite tired, glad we were almost done, and close to the car. I looped Pardner's bridle around a thick bamboo stem and went into the opening and down the slope to follow.

Despite the diffused light of the solid overcast, the opening in the canopy over that road made it easy to see. In five paces, you were at the height of the ridge, which then fell away sharply down the road south and curved left. The smell was back, and the air was thick with it. Mixed in was the smell of fire and smoke. Two more steps down, and I saw Arthur and Cleo twenty yards ahead, where the road leveled briefly before continuing its descent. She was bouncing around, animated, but he stood still in the middle of the road and seemed to be talking to someone. His arms were raised.

I took another step and could see another of the white farm hands, Raymond Crick, holding a rifle leveled at Arthur's chest. My gun was up the hill behind me where I had just leaned it.

Cleo saw me and bounded up the hill.

Raymond looked up at me, and in the same instant, Arthur tore the rifle away with both hands and cracked him hard in the chest with the stock. Raymond went flat on his back; the wind knocked out of him.

Arthur jacked the lever underside of the rifle, and a cartridge flew out. He tossed the weapon on the ground behind him.

When I got down to them, he was on one knee beside the unfortunate Raymond, who was heaving and spitting a little blood at his mouth's corner. His eyes were wild and red. He wore only a grubby sleeveless undershirt and overalls in the cold, hitched to his bony shoulder by only one strap. A small circle of blood stained his undershirt where he had been struck.

"Fuch-king nigger," he spewed. He only had teeth on one side of his mouth, so his long face caved in some on the side that had only gums. "Sloufing nigger, you HIT ME!" He arched like he was going to spring up, and Arthur put his hand on the chest at the spot. Raymond screamed, "I'm gonna skinna black off'n you!" Arthur pushed again, and Raymond's head jerked back violently, smacking against the ground.

"Thas gone be tough from jail," said Arthur. Raymond jerked his head about, and his eyes rolled. "Yo ribs is prab-lee broken. Be still."

The smell was back full bore now, with maybe a hint of burning rubber.

I was just opening my mouth to ask what the heck was going on when Arthur said, "Where's the still, Raymon?"

Shuffing flithgrr," Raymond wheezed, calming somewhat. "Fuff you, thigger."

Arthur got to his feet and picked up the repeating rifle he had been accosted with, handing it to me. I closed the breach, and another round went into the chamber.

"Mr. Chahlee wone 'preciate moonshinin' on his propity."

Raymond wasn't moving, but his eyes were rolling back, and it looked like foam at the corner of his mouth. He looked rabid. Dad said he must be the spittin' image of Ichabod Crane. I didn't know about that, never having met Mr. Crane, but he had the spittin' part right. I imagined Ichabod Crane was tall, was skin and bones like Raymond, his Adam's apple was the size of a golf ball, he drooled tobacco juice and had the worst breath I had ever smelled, and had the ugliest, fattest wife I had ever seen, like Raymond. Subordinate to Mr. Jenks, Raymond was still part of the white "management," already living and working the place when Dad bought it in 1940. Jenks said he wasn't but about 35, so he should be off fighting, but the Army spat him back to Hardeman County after a week on a '301 Disqualifier'... meaning, Jenks said, he was too stupid.

"He was gonna kill you," I said.

"Don't think so."

"Do you know what's going on? Why did he point his gun at you?"

"I surprised him. They is makin' whiskey. That's what you's smellin'—the mash."

"Where?"

"Careful with at gun! Aim it down and run nat lever a bunch of times."

I shucked five more cartridges out of it onto the ground until there were no more and started collecting them in my hand.

"Follow yo nose," said Arthur.

Arthur picked up his gun on the ground behind us, where I guessed he was forced to drop it, and went into the woods right there, stepping over a creek just off the road, then back up a bank into the thick woods towards the homestead and graves, and the field that we had walked from the north line.

Raymond had stopped moving so much. His eyes were closed, and he breathed popping bubbles. I stepped around him and followed. We hadn't gone 30 yards when we found a metal boiler sitting atop orange coals, which had all sorts of long pipes coming out of it, especially at the top, ending with drips into a much smaller vessel. It looked to be hammered from tin.

I had forgotten a creek ran through here. One of the pipes was a hose that dropped down from the underside of the boiler into a pool made by a dam of rocks.

On a long plank were several bottles, jars, and pots, no two the same. The glass ones looked mostly full of liquid varying in clarity from clear to brown, like weak tea.

Arthur picked up one of the smaller glass ones with a cork. He took a whiff, and his face was seized with a grimace. "C'mon, les get out of here."

28

Raymond, again

I had never been so damn glad to be out of school after the lockdown late winter and icy spring of 1946, not having been home for Easter—"too short a break for the two-day train ride," Mother said. The real reason was Mother had her hands full: Big Charlie was in New Orleans, and she wanted to get Billy looked at by another doctor, not to mention Lindsay had just broken her arm, Denton had an earache which would turn out to be tonsillitis, Mac was in full-bore-terrible-twos, so I had been stuck in Alexandria since returning from Christmas break in early January!

Honestly, my brother *had* awakened gasping a few times, and the infirmary doctor at Episcopal said he had mild asthma. So, on Maundy Thursday, Mother sent him up to Washington to see another doctor, who confirmed this and prescribed the dry climate out west. *So that's why he had to leave school.*

Arthur always said, "Tell it all, if you gone tell it. Leavin' out part of the story is jes like tellin' a lie." New Mexico or Arizona might have been good for Billy, but in truth, the energy he put into his scholastic work had never been high. He collected demerits rather than honors.

As none were to be found on campus, of course, girls were the prime draw, and the easiest place to find them was to ride into Washington on the train. But, unless it was a holiday break or Parents' Weekend, students were expected to be back on campus by 8 pm. Because they were back in bed before sunrise, Billy and buddies from his dorm were emboldened by their after-hours adventures across the Potomac. And when they discovered parties on campus at Georgetown their excursions became routine. My brother returned talking of a college girl, Tricia Weeden, and connived to see her.

The Saturday afternoon before Easter break, he went alone. Dawn on Palm Sunday, as the sun began to brighten the eastern sky, traffic began to pick up— better chance of a ride. He put out his thumb. A blue Buick Century passed, slowed, and reversed. It was familiar, and Billy said he got a pit in his stomach. Reaching across, the driver opened the door and shoved it toward his prodigal student. Professor Tompkins had recognized Billy in his heavy car coat and pulled up alongside.

"Where are you headed, Mr. Walterlane?"

Tompkins was a baseball coach and professor of History known for complete intolerance of distraction in his class. His aim with a piece of chalk was legendary.

Billy smiled the kind of toothy smile Daffy Duck does when sweat leaps from his forehead in great drops. "With you, sir!"

He got 100 demerits, which was 100 more than he was allowed to get and remain for the semester, and so asthma and a convalescence out west became a convenient if perhaps not completely forthcoming explanation.

One of Billy's great gifts was the ability to fit in and endear himself and be happy wherever he was. He wrote he had a best buddy, Robin Cross, from near Turanza, Arkansas, near Menashay of all places. Well, there was a school there, and he wouldn't be home until the end of June.

June 5, 1947

Arthur and I went to the farm.

Arthur said Dad had the Hardeman County Sheriff come out and pull Raymond's still off the property. Big Charlie knew Raymond wasn't remotely clever enough to assemble a recipe to turn sugar and corn into alcohol, much less engineer an operation like a producing still, so he knew Jenks was probably involved and may have even confronted him about it, I don't know. But he didn't tell the sheriff it was being run by the farm hands, he said Arthur and I stumbled across it, which is true but not quite the truth. Arthur must have said dozens of times over and over that leaving out something important to a story was just as good as telling a lie.

And neither did he get rid of Raymond or Mr. Jenks! I thought this was amazing, but Arthur seemed to think it was because country people were clannish. "Mistuh Chahlee say he don't want to meet the rest of Raymond's family, and he ain't got nowheres to go." Well, I think it was surely also because the county was thick with Jenkses.

I had told Big Charlie exactly what happened that day too. He was in New York with Mother, but we talked on the telephone, and he even talked to Arthur on the telephone (unusual), and Arthur told about how Raymond was drunk and spitting, pointing a rifle at him (I added about calling Arthur names). I told the details of the plumbing and the smells and how Arthur said the whole operation was a still.

So I was pretty surprised to see all the same players. Mr. Jenks was his same glaring, asshole self, which reminded me of the animosity in the scene when we showed up last fall before any of the stuff of the last season happened. I must ask Arthur what that was all about... Then, I had a curious thought.

"Arthur, did you know about Raymond's moonshine before we found it?"

Arthur didn't answer. We pulled up slowly past the Jenks's house. I don't think he wants to speak to any Jenks any more than I do. It wasn't the wandering, vacant scene of chickens and children a few months ago; a couple of kids are milling about. I don't remember them being so big!

Jenks's wife Wilma burst from the screened porch. Before the screen door could bang shut, a tall girl followed. They strode to the clothesline– wires stretched across T poles like a power line, converging at the sheets, which they began to fold in an orchestrated motion. Then they recovered garments until their baskets were overstuffed.

The girl's shape so pleased my eye it had no choice but to follow her. I had just begun to notice this phenomenon, but my eye still had not learned of it.

Arthur and I went down to the lake you could see from the house at the top of the hill. Always muddy from the cows, it would still yield the occasional big bass before the summer heat shut them down and could always be counted on if you had some crickets to tempt the shell crackers. We were catching them. With a short paddle in the crook of his arm, Arthur moved expertly around the pond from one honey hole to another, saving the best for last... a deep spot where a wooden boat was said to rest on the bottom, a casualty of some unlucky excursion a decade before— guaranteed pay dirt. I missed a couple of big strikes.

Arthur said, "Are you payin' 'tention? No, you ain't."

He looked at me like he could read my mind, and I thought, if he could, he would have seen the image I was tending of Jenks's daughter in her clinging sundress.

When we gave it up, Arthur cleaned our fish on the stone picnic table that was on the brick patio, near the hose. Trying to match his technique, I made a big mess of the three-pound bass I caught, so I suggested maybe he could clean the rest, and I could take the car to the barns close to Jenks's house to gas it up at the farm's pumps. I think he knew this was a transparent offer but allowed it, and I pulled around behind the stables opposite Mr. Jenks's house, hoping not to see him. I stood filling the tank. The rusted sliding door to the barn that sheltered the farm's new Allis Chalmers tractor (and other farm machinery) slid open slightly with a squeal, and Raymond poked his dandelion-on-a-stalk head out, looking left and right. The Woody was still running, and the gas pump clicked noisily, so I was sure he would look, but he did not, and I stepped behind the diesel pump, which hardly offered cover. I thought— any idiot would have noticed the car being fueled, the boy standing in plain view 15 yards away, hardly hidden behind the two column-like pumps. Raymond must be a very special idiot. A moment later, the rest of him emerged, no shirt, his overalls held up by one strap. This wasn't unusual; what struck me was he pulled on the other and brushed himself off as if he had fallen into the grain elevator. He slid the door closed and started to fast-walk toward his house in the opposite direction. Before he rounded the corner out of sight, a door on the side of the barn facing the house banged, and the young girl who had cluttered my mind all afternoon dashed across the yard and went inside the screened door.

I could not think of any reason for them to be inside that barn at the same time— that made sense. Arthur made me tell him this account twice, and he hardly spoke during our trip to Memphis. The shadow of his hat landed right under his nose, darkening the lighter upper half of his face in great contrast to the skin below. Intent eyes stared ahead. He rolled a smoke one-handed at 45 mph. We went on that way for a few minutes until he flicked the stub out the window and started to make another.

"Roll me one."

"No."

"Then let me roll it. I'm almost fourteen."

He said nothing, and so as soon as he set them between us, I took up the King Edward tin and papers and made a loose cigarette, twisting the ends closed. Tobacco flakes seeped out along the side, but it was more smokeable than the bass I cleaned earlier was edible, and so I was pleased with it. I struck a match on the dash, feeling ten years older.

"Was she playin' in there? Do you think... what were they doin'? Do you know what her name is?"

"You doan need to worry 'bout that. Hit wasn't nothin'." Arthur declined to participate in a conversation this way. I knew he would say no more.

Well, I forgot about this scene eventually, and it must have cured me of the image of the girl's sudden sexuality because within a day or two I did not think of her anymore either.

29

Tele-vision

August 1947

Big Charlie had a massive telescope made by Edmund Scientific in the house because the moon and the stars could be so incredible at Skytop. That's why he called the farm that; he built our little house on the very top of the hill looking north; you're at the perfect center of a blue dome reaching to tree lines lower than your feet on all sides. The two-acre pond about a quarter mile down the hill is the centerpiece of the view; the blue horizon drops down below the levee road on the far side. One night in early summer, when Billy and I got tired of trying to keep up with the moon, which wouldn't stay still, and moved across our field of view, he pointed the telescope at the brightest star. After a few focus struggles, we looked closely at the planet Jupiter, which we knew because we could see the big red spot and the four visible moons, strung out more or less in a line: Io, Europa, Ganymede, and Callisto. We could even see tiny shadows cast by the two center ones (neither of us knew which was which).

Clear days you could see for miles. We used to peer way north over the trees at the prison, imagining we'd witness an escape or see a guard with his machine gun in one of the towers. But mostly, all you could see was walls and a glimpse of something that might be a tower. Who said it was a prison anyway? Neither of us could remember.

We played the game of "Shit Breath." One trained the Edmund on a distant cow. At "go, you took a huge breath, and if you could find a cow taking a shit before you had to let go and breathe (proved by focusing the telescope, then sharing the glance), you won a nickel. You had to be long on change to play the game because cows shit so much. It wore us out when they would do it in transit, sometimes swatting at a violent spew nonchalantly with their tails. Hippopotamuses do that— we learned firsthand at the zoo.

A cloud of dust drew our focus to the source-- Raymond on the red Allis Chalmers tractor. He was engaged in pulling discs across a dry field. Clods jumped into the air behind him, and a slight breeze pushed the dust cloud away. I went back to the cows when it was my turn. Billy produced the build-ups and deftly rolled a cigarette.

I had not thought to tell Billy of my experience seeing Raymond and the Jenks girl leave the barn within seconds of each other and was suddenly seized with urgency. I stepped away from the telescope and related the story.

"Damn! He is a horny bastard," said my brother.

"Do you think he was doing it with her?"

"Shit, what do you think? Did you tell Dad?"

"No. I was going to, but he was gone, and I forgot. I thought Arthur would tell him. Maybe he did. He sure didn't want to talk about it the day it happened... said it wasn't any big deal. "

Billy took a look for a minute. Suddenly he said, "Oh shit! Look now," and jumped back. Raymond, cigarette in mouth, one hand on the wheel, was quite literally enjoying himself with the other, his overall pants bunched at the knees, under the wheel. Our faces were stretched in laughter like cartoon characters, and we started jumping up and down and screaming to see if we could get his attention! Of course not. The tractor bucked, and black smoke billowed from the exhaust, and his skinny naked ass was thrown into the air up off the seat like pocket change, reminding us he heard only the diesel engine, and he went on taking matters "into his own hands," until he turned and the tractor angle was no good, and his back was to us.

Later in the afternoon, Raymond came chugging up the road from the field toward the barn, and we happened to be there pulling saddles from the tack room for a late afternoon ride.

"Hey Raymond," said my brother. "Do you like the new JACK-ter? How's that JACKter handle?" He thought this was immensely funny.

"Hit's fine," said he. "Mistuh Chahlee don't want youns messin' round with it now. Y'all go on."

That was the last time either of us ever saw Raymond.

30

Catfish Project

September 1947

Dad was starting a project to stock the ponds at Skytop with catfish. On their way to the farm, he and Arthur dropped me at a little bump along the track where the train always stopped for a minute, Grand Junction, not too far from the farm. I was a little down about going back to school but somewhat ambivalent about the journey, planning to distract myself so I might master one of Arthur's greatest tricks: he could roll a quarter, end-over-end, back-and-forth across the back of his hand. The coin seemed to travel on its own, just forward of the knuckle over the fingers from index to little finger. It could only be done with perfect timing; you move your fingers like piston rods. Arthur could do it with amazing speed, and I was determined to master it. Once we were underway, I practiced with an oversized washer. The challenge infected the Memphis guys going to Baylor, and by nightfall, quarters were in short supply. By the time we dropped them in Nashville, it seemed as if every kid on the train was working on it.

Last trip back to school, I played poker with them and lost $25. They left the dog-eared deck on the table when they got off, and I snapped it into my travel bag's outer pocket— where it was when I arrived in Memphis the following December. Arthur showed me how it was marked— tiny nicks in the edge, made by a fingernail, one for an ace, two for a king, one on either side for the queen, one on the top for a jack. Fuckers.

Like beekeeping, which he would undertake years later, the catfish project was another of Dad's "temporary" infatuations. I think he got the idea once he learned of Arthur's experience with catfish farming 20 years before in Indianola, Mississippi.

The plan was for Arthur to supervise Raymond Crick, and they worked side-by-side for a week to berm up the levee at the east side of the tiny pond near the entrance, so it might be deepened to support catfish. The lake in front of our house was already deep enough, but it took another two weeks to dredge and install a drain and emergency spillway on each. It was still warm by late September, and Arthur met the county agent and a one-armed catfish farmer called Nubby, who brought four thousand fingerlings in a huge tank with 100 adults that were supposed to help keep down losses from turtles.

Nubby backed the truck wheels right to the edge of the high west side levee and opened a valve. The four thousand fingerlings splashed into the pond, which boiled for a few moments until they dispersed. Another tank holding the adults would have to be lifted off the truck and manually emptied. Arthur said it weighed probably 500 pounds. Nubby was no help, and the three other men could hardly budge it, so they enlisted Wilson Jenks and Lucas. The tank landed hard on the ground, and a dozen of the big fish flopped into the tall grass. Instead of securing them with a foothold, as did Nubby and the agent, Raymond seized a four-pounder with both hands and was barbed in the meatiest part of his palm with its poisonous dorsal. His hand swelled grotesquely, and he cried like a baby.

I would have liked to have witnessed that scene. No love was lost between the farm hands and Arthur after all they had been through. I understand another installation was undertaken later, at the lake in front of the house, without mishap. Never questioning anything he was asked to do, Arthur spent a good bit of time out at Skytop that fall working on the catfish project... which ultimately would not serve him.

31

The Tennessean

December 19, 1947

Mother and Big Charlie spent a lot of time that fall in Linville, supervising the construction of an addition to the wrap-around porch, playing golf and bridge, and cocktailing in the evenings. On the way back to Linville for Thanksgiving, before real winter would exile them back to Memphis for the season, they made a side trip to see me. I had not been home since August, and my almost tearful entreaties to accompany them for the Holiday weekend were not received warmly.

"Uncle CD is very ill," said Mother. "His smoking..." Her eyes filled with tears. Big Charlie went on to tell me they found spots on his lungs. "You can help us best by concentrating here. Aunt Katherine has her hands full with two still in diapers."

The gravity of this exchange did not reach me. I had hardly seen Uncle Deane since the wedding, and though he was thin, he looked strong. It was a cold he would get over.

My first high school Thanksgiving break was spent in study at school.

All semester our teachers colluded to overwhelm us. The work seemed interminable, if not impossible. On the first day of class after summer break, Omundsen, the chemistry professor, demanded (by class the next day), a solution to his problem:

"*Determine the thickness of a molecule of oleic acid.*"

This was supposed to be a hint:

If the film has one molecular thickness, then the thickness of oleic *acid film will directly give the approximate size or diameter of a molecule of oleic acid: The value comes out to be of the order of 10^{-9} m.*

After a tough few months, we couldn't wait for the Christmas holidays. I was pretty excited to see everybody and of course, hunt with Arthur and Big Charlie. Depending on the weather, Mother might even go— she is a fine shot. She sent me a ticket on the *Tennessean*, the Washington to Memphis train that ran back and forth every 36 hours, with dozens of stops. Sometimes there was a sleeper car. Mostly though, too many stops to make that worthwhile, and passengers instead gravitated to the lounge and dining cars. I got over the excitement of riding the train on my first trip and preferred my seat. I could sleep there better than in a noisy bunk with a curtain separating me from a snoring fat man.

At dawn, Professor "Crotchit" was waiting to take me to the station, chipping away at the passenger windshield to remove the remaining ice. Having failed to find alternative transportation, I dreaded the twenty-minute car ride more than the 18 hours it would take to get to Memphis. The musky BO smell in his car was made worse by the heater blowing full blast. The moment we left the campus, Crotch spoke to me in a way that was uncomfortable, too familiar, as if we were friends. Earning barely a passing grade in his English Lit class, I preferred to maintain my grudge and the respectful distance of our ages.

"So, Mr. Walterlane, what will you do over your Holiday break? Is there someone special... a young lady? I had a first love in Memphis..."

And so I heard the story of his tame first love experience, an arranged meeting at a dance. It was hard for me to imagine my English teacher being young, much less attracting girls. Whenever he says his "ee's": "theese,"... "weeeeks,"... his teeth show far yellower than is apparent in class. Always in a threadbare tweed suit and scarf, Professor Thomas Alexander Kotchet made us think of Dicken's Bob Cratchit, frozen in that time when access to baths and clean clothes must have been very limited.

Crotchit pulled up to the crowded station. We couldn't get very close. I gathered up my satchel, barked a quick thanks, and practically ran out of the car. Standing in line at the platform waiting to board, I saw his car pull away and remembered the stack of books I hoped to read, bound by my belt, still in the trunk.

Dime comics carried me as far as Strasburg. Mercifully, I passed out for a long while and awoke just as we rolled into Knoxville. I woke up thinking about Arthur and our odyssey with Uncle Deane. Now, he had Aunt Katherine, Janie, and the twins Donovan and Day.

"The train will depart precisely at 11 am," said the conductor, walking the aisles. I could hear his warning in the car before and in the one behind. In my experience (three trips by myself to Memphis), the train had not once run on time. I had forty-five minutes at least. I got up to find something to eat at the station but quickly sat back down. The lady in the seat in front of me was just offering her infant a tasty bosom under a blanket, and I could see all of a creamy swell right to the nipple. I stood again and shuffled my knapsack in the overhead for as long as I dared, freezing the image in my brain, recording changes in the perspective, finally exiting my seat ever so slowly.

With a twinge of disappointment, I stepped out of the warm train and into the cold; the image of suckling and delicious breasts blocked the light from my eyes. Turning my thoughts to the pending break and shooting ducks with Arthur and Billy, I could almost smell the sulfur from just-fired shells... Suddenly, I was quite hungry.

The Knoxville station was also packed. The sights and smells brought me right back to the same scene my first spring: the coffee in the greasy spoon was mostly foul-smelling mud, and I could have patched my shoe with the fried eggs.

A long line at the station diner pushed me back out the door, looking up and down the street for alternatives. A biting wind chilled me to the bone in just my sweater— my heavy jacket stayed in my seat.

The clock above the ticket window read 10:25– still plenty of time. I stepped up on the platform between cars, looking up and down the other side. Some kind of eating establishment or newsstand was visible almost at the end of the train. Surely I can buy a Danish at least, and maybe a decent cup of coffee. I hesitated a moment... really ought to grab my jacket and step back to the station side. The lady in the seat in front stepped down from my car, her baby buried in blankets clutched to her chest against the cold. I stared at the bundle with envy. She hurried off in the direction of the restaurant at the end of the train, and I found myself a few steps behind her, the jacket momentarily forgotten. Hopefully, the baby will still be hungry when we get back on the train.

When she finally ducked into the ladies' room almost at the end of the station, I could see that the newsstand was actually part of a large market, and good things were for sale everywhere. I had my first sausage biscuit this day, bought one for later, and tucked it into my pants pocket in a napkin.

The newsstand had the new *Batman* comic book, and I flipped the pages... *Superman* was my guy, but they didn't have any issues I had not read. Standing there, I read half the thing, flipped to the end, but bought it anyway, anticipating the story might unfold in more detail back in my seat (as if I didn't already know it). The sausage biscuit stirred in my bowels, and back into the station, I went in search of the men's room.

I sat there and read the last page, experiencing another disappointment- it was a two-parter (I HATE those). Robin (wimpy sidekick Robin, another reason I don't like Batman) was about to be bisected by the Joker with a huge band saw, unless... *11:05 by my watch.*

On my way out of the bathroom that day, the smartly dressed, kindly attendant asked me something about my book. He loved comic books because the pictures showed "full the actshun." But when I opened to the page where The Joker was lowering my hero into hot oil while shouting,

"BAT SOUP!", (the very climax, I thought so far), he didn't say anything, and I thought he couldn't read. It made me a little sad for a second.

The *Tennessean*! I snatched closed the magazine. "Sorry, gotta go" and ran outside to see my train already slowly underway.

I ran. No way to catch up to the passenger cars, almost a city block ahead, but I made it alongside the silver caboose. At a full run, I might be able to jump aboard the open freight car, which was fast approaching the throng looking forward, waving to the departing coaches. The biting wind I felt leaving the station was at my back, but freezing air pained my lungs. Just a couple of strides more... I ran harder. When the gravel apron turned to the platform pavement, I saw myself gaining. Almost aside the lower step, I grabbed the rail, then my arm was seized in an iron vise, and I was yanked two more steps up.

"WHAT the hell, son?"

A very tall fellow, his face framed by a fur hat tied at the chin, looked at me with disdain. He was buried in a heavy coat with a fur collar, and thick gloves clutched my upper arms. Patches on the shoulders said UNITED STATES POSTAL SERVICE. I've been pulled aboard the mail car.

"You tryin' ta-get yourself killed? What're you doin'?"

"I... I have a ticket." was all I managed, and he laughed.

Stiff with cold, teeth chattering, I couldn't feel my fingers. Then Mail Man said the car wasn't heated. Insult to injury: "And there's a porthole that stays open so we can visually check to make sure the mail is recovered." In rural areas, between stops, a hook arm sticks out from the train to snag the mailbag as we go by. What do they do if the catch is missed, hope the next train has better luck?

He settled me in a wooden chair under a piece of a thin blanket and turned back to his business, moving newly snagged sacks, pulling out boxes and items larger than bundles of letters, and tossing them into labeled bins. Under a clipboard manifest hanging on a nail, detailing stops and bags (successfully) taken aboard, I spotted a stack of newspapers on a countertop where Mail Man has his "office." It's Monday's news, five days old, the front page section adorned with impressions of coffee cups detailed the rebuilding of Leningrad, the Cold War, the Hollywood blacklist, "Robinson joins the Dodgers...." No one will miss it. It goes up my pant leg, over my socks, under my shirt. Another section headlined "Riots in Palestine and growing violence throughout the region".... "Britain and the partition of Palestine" earns a spot down the back of my pants. I burrowed down into sacks of mail, thinking maybe I was warming up just a little.

It's a trick I learned from Arthur. The time he and I were hunting across the levee at Akabutla, it got dangerously cold. We had a close call.

The afternoon hunt was a good one. We stood waste-deep in chest waders in the thick of the willows between the woods and the open water, shooting wood ducks so long my arms ached from holding up my gun. The temp was probably in the thirties when we started mid-morning, but it dropped steadily all day. I marveled at the thin insulation Arthur could operate with: an oiled canvas coat that had belonged to Uncle Bill, over one layer of long underwear (also hand-me-down), and over that newspaper. Arthur would fold newspaper around his body, over the thinnest socks, into rubber boots Big Charlie once wore, which were suitable only for keeping feet dry in the summer, or stuff his waders almost so that they looked inflated. This he did all over his body, and I have never once heard him mention cold nor even comment when we fussed about it.

What kept me warm was wading to recover the kill or chase a cripple. Sometimes it was a long back-and-forth journey. I would forget what landmark I referenced when I knocked one down. The action, the chill, and the movement kept us alert; I did not realize how tired I was, so maybe we dallied perhaps a bit long as the gray afternoon light faded. When we got back to the car, which we left inches deep in mud at a steep down-facing angle (just over the levee), it was stuck solid, frozen in mud-turned-concrete. This might not have been such a problem if it had started, but it barely turned over. Minutes passed. The freezing rain began. Shortly, it would be dark.

I had not experienced relentless cold like that, nor have I since. Dadgum car door was frozen shut, and Arthur had to yank on it a couple of times, but finally, we could toss our game and guns in the back seat and heave ourselves into the worsening elements over the frozen levee. When we did, the wind pelted us with sleet. At first, you just heard it on your hat, like birdshot shot raining down when someone would shoot too close in your direction, spraying you, except it was sustained.

"Cahlo." Arthur's voice somehow warmed me. "C'mon," said my trusted friend. "I know a house..."

"SONOFABITCH!" I shouted. The wind has a nastier bite suddenly, and my chin seeks refuge below the collar of my turtleneck. I am not moving well.

"We'll jes walk up the road a bit."

I might have asked Big Charlie, "What for?" or "How far?" But, with Arthur, you just knew he had something in mind.

We started a long walk on the hardened levee road, crunching deepening sleet, pelted in the face, almost blind, except I could make out the moats of water left and right. Free-flowing channels when we arrived, they had frozen. The buildup of ice and sleet reflected a hint of moon glow from the east.

Far ahead, there was a flickering light. We finally came to a shack I hadn't noticed on the way in (not that I knew exactly where we were). Arthur knocked at the door.

I was numb, but standing on the floorboards of the porch, I felt the commotion inside. There was much scurrying, and the door opened to a silhouette outlined by a (blessed) fire. In we went, and the colored man shut the door behind us. It was a great relief, but in a moment, I noticed the wind whistling in the walls. Little was solid about the house except the brick fireplace, well-tended and roaring.

The firelight showed the face of our host. I noted his red, tired eyes.

The man said to 'getyoself' warm. Cold as my fingers were, when I pulled off a glove, a colder, dry hand seized my hand, and I mumbled my thanks. "Rodney," I think he said and slipped behind the only other door, but not before several little bitties emerged. They were gruffly corralled to follow.

Then it was just Arthur and me, freezing in our clothes, standing in this man's tiny house, hoarding his heat while we gawked at each other.

"Git yo clothes off," Arthur said, already having done much the same. Mine was a two-foot heap of layers of clothes. Arthur made a neat pile of his clothing topped with carefully folded newspaper, the wet sheets draped over the top to dry them in the heat.

He sat up straight, facing the fire Indian style, legs crossed under him, bare from his waist up. Arthur is an imposing figure, powerful, his back an inverted pyramid. I was so tired I took a chair against the wall. The heat in the room began prickling my frozen skin. We sat for a long time like that.

Just when I wondered if we were spending the night, the door beside me suddenly opened out into the room, blocking my view of the entrant. A few seconds later, I heard a woman gasp, "ARTHUR CAMPBELL!"

When Arthur turned, the firelight defined his profile and was reflected in the whites of his eyes.

"LAWD in heaven," she ended in a whisper and in another beat, stepped back to shut herself out of the room. From behind the slammed door, there is suddenly much more commotion, shouts, and cries from both adults and, shortly, crying children.

It took me a moment to realize the woman recognized Arthur's naked torso, in the dark, from behind.

I don't feel very welcome suddenly. Arthur, a black silhouette against the firelight, is already gathering himself, already standing, stuffing newspaper back into his waders.

We slipped out the scant door in the direction we came.

"She knew you," I said.

"Yes."

Arthur said when you come to the end of your rope, tie a knot in it and hang on. He should know a lot about being at the end of your rope, from what he had told me of his humble, adventurous life.

I could shove one of the heavy bags against the porthole and cut way down on the draft, but I couldn't cut the chill. I must not have Arthur's technique because I could not sense that the newspaper insulation was working.

Mail Man had come in a time or two and seen me trying to bury myself under bags of mail but seemed to take little notice, which encouraged me to burrow deeper. I remembered the sausage biscuit and wrested it from my pocket, scraping knuckles on the hard canvas of my mailbags cocoon. The biscuit was hardened to tack in its protective paper wrap, but it tasted wonderful.

"DO YOU REALLY HAVE A TICKET?" was what I heard next, waking to Mail Man's tug on my sweater. "Train stops in five minutes, and you can get back on a passenger car."

Many hours later, I saw the Woody before the train came to a stop. Arthur was waiting for me, as always. I told him about the mishap on the train and how I stuffed my clothes with newspaper like he does: "Doesn't work. How do you stay warm with newspaper?"

"I ain't really warm. I jest put my mind to what's befo' me. If we is huntin' or fishin', I don't thank on it." Arthur Campbell, the stoic, immovable object.

32

The Great Sand Ditch

Spring 1948

Mr. Walterlane had not confirmed their appointment. Hoping his trip was not for naught, Dex McCullar turned left on Chapleau FR12 from Highway 57 and rode five miles down a potholed gravel road that suddenly turned hard right at a closed gate, where stood a new wrought iron sign painted white: 'Skytop Farm.' Finally. He took the truck out of gear and unhooked the chain from a nail, swung the gate wide, and drove through. To the right was a thick forest behind croppers' shacks and a cinder block house up the hill. He didn't see any livestock in the great open field to the left, nor near the little pond that could be seen at the crest (where Dad's catfish undertaking had begun), so thinking he might be back through momentarily, McCullar left the gate open. He nosed on up the hill to the two-story red brick house next to a couple of green barns and a gas pump. Two shiny silos were to the west, behind the house, where now he could also see about a hundred head of cattle making their way to the pond in the very direction of the open gate. Hmm, I better—

"Kin I help yew?"

He spun around. A sallow-faced woman with a thick brow and bony frame was there, holding a basket of clothes. She had been attending to the clothesline that went around the house. She eyed him up and down but stared at his steel-toed cowboy boots.

"Yessim, thank you. Hi, I am Dexter McCullar, with McCullar Lumber Company of Bolivar, and I am looking for Mr. Walterlane." He handed her a card that said all of that, and it also said McCullar Lumber Company was a 'PROUD MEMBER OF THE NATIONAL HARDWOOD

TIMBER ASSOCIATION'.

She looked at it for a second, then tried to hand it back to him. "Ah cain't read."

Probably not Mrs. Walterlane, he thought. "Oh, no, ma'am, that's for you to please give to Mr. Walterlane... or to your husband to give to him. Unless... is he here? I think we have an appointment."

"Ah ain't seed him inna month uh Sundays. He ain't been out here but a few times since the war's over."

The screen door to the house slammed, and Dex saw a tall girl with a sad face, who changed direction when she saw a stranger and hurried around the house to the clothesline from whence came the woman who stood before him. Her clothes hung on her, though her belly was distended— she carried a baby. He swung back around. "May I ask your name, please, ma'am?"

"Wilma Janks."

"Uhm, is Mr. Janks home?"

"JANKS," she said, "J-E-N-K-S... Janks."

"Yessim... Mr Jenks. Is he home?"

Out of the corner of his eye, he saw a vehicle kick up dust and spray gravel, stopping just inside the open gate. The door flew open, and the driver leaped out and pulled it closed just before bovine curiosity was upon him en masse.

"Thass him." She went around his pickup and into the house. Feeling a bit intimidated because of his carelessness, and not likely to get much of a recommendation from Walterlane's ranch hands, Dex stood wiping dust from the chrome grill of his new blue Chevy.

Jenks pulled up in his battered white truck. "You leave my gate open?"

"I did. I'm sorry, I didn't see any cattle, and I only planned to be here a minute."

Jenks suddenly spat a brown jet that kicked up dust in the drive like a round from a six-shooter. "Whuddyewwant?"

"I'm looking for Mr. Walterlane. I'm with the McCullar Lumber Company."

"Like your truck says."

"Yes!" Dex fished out another card. "McCullar Lumber Company is a member of the National Hardwood Timber Association. I've talked to Mr. Walterlane about buying some of his timber. We have an appointment."

"He ain't here—"

"Yessir. Well, I hope he may be expecting me. Mind if I wait?"

A squeal of brakes turned their attention to the entrance gate. A large fellow swung out of a topless green Willys Jeep, shooing cattle away as he approached from outside.

"Well, yer in luck," said Jenks. There's yer appointment. F'yoo come in again, don't leave my gate open, lessen' you wanna spen' your day roundin' up cows." He spat again and walked inside his house.

"Nice to meet you too," muttered Dex.

Charlie Walterlane unhooked the nail and swung the gate wide, drove through, and quickly closed it behind. In a moment, he pulled up to the blue truck. He extended a meaty hand and bade Dex to follow him to the white house at the edge overlooking the valley.

Dex sipped gratefully on a cold Budweiser and took in the stunning view north through a plate glass window. Charlie opened side windows for some air, sweeping dead wasps from the sills. "I'm glad I could get out here today. I have been traveling so much I have not had much time to enjoy this place."

"I hear that. It's beautiful..." said Dex. A live wasp bounced off the wall near a small comb nest in the fold of the curtain above the small window to the west.

His host continued: "You want to survey. Well, rather than do it by Jeep, I think we'll saddle up a couple of horses and take a ride over the spread. We can go into the woods, and you can get a better idea of the tracts I think are most overgrown, where we won't miss anything. There's an old lake in the bottom too, where a snatch of pine would help attract deer, I think." Charlie referred to the reforestation program McCullar sold him on as part of any timber harvest.

They rode back out the way they had driven in, taking a right past the Jenks house. Children ran around. Wilma Jenks yelled something at an older boy, who seized the nearest rooster and held it. He then wrung its neck expertly, its sharp spurs flailing empty air. In the shadows behind him, the tall, possibly pregnant girl Dex had observed before eyed them from the corner of the house.

Charlie Walterlane said. "There isn't much I understand about the Jenks, but Wilson is a pretty good foreman, responsible, helps keep the farm hands to task. Guess he can't account for them all; one of them disappeared at the first of the year."

"Disappeared?"

"Vanished. Without a trace." His wife lives here. She thinks he ran off with another woman, but... well, you haven't seen Raymond."

"Hmm."

"It's a mystery. One of my men from Memphis and my son, Carlo, found Raymond running a still. We will ride past that spot on the way back. He pulled a rifle on Arthur, but Raymond was so drunk Arthur took it from him without much trouble. Raymond is short on intelligence, so I'm sure Jenks had a hand in that still, but Arthur just told him what happened, and Wilson Jenks collected Raymond and took him home.

"Were they selling corn liquor?"

"I imagine. Strange, though... Raymond disappeared not too long after... about mid-January, I think. If we find out what happened to him, whatever it is, I doubt it will surprise me. These damn country people..."

Dex let out a snicker. They rode down past the silos on the left.

"We put those in to store corn for the livestock," said Walterlane. "A new worker climbed up those rungs and fell through the door into the one we'd just filled. He suffocated his first day on the job."

Dex was about to comment when Walterlane said, "I mentioned Raymond's wife? She's as big around as a house. She thinks he has a girlfriend. Raymond looks like a turkey, with an Adam's apple the size of a baseball. If there was anything in those silos right now, I'd say that's where we ought to look for him!" Both men laughed.

They passed down into a field in fallow, either side of the muddy road bound by weed grass the height of the horses. Rounding a slight bend, they surprised three turkeys, hens strutting out of the reeds to cross the road. A half-dozen poults as big as chickens took to the air and settled back in well across, safely anonymous in the tall grass.

They rode through a 10-acre forest of oak, pin oak, and poplar trees before the woods gave way to a clearing and a lake. An insistent whippoorwill called to its echo across the lake. Dex noted the acreage and approximated the available millable timber on a pad. By mid-afternoon, they had circled around to way north of the lake along the fence marking the property line. There, at the center of the tract, the view north took you down over the tops of trees almost far as the eye could see. Tips of church steeples indicated "the God-fearing community of Whiteville," said Walterlane. They made their way along the fence line of the periphery to the east until it went back into the thickest woods. It was this part of the property that most interested McCullar, and he wished the aerial photos he had commissioned had been available today.

They punched into the woods along a critter path, which found an old road. Downslope they went until the road eroded into a steep ditch, a challenge even for the sure-footed horses, to a decayed wooden bridge. It was able to support their crossing but unlikely to hold an automobile, though that may once have been its purpose. Dex tried to reason why here.

Charlie Walterlane said, "There was a log home in here around the time of the Civil War. I think it may have been burned by Union Troops on their way to Memphis. There's part of a chimney, soot-covered field stone with mortar on it, somewhere under those leaves and vines between here and the fence."

They crossed up to the other side. The ground settled into a ridge that ran north and south for a hundred yards before snaking left and right, down and up, cut and formed by the main drainage system of ditches. One of these was twenty yards across with a smooth bed of pink-orange sand common to the area. Trees of three feet in thickness were numerous along and just beyond its banks. As the ridge held and the riders could stay atop, their walk led around the great trees, half out of the walls of the ditch, most still-standing, though their roots were exposed, the soil gouged from the red clay banks by the fury of the stream after the heavy spring rains.

"You can see it will be a challenge to get them out, but this is why I am interested in selling you this timber— they're doomed anyway."

"I think we will be interested in the whole area, not just the ones that won't live."

"Of course. I want to level this land and create a single drain. Loggers will do a lot of this for me and help me pay for it. Take all of them here. I don't care. I'll show you the boundary I want to leave completely forested."

They kept moving north as long as the ridge was passable, then it came to an abrupt drop-off. Back-tracking to a path down into the ditch, a gradual slope where animals had crossed, the horses stepped onto the soft sand, and the men experienced a moment's relief— pillows after walking on cobblestones.

"My boys call this 'The Great Sand Ditch.' It is an ideal spot to slip along hunting without making a single sound. I taught my oldest to squirrel hunt in here. We've shot big fox squirrels in these trees. Gave them to Raymond. His wife makes squirrel soup. It's really not that bad."

Dex was counting, making notes, trying to figure an average per quarter acre. You couldn't much think of this chopped-up place in terms of whole acres, but the trees were numerous on either side of the ditch system where it was more or less level to get at them. As they made their way north, Charlie hadn't said stop yet. He just wanted to know how much the ditches broke up the land once they penciled in the target area on the map.

"But after a big storm, this is no place to be, " said Charlie. "When it's wet, I don't even know how deep the sand is. Once, when I was in here trying to slip along turkey hunting, I stepped in a pool that looked like tomato soup and was right up to my navel."

The sand was firm, and the horses were having no trouble with it. But, the path was not straight for more than a few yards. The drain bed zigged and zagged yards to the left, then yards to the right, staying at the same level elevation regardless of the rise and fall of the forest floor above. The cliffside on the right rose to twenty feet, then the passage narrowed and the downfall thicker. They rounded the corner, ducking under thick brush. Completely blocking their path, about chest-high on the horses, a great oak had recently lost its grip on the west bank, and the ton of soil still in its root system cast the sand before them into shadow. The top rested on the opposite bank, just missing a cross gully, leaves still green. The branches were jammed into the sand like pilings.

Big Charlie rode right up to the massive trunk and said, "Oh, Jesus."

Dex sensed his host was over his amazement at the deadfall and stood up in his saddle to see past. On the other side of the tree, in undisturbed sand, rose a skeletal hand, a human finger pointed skyward, and the top of a skull with one eye socket visible. Between the two, frayed strips of red and black flannel disappeared neatly into the sand, a shoulder perhaps.

"I'm going to bet we have found Raymond."

33

In his own words

April 19, 1948

Big Charlie and Mother had just arrived in Italy when a Memphis Police cruiser and one marked Hardeman County Sheriff pulled up the drive on South Parkway. Arthur was in the kitchen with James Anna. They arrested Arthur for Raymond's murder and hauled him to jail in Somerville. Uncle Cliff reached Dad after several days, and at Dad's request, he drove out to the Hardeman County Jail, but (somewhat to Cliff's relief) they would not let Arthur see anyone.

They told him, "Mr. Campbell has made a statement implicating himself."

Weeks passed. Dad sent his attorney, Smithwick Cox, out there to demand due process. He learned they held Arthur on evidence provided by Wilson Jenks. What evidence? I knew Arthur didn't kill anybody. I wrote down every piece of the story I knew: the still incident (self-defense), Raymond's suspicious behavior around Jenks's daughter, and his masturbatory tractor ride, and sent it to Dad to give to Mr. Cox. They got me out of my calculus exam to talk to him on the phone. He asked a lot of questions, especially about Jenks's daughter, whose name was Dedee. Dedee was fifteen and had just given birth to a girl. Had I seen Raymond and Dedee together on any other occasion?

What the hell? I was consumed by the need to get home and probably flunked that exam.

May 30

Dad picked me up at the train station. "Jenks swore he saw Arthur and

Raymond go off down into the bottom one day between January 15 and the 20th. He said he heard gunfire, but that's so common he didn't think anything of it. He's seen Arthur out there a lot since, but not Raymond. Since Raymond disappears from time to time, again, that's not so unusual. Coroner says that could be consistent with the time of death, hard to tell. The body was burned. What was left had teeth marks indicating the coyotes and other predators picked it clean, down to the bones. He guesses the exposed skull and hands bleached over two or three months."

"Bullshit!"

My father looked at me with surprise, then laughed. "Don't worry, son. We will get to the bottom of this. You know I don't think Arthur had anything to do with that fool's death. But we have to go by the law. Unfortunately, they're gonna take a white man's word over a colored man every time. S'way it is. Burden of proof's on us. We'll get there."

"Raymond was messing around with Jenks's daughter. He found out about it and *killed* him. That's what happened."

"It's an interesting theory. From what I know now, could be. But we have to find a way to prove it."

"Is Mr. Cox investigating? Asking questions of all the farm hands and their families?"

"I understand he has. No one offers anything to contradict Jenks's account of the story. But he is confident that the evidence is circumstantial and will not be enough to convict."

I had a sudden thought. "Professor Tompkins is a shooting enthusiast. If we ask enough questions about a subject he likes, he'll keep talking about it during class time, even if it has nothing to do with the lesson. Last month we talked about the science of 'forensic ballistics' and ballistic fingerprinting. Do you know what that is?"

"Yes. Sorry, no bullet has been recovered."

Can you ask Mr. Cox to have the Sheriff take all guns owned by farm hands, in case I find one?"

I'll never forget the look Big Charlie gave me then. After a moment, he said, "Son, I imagine he has already done that, but if he hasn't, that's a damn good idea."

June 2, 1948

Dad and Billy, and I went to the farm, and he took us to the spot where they found Raymond, just the other side of the huge oak that had fallen across. It had rained often in the weeks since they pulled the body out, and the freshly disturbed hole I expected was barely a smooth depression. "Boys, listen to me. Be careful about that ditch. It's dangerous. And you might better not disturb that spot. It's a crime scene. You won't find the bullet there. They think the body was dragged by animals or washed into the ditch during spring flooding. If I were you, I'd look along the banks north. We know the water flows south when there's a heavy rain. You are looking for some evidence of burning. I'll walk up the bank a bit, and if I don't see something interesting, I'll come back and get you in a couple of hours. I'm going to see Arthur in Somerville and talk to that damn Sheriff."

We were excited as thieves. Billy crossed the ditch to the other side, and I started looking hard at the bank where we stood. We ignored Big Charlie's warning to stay out of the ditch because it was easier to examine the bank. We just started on the other side of the tree to avoid spoiling the crime scene.

I looked hard at the bank just under the surface of the leaves for any blackness. I thought of my geology class when we learned how layers of rock were laid down over the eons. Diagrammed pictures in the book had call-outs showing geologic periods and the estimated ages of layers. A thick black layer indicated possible volcanic activity. Below that, an arrow pointing to deeper layers led to a blurb saying dinosaurs walked the Earth during the millions of years of the Mesozoic Era. *Millions* of years. In geologic time, that was supposed to be fairly recent.

We moved slowly. In an hour, we may have navigated fifty yards. The light was dimming as afternoon approached. We decided fifty yards was a long way for waters to carry a body around such a snaky passage riddled with snags. We got out and worked the cliff edge for ten yards out, scraping the leaf bed gently, like turkeys scratching for insects, to expose any evidence of a burn that might be only months old. We were disappointed when we got back to the starting point, finding nothing. Big Charlie was there almost immediately, and we gave it up for the day.

That night, Billy said, "If it was dragged by animals, they wouldn't have to go north or south... or wouldn't think to."

"Or the murderer," I said.

After a time, Billy said, "During the time Dad was gone, Arthur taught me to make shells, and I worked all afternoon one day making them. I think I was... twelve. Do you remember that– I think you wanted to make some and screwed them up, and Arthur convinced you to let us do it, and you cried. When I finished a whole box, I pestered him to take me duck-hunting. Anyway, whether it was that time or another day, we went to Horseshoe."

"I cried when you left without me– I was asleep. Arthur said I was too young."

"Yeah, right. Anyway, on the drive over, I told him the story of Huck Finn and Jim, on the island, and in the cave... about how I was like Huck, and he was Jim, and finding the dead body. He wouldn't let Huck see it." We looked out for each other... I called him 'Jim' that day a few times, and he laughed. I don't think I have heard him laugh before or since. He really liked the story, and I promised to read the whole thing to him, but I never did. Damn."

"What made you think of that?"

"I dunno- Raymond, dead body, Arthur accused..." Billy had a tear in his eye. "It just pisses me off."

We hardly slept that night for wanting to get back into the woods in the morning.

At dawn, Dad was off somewhere, so we walked down to the bottom, passing Raymond's dilapidated house. Window shades were pulled down. Except for the laundry outside on the line, blowing slightly in the breeze, you wouldn't know anyone lived there.

Billy said, "Raymond's wife must be as stupid as he is... I mean *was*," he corrected. We snickered. "That laundry is probably soaked with dew."

The statement Arthur gave on the day he was taken into custody, witnessed by Big Charlie and Smithwick J. Cox, was tape-recorded, thanks to Cox:

"I ain't killed a white man... on purpose, det I know of...

Raymond was breathin' jes fine when I seen him lass. Mistuh Chahlee say we-uud figguh it out, in due time, an then they come'n get me. Well I been sittin' in dis jail in Bolivuh fuh fo weeks' 'due time', waitin' tell they figguh hit was Janks, that kealt'im. I thought hit was, but I din' say nothin' cause... nobody wuud b'leeve me. An, I wuud'n either, sho' nuff. But what Raymon was doin' to Janks' chile... Lawd! Can't nobody blame him.

Right befo' the flood, jess a coupl-a days befo', the levee blowed out fum under us, I took de fireman's shovel to Jon Wilburn's haid when we was woikin' out there. Well he was about to tho-a nigger in the rivuh, jes 'cause he hurt. Had to hit him to save at nigguh's life. He went down into the mud, yassuh. B'om-tellin' ye, he could get up again, an he walk out tat place. I din' killeem, an didn't nobody come afta me neithah. Dey wu'nt 'neeway. Them white folks was crazy. It was thousands and thousands uh nigguhs woikin' on nat wall. We all knowed it wuddn't hole, but de white folks had guns and boats an aihplanes an money. When it blowed, it kealt'a bunch uh peoples white an black. Rivuh don't cayuh…"

Arthur looked down at his boot and pulled at tiny straws sticking out from the dog-eared sole. "White folks is still crazy," he said.

After another beat, as if walking back the statement, he said, "We all crazy, heh heh." He stared ahead for a moment, then his eyes fell on the recording machine— its two small rotating platters.

"Went up to Beale the yeah befo dat, Manfred an me." Nobody had ever called him that but Arthur.

"Lawd. You ta'um 'bout some crazy peoples. Well I doan' thank 'bout dem times too much,.. 'bout de womenz, and de drank'n, and de dope. What I want to remembah is de blues music, and I cain't. I remembah Lizzie what got famous, cause she could play, but she played me, sho did. She toin'in tricks. She got famous, Memphis Minnie. An I remembah fightin'… an winnin'. I din keep none 'o my money, tho. I was a drunk.

Well, aftah awhile, I had enough uh them people, an I jess went back ta de club, an jess stayed. Din wanna see noo-body. Cu'un fine Lillibelle or huh Momma or huh Daddy, no place, an you can bettuh believe I looked. I look up and down nat whole countywide where dat wattah went down. Hit wuddin' nothing but wattuh. Not nuthin' in Leland but de 'lectric towah, whey dey was figna put tat powah line. Time I got deah, hit was jess dat last towah, an de tops uh some trees and nothin' else… but wattah.

Well, bout 1942, de club shet down. Hit wuud'n many peoples comin'… 'cept older folks…"

Billy and I started at the tree and crossed together at the point where we had started yesterday. We decided to fine-tooth the bank together; we could focus on a wider swath, and make a full circle back to that spot up the west bank when the sun was brighter, the more logical side for a killing to take place. In about 90 minutes, we were so far down from the point we started you couldn't see it, so we crossed the ditch and started north on the west side. By then, it was about nine, and the sun, through June's full canopy, spotted the forest floor in splashes of bright and shadow. The summer was young, and heat and bugs were at a minimum— good detective weather.

We moved ever so slowly, pulling back the leaves. It was hard going. I felt a tickle and pulled a tick from under my ear, hoping it was before his head was buried. My back was beginning to hurt a little from the bent-over position. Sometimes the ground was very uneven. Here and there a tree, torn from the ground by a storm or no longer able to sustain itself in eroded ground so close to the bank's edge, retired with its entire root system intact, leaving a gaping depression where it had once stood tall. Stepping down into one, I tripped on a thick root. It was black… burnt. We peeled back the accumulated leaves, and there was a fire pit with burned logs. Picking through it like archaeologists, we turned up beer cans and a belt buckle. We ran all the way back to the house.

Dad called the Sheriff but wouldn't let us go back until the deputies showed up, at about three o'clock. We piled into the jeep and rode down to the Great Sand Ditch. Excited, breathless, we led them to the spot.

"Could be," said one of the deputies, a tall skinny man with a buzz cut. 'Briley,' his shirt said. His sweaty tan shirt stuck to his bony chest. Huffing from the walk, the other lawman, with huge sunburned ears and a belly spilling out over his belt like a laundry sack full of water, surveyed the scene. He lit a cigarette. "Don't prove nothing, tho."

Big Charlie said impatiently, "Well, don't you think we ought to sift through it carefully in case this is relevant?"

" Uhm… yeah… 'Course."

The wall of roots at the foot of the fallen tree now cast a shadow over our find. I noticed a six-inch millipede crawling along one of the branches. I leaned in for a closer look.

"Boys, y'all keep back as this heah could be… ah, could be pertinent to the crime," said the fat one. The millipede made its way into the center of the tree past something shiny. A shell casing caught in a thick snarl of small roots. "Look!"

Briley stepped in to retrieve it. "30-30. I'll be damned."

"Raymond has a "30-30 repeater," I said. "Arthur took it off him the day we found him tending their still. You have to run the lever for the shell to come out."

We stood around then, trying to figure out what direction the killer might've shot to cause the shell to eject that way.

"Mr. Jenks has one too. I have shot it," gushed Billy.

Dad said, "Just a second." To the officers, he said, "How many bullet holes did they find in Raymond? Could the killer have shot again?"

"I don't know, Mr. Walterlane," said the fat one.

"I do," said Ears. "Hit was one hole in his head. That's all I heard about."

"One hole," said Dad. "Then they ought to have found that bullet in his head."

"No, sir. Not necessarily. Coroner thinks he was shot through the eye, point blank. It's a big hole in the back of his head. Bullet took away a good part of the back of his head."

"Billy! When did you shoot Mr. Jenks's gun?"

Billy looked down at his feet. Borrowing the help's property was something Big Charlie had told them never to do.

"C'mon. Did you shoot it or not?"

"Yessir."

"Is it a side-eject gun?" Older lever-action repeaters throw out the cartridge out of the top, over the shooter's shoulder.

"Yes, sir!"

"Fellows, I'd say it's a good chance your bullet is in the ground somewhere on the left side of the roots of this tree. Maybe it's even in those roots."

My mind was working furiously. "If he just shot him once, why eject the shell?"

"Habit."

"What if he gut-shot him and finished him off with the eye shot?"

We stood there thinking about that for a minute.

I said, "If he was shot once, he might be down on the ground, which would be easy to put the gun right up to your eye and pull the trigger. He could have been facing this way." I looked to the south holding my arm down like it was a rifle trained on my victim on the ground. Then, I got very excited.

"Plus, the gun would be aimed down, or you're about to shoot this guy lying down, looking this way. You run the lever to load another bullet, which would throw the cartridge at this wall of roots."

I had everybody's attention. "Maybe the bullet's right here."

"I'll be damned," said Briley. "Maybe... Boy, you a lawyer?"

"Can we look right here, please?"

The Sheriff's deputies looked at each other. They were caught up in it now.

"Wouldn't hurt to rule it out... Earle, what do you think?"

While the fat one sat on the log, smoking, Sgt. Briley drew a line down the middle, and one perpendicular to that, and each of us took a quarter, reaching over the ground so as not to compact anything anymore. The four of us fell on the spot like ants, picking apart leaves and sticks until the ground was bare. We turned the moist dirt with sticks. Within five minutes, Briley dug out a heavy dirt-clogged, mushroomed lump.

"Son of a bitch," said Ears.

In another week, the Somerville County Sheriff arrested Wilson Jenks for the murder of Raymond Crick. They said they shot his repeater, and the bullets matched, which wasn't exactly true. The round that Earle found was so deformed they could not get marks off of it, but the Sheriff thought it was worth trying to see if he would confess, and he did. They released Arthur with their apologies and an admonishment to keep his nose clean. That wasn't quite good enough for Big Charlie, who I think was feeling like he didn't do as well as he could have by Arthur. He wanted to have Mr. Cox sue for unlawful imprisonment, get some money or something.

Mr. Cox just told him he'd be wasting his time. "These backwater country courts give less of a shit about a negro's rights than law enforcement in Memphis. They'd just as soon lock one up with zero evidence, much less the sworn statement of one of their own. Charlie, let it go."

Dad gave Arthur five hundred dollars as a Christmas bonus in September. Arthur would have been OK with it either way.

Jenks said he had shot Raymond two times, the last being the headshot. He burned the body and covered the scorched earth with sticks, dirt, and leaves, and dragged what was left 100 yards to the closest bend in the sand ditch. It was getting dark then and starting to rain buckets. He hadn't thought to bring a shovel. He said he was too spooked by the whole thing to come back and bury him, so he covered up Raymond's charred corpse in the ditch, probably thirty yards upstream of where it was found. When he went back in the morning, it was gone. It was still pouring down rain, and the spot was soup. He figured nature was looking out for him and buried the rapist of his daughter for him.

The trial was set for December 5th. I was glad and hoped that Dad would let us go since we'd be home from school soon after that, and Billy and I were sort of heroes, we thought because our detective work proved Arthur innocent. Hardeman County was stuffed with Jenkses, though. That story was nowhere near over.

34

House of Sticks

June 1948

If Wilson Jenks had any redeeming quality it was that he knew Skytop and managed the 2,000-plus acre working farm more or less without serious problems. We didn't like him much, but I understood after he was arrested why Big Charlie didn't send his bony ass packing after the moonshine debacle. Getting seed in the ground on time, cutting the corn and beans when they were ready, piling brush and stumps into the ditches where topsoil was eroding to the clay during torrential rains in the off-season… there were a million things not just anyone could or would accomplish. Lucas and Jem, and other of the colored worker residents, would have some idea of when to do what, but they were used to being directed. Arthur and Billy and I were there a lot more that summer until Dad could find a replacement. With Raymond gone, and Wilson Jenks not likely to return, the farm started to show neglect in a few short weeks.

Then, Uncle Deane died.

The Walterlanes and the Smiths, and prominent folks from all over held us together that weekend, especially Mother, Nonna, and much more visibly, Cooker. Billy and I were still teenagers at this point, and so not invited into a lot of adult conversation. But, a couple of encounters I had were memorable. During one of the few calmly conversant moments Cooker had that day, she said Arthur told her more than once Uncle Deane would come home, but not for long. She thought he was being reassuring, and that meant he would move away or something.

Joe Bisahalani, the Indian Sergeant we met in Arizona, showed up for the funeral. We talked afterward, in the great paneled den in our home on East

Parkway, a scene very like the one when Uncle Deane asked me to come on the road trip out west, complete with all my uncles and aunts and the effervescence of vodka and lemon.

"Your Uncle lived with so much death," said Joe. "So much. Too many *chindi*." 'Chindi', I learned, is the ghost spirit that carries away the residue of life when a person dies– everything that was bad about the person. "*Chindi* infected and killed him," said Joe. I did not think this bodes well for POW survivors anywhere.

Aunt Katherine was there for a time. I hardly knew her. She was beautiful, elegant, and amazingly composed for having just lost her second husband. She told me Uncle Deane was about to send Arthur back home when we had broken down in St. Louis, but the dream he had that night changed his mind:

"He stood beside Arthur on the bank looking across the Mississippi River during a terrible storm. A small boat containing two people took on the water with the crash of every wave. The man was knocked out of the boat by a huge wave. Arthur dove in after him. The boat came toward the bank on another huge swell, and Deane dove in when he saw that I was the other person.

Before Deane died, he told me the first time they met, Arthur predicted he would survive the War, years before anyone knew there would be another great War. Deane thinks Arthur is a prophet."

In late June the flies infected every one of the 85 cattle with pink eye, which got so bad their eyes turned into leaking red ulcers and they started to lose weight. We thought they might have to be shot. It was Friday afternoon before the vet in Bolivar could get out there. He said the only thing to do at this point was to corral each one, inject their eyes with penicillin and sew them shut. We could not understand how any creature could live or much less regain sight after that repulsive disease, or the treatment.

The doctor just laughed at the looks on our faces, and said, "Boys, it ain't so bad. S'justa job. This mornin' I hitched a come-along to a fence and winched a stillborn foal out of a big dun mare. She didn't like that and kicked down the post she was tied to. My lab ate the afterbirth and it came up on the quilt my wife just made to cover our couch."

Big Charlie was despairing: "Goddamit, how are we going to do this?"

The vet showed up Sunday afternoon with his brother-in-law, Wilson's cousin, Lonnie Ray Jenks, and four other men in a pickup and another large truck with double wheels on the back, hauling a trailered squeeze chute, a vise to keep livestock animals "still" for treatment. One by one, we herded and clamped them, bucking and snorting, into the thing, and in two days almost a hundred cows were comically stumbling about with purple antibiotic gunk on stitched eyelids. They all looked to be wearing masks. Problem under control, for now.

Well, Dad was pretty grateful and they talked about having Lonnie Ray come out and run the farm.

Lonnie Ray listened to Big Charlie's offer and promised to think about it. Then he looked across the field to the barn where Arthur was closing the barbed wire gate behind the chute truck. "That the nigger that shot Raymond Crick?"

After that, Dad decided he would make a clean break from Jenkses.

The strips of trees that bound the front yard on both the west and east sides, framing the view of the lake to the north, hid small zig-zagging drainage ditches that reached a quarter mile way down to the valley, to spill out across the fields at lake level. You could slip into either ditch a hundred yards from the house, and hunt squirrels until you tired of it, or until almost dusk, when the shadows of the tallest trees reached completely across the front yard to the east line, and the squirrels stopped moving so much. It was good in the later afternoon to start that way on the west side.

We flipped for it, and I chose the west ditch, and Billy and I took our guns to our tree lines, each of us pretending on the way it wasn't a contest, but *of course, it was.*

It was not yet the stifling heat of summer, but the bugs and spider webs were thick. I stumbled down into the ditch, spilling shells, scraping my arm on a mulberry thorn. Even for the thick brush and strips of woods on both sides of each ditch, the sometimes torrential rains would eventually carve them as wide as the Great Sand Ditch way down in the east bottom. Natural refuse in the path, brush, and trees that succumbed to the constant gnaw of the waters on their roots, made the hunt slow.

In just a few steps, commotion in the top of a tulip poplar focused my attention and I slipped around and over obstacles while watching two big fox squirrels engaged in a chase around its trunk. No shots heard, a double would put me in the lead... I might be close enough for a shot at the next snatch of thick brush. As I eased forward, there came a "BOOM" from across the front yard. Dammit!

The squirrels were undisturbed and continued their pursuit, but in the opposite direction, north towards the lake. For the next ten minutes, I slipped along after them, over, under, and around, moving slowly. My forehead dripped with sweat. Then a breeze from the east brought slight relief, along with the sweet smell of skunk. Before another minute had passed, the smell was so strong I wondered if something nearby had been sprayed.

My squirrels barked and fussed and one jumped off to the left at a steady clip, disappearing into a perpendicular tree line that separated the two fields west of the ditch. I picked off the jilted lover when he presented himself in easy range, looking contemplative, frozen in profile on a branch facing that direction. I recovered the shell and inhaled it deeply... the pleasant smell of gunpowder on my fingers was a welcome relief. After that, the hunt was the thing, and the skunk scent slipped my mind. But in the hour it took to travel the length of the ditch, a mere five hundred yards, no more squirrels presented themselves for execution. Walking back up the hill in the almost dark it occurred to me I had heard only one shot, and so I smiled- at worst, we were tied, and... maybe my brother missed.

Halfway up the hill, my nose was again assaulted by the clinging, burning rubber smell of skunk, more pungent with every step. Way up the hill at the house, in silhouette against the great window and the inside lights, two figures on the brick patio moved restlessly. By the time the yellow light from the living room fell on me I could see Arthur on the patio hosing down Billy, arms outstretched. Arthur held a stick with a sponge tied to the end which went into and out of a bucket of foamy soap, and onto my brother. He would stay with it for half an hour, but progress against the toxic stench was wishful thinking and... useless. Billy would spend the night in the barn. But Arthur said that first there was unfinished business.

Billy was lucky it wasn't a direct hit. He said he was making his way past a particularly deep spot down in the east ditch, where the eroding red bank rose up twenty feet when he spied the striped critter foraging way up on the lip of the ditch and shot it before he gave that a lot of thought. "Not much clevah, " said Arthur. "Whud'jew want to shoot a skunk, fuh... what he done to you? Serves you right."

"She."

"What?"

"She. It was a momma and she had babies."

The skunk was knocked out of sight by the blast, and Billy climbed out to see what he had wrought. Four baby skunks circled about their wounded mother, who began to hiss loudly like a cat at his approach. The juveniles spread out quickly. Her last act was to raise her tail and let go in the general direction of her attacker.

"You already smell like skunk, an I doan' think hit's much they can do. You gone catch the young'uns. C'mon." Hunting with Arthur, you looked for your kill or cripples until you found them, or the terrain became too impossible to effect recovery. You knock down eight, you pick up eight. If a dove or a duck is flying over a snake-infested swamp, don't shoot it. Be responsible, be respectful. Big Charlie was fully subscribed to that philosophy, but even he would give it up sooner than Arthur would.

"ARTHUR! What are we going to do with baby skunks? No!"

"I doan know. You worriboutit." He let Billy stew on that for a minute and said, "eff we can even find them, it prob won't be but a couple leff. Owls and coyotes gotta eat. C'mon."

Arthur said it wouldn't do to just catch one- if you got two or more they probably wouldn't spray each other. They took a flashlight and came back in an hour with three baby skunks in a burlap bag. We turned over the peat under Mother's tomatoes for some night crawlers, and Arthur pulled off a couple of big ones, and said to Billy: "Take them into the tack room and fine some hay and a tin of water', an put 'em in that wood box where the bits and bridle parts are." Then break these tomatuhs open and scrub yo'sef with'em, til you's wet wid juice… hair an' everthang. Then we'll hose you down again. You got 'nee-more clothes?"

By the time Arthur got back to the house, he was almost ripe as Billy, but he changed and it went away. The next morning the three baby skunks were out of their box and nowhere to be found.

July

Skytop is a place of magnificent extremes.

Not long after Uncle Deane passed, and we got the cattle settled, all of the Walterlanes, sans servants, spent a rare night together in the house on top of the hill. The seven of us arrived packed into the Woody for the July 4th weekend, pulling up to Mother's tomato patch. We were immediately struck by the volume of distended, almost bursting tomatoes on the vines she and Arthur planted only two months ago.

In the early evening, after an afternoon of helping her collect them, Big

Charlie built himself a three-finger scotch, and Mother a vodka. She was still delighted with her tomato patch, and the moment and the infectious spirit took hold in the dusk.

They rocked gently in chairs of wrought iron, nursing their cocktails, watching the shadows of the tallest trees creep left to right across the great north-sloping four-acre "lawn" that fell away gradually to the lake centered a quarter of a mile below. Over the woods to the west, cirrus fingers spread gold and magenta across the sky, changing every minute. Big Charlie had often said what a wonderful nine-hole, three-par practice course the gently undulating field surrounding the house would make, if it could be kept up, of course. Between sips, his mind returned to its design. We ran about playing games with our little brothers and sister, sometimes two hundred yards down the front hill, almost where it equaled lake level. Just before dark gained the advantage, the eye caught a spark, then another, and another… until everywhere were floating, swirling sparks… the annual dance of the fireflies. But, we had never seen such a spectacle as this. Suddenly, before the last streak of gold in the sky gave way to darkness, there were millions in every direction, strobing bug love occupying every square foot of air, thirty feet tall, in every direction.

All children froze in stunned wonder where we stood, speechless, whatever thought in our minds displaced. Mother would later comment on her surprise that all appreciated the spectacle, but more so… our almost simultaneous notice of the display.

Almost forty-five years later, I'd sit on this patio with my sons, Will, Chas, and Wes, grilling duck breasts on the eve of the opening weekend of Tennessee turkey season, as we marveled at another ethereal miracle in this very sky: the Hale Bopp comet, an immortal snowball pulling a fading veil, an unearthly glimpse of the universe that does not recognize the human (earthbound) concept of time and space. It will bounce around our solar system at 50,000 miles an hour for twenty years or so until finally, it flings itself out of bounds, again, in a gentle orbit, not to return for twenty-five centuries.

The storm that came that next day in 1948 arrived about when Arthur drove up to the farm in the Willys Jeep.

Immovable object Ocie Hartley had been convinced to take Arthur to Moscow to pick up the Jeep only when his master (Nonna) finally confirmed it was the will of her son-in-law. During the hour's ride from Memphis, not a word passed between them, and Arthur suppressed his scintilla of a smile, relishing for a moment the power to introduce serious apprehension into Ocie's precious, proud "career" world should Mistah Chahlee come to know of the chauffeur's stubbornness. Being Arthur, he would never think of it again.

Arthur drove the roofless vehicle the forty miles distance from Moscow (where it had received a new fuel pump). After a few minutes, what began as a misting rain became a drizzle and soaked his hat. When it became stinging, he pulled over to swing up the windshield. The windshield helped, most of the water flew over him. But he was soaked to the bone in the first minutes, and thus very thankful for warm temperatures. An hour later, when he drove through the gate at Skytop, wind, and lightning were the featured players, and the rain was more or less horizontal. He pulled into the shelter of the first barn, knowing he might find horse blankets in the tack room. He would clean up as best he could, before presenting his current disheveled picture to the family.

Billy and Lindsay and I and the little boys played outside even in the drizzle, hiding around the house in obvious places from Mac and Denton. The first place they looked was the storm shelter, sort of a giant shower stall with a door on it, sunk into a berm off the back corner of the house. Because after initial inspection they had ruled it out, of course it was where in subsequent rounds, we all hid, giggling. Then Mother called us in. She saw lightning strike a power line on the far side of the lake.

An evil-looking sky, dark as smoke from burning tires, rose above the tree line straight down in front, over the lake. Trees at the ditches left and right of the front lawn undulated and bowed over halfway, violently choreographed.

"Look at the flag", said Denton. The heavy canvas flag atop the pole out back stood straight out horizontally, with barely a movement. Then, as we watched, a piece tore off and flew away, and what remained suddenly wrapped completely around the pole.

"THAT'S IT! EVERYBODY GET TO THE BACK OF THE HOUSE." Naturally, we all looked at Big Charlie for an explanation of his alarm. Out the big window past him, half the distance down to the lake, pieces of the great oak tree that had been in that exact spot circled, off the ground, and bushes and trash were sucking up into a huge black funnel cloud, while at ground level it tore up fence posts and wound up the barbed wire fence as fast as fishing line tangling in a boat motor prop.

"GO! GO! GO!!!"

Dad grabbed Mother and Lindsay, and Billy and me, and we each took a little brother, and we packed into that shelter. Our father had to use all his strength to hold closed the door against the roar of the wind, and all seven of us crouched down in the darkness, the only light coming in slivers as he and the wind wrestled. We had swept out the spiders in the front playing hide and seek, but as we only got in the front edge, I couldn't be sure about the back, where we were. Something was surely crawling on me! Then the noise was so great, all our ears popped. Lindsay screamed she couldn't breathe. Sure enough, we all gasped and cried for about a minute, it seemed. There was simply no air. Until... we could draw breath again.

When the twister took the barn, Arthur had just got his pants back on after squeezing them out and patting himself down. He stepped down, out of the opening of the tack room where the saddles were kept, to the dirt floor. At that instant, the tin roof curled up on the north side, and then it was gone. As if yanked by a chain, the jeep jumped ten feet into the air and was flipped onto its hood, exploding a cloud of dust— the last image Arthur would recall until he came to— far across the farm.

Two hours after we entered the shelter, when the thunder ceased except for low rumbles in the distance, Big Charlie relaxed his grip on the door. Exhausted, he pushed it open slightly, and we saw it was almost dusk. Then it was pulled from his fingers, and we looked up into the face of Arthur Campbell. He was covered in thick mud, lighter than his skin, even caked under the brim of his soaked fedora.

He told of being in the barn, last seeing the jeep turn over as the roof was torn off.

"But den— de Lawd set me down in the bottoms. I woke up and dream't I had been flyin', an 'nas what I done, cause I was inna middle 'o dat field where we cut de cotton, but next yeah set in de corn. An hit was rainin' ha'ad, an I open my eyes, an de Lawd set me down an carried that toin'in cloud away onna bolt a lightnin'. An I walked up at road past Raymond house and I figuh'd y'all might be in heah."

Mother said, "My goodness, Arthur! We are all blessed."

Big Charlie lifted out Mother, Denton, Mac, and Lindsay, planting an uncharacteristic kiss on each. When we were all standing on the ground finally and beginning to relax a bit in the cool calm of the exhausted elements, Dad said, "Now Arthur, you are pulling our leg. You rode a twister from the barn to the bottom, without even losing your hat?"

"No suh. I walked up on my hat in de middle of the road."

The story made its way around the county.

35

Assumption

August

"My boy is done. His life is over." Lytle sobbed. He had never been much for Bible study, but the men's Morning Disciple Group at Second Baptist Church offered a shoulder, and to their collective surprise, Lytle Jenks seized it.

"He'll spend his life in bed. Cain't walk. Cain't get up and piss. I've been wipin' his ass for a month an I cain't... I cain't get... ah'm havin' trouble gettin' used to it."

Hickory Valley is a tight community. They felt Lytle's pain. They empathized with him. But, there wasn't much getting away from the fact that it probably should have been Lytle the tractor turned over on, not his boy Hank, who today felt nothing below his chest.

When he did sleep, which wasn't often, Lytle Jenks went to sleep angry. He woke up angry. Wouldn't be this way *if it hadn't been for the nigger trial.* Lytle had taught his boy to drive the tractor like he wanted. And he was a good driver for thirteen, and he said he could handle it. Lytle *knew* he could handle it, right? Hank had proved that and wanted it, didn't he? Of course. Hank could cut those beans in the field, Lytle could go to his cousin's trial for shooting Raymond Crick— for moral support. Everybody knew the Walterlane's nigger did it. The truth will set you free.

Then, the case turned completely around. They said Wilson killed Raymond, and suddenly here come a high-dollar lawyer from Walterlane that got the nigger off, and they said it was Wilson that done it! Now the nigger walked free while Wilson was rotting inside! *Aaargh!* It just burned him up. Wilson wasn't no killer. And he made some of the best whiskey for the money Lytle had ever tasted. Not that he'd know good liquor, but it had to be good. It worked way faster than beer, and it was the only thing that helped him get the whole thing out of his head.

Lytle and Jimmer Rhymes, distant relatives of the Cricks, spent several afternoons drinking beer in their pickup backed into a dead-end dirt road, behind a big fur tree fifty yards from the entrance to the Chapleau's driveway, by which all vehicles entering or leaving Skytop farm would have to pass.

"Unbelievable times," said Lytle.

"Well," said Jimmer, "the Walterlane's nigger might escape the law, but he ain't goin' escape justice."

Sometimes, they forgot the mission by dark. Tipped off by Mr. Chapleau, who could not believe two country boys parked in the same place nearly every afternoon for two weeks drinking beer (until they passed out) could be up to any good, Hardeman County Sheriff's Deputy Earle Briley nosed his cruiser into the drive when they were both "napping" and hit the siren. Hank hit his head on the back window jumping out of his skin.

"WHAT THE FU—? What the hell, Earle?"

By then, seeing Earle coming around to the driver's side, the occupants quickly shifted and fidgeted guiltily, and a dozen empty beer cans tumbled noisily onto the floor. Earle was disappointed to see Jimmer Rhymes on the passenger side. Jimmer was every bit of 200 pounds of mean redneck, thick and stupid as a bull. Earle had to lock him up a couple of times, most recently for injuries to his wife, which she could no longer deny when an argument spilled out the back door and a dozen neighbors standing around a charcoal grill saw him punch her lights out.

"What are you boys doing out here?"

"Nuthin' we ain't 'sposed to," said Jimmer in a low growl. His eyes were bloodshot, and he looked about to snort smoke and stamp like the cartoon longhorn.

"Smells like a brewery in here. Unless you want to spend the night at the courthouse, y'all go on home. If you can. Remember where you live, Lytle?"

But, he was afraid he knew what they were doing out there. Troubled by the rising incidences of the misplaced retribution of the Jenks and their numerous relations, widely populating Hickory Valley and the surrounding counties, harassing Arthur Campbell, or sometimes negroes mistaken for him, even reportedly staking out the entrance to the Chapleau road leading into the Walerlanes' farm and the gate of Skytop itself, Deputy Earle came to believe he must constantly surveil the male members of the Jenks family, lest one or more kill or maim Arthur Campbell, as they did to a ringer at the CO-OP in Hickory Withe, in a case of mistaken identity. Earle confiscated Jimmer's rifle and warned them not to be there again. Lytle just grinned his grin, sitting over his grandfather's massive Colt six-shooter under the seat.

Earle advised Charlie Walterlane, who passed it on to Arthur: "Arthur, this will go away eventually, when Jenks has been in prison for a while, but we need to be careful. You keep a lookout over your shoulder. I am going to find some help out here, and then we'll stay in Memphis until this area cools off."

But Arthur knew whatever help Mistah Chahlee could find wouldn't come from Hardeman County and maybe not the ones outside it. Skytop wasn't going to get much support locally.

The following Friday, Arthur and I went out to the farm. Arthur had to take some of the biggest catfish from a seine and we'd move them in big barrels to the lake in front of the house. Dad also said the horses were getting so much freedom we should ride them a bit if we wanted to get any cooperation out of them during quail season. It was too hot to run the dogs but we could visit the best points and see if the coveys had moved.

We turned onto Chapleau Rd from the highway at about four o'clock. Parked nose out, in the gravel drive of a crumbling shack, was a rusted blue Dodge pickup with the windows rolled down and two people open-mouthed, eyes closed. We were close enough to hear the driver snoring.

"Hey Arthur, did you see—"

"Yep. Doan worriboutit." We went on.

We pulled into the shadow between the great oak and the gas pump (behind which I had been invisible to Raymond, exiting guiltily from the barn) which was catty-corner from the Jenks's house. Arthur said, "C'mon, show you sumpthin'" and dug off down the hill behind the pile of rubble that had been the barn, toward the kennels. The dog kennels against the edge of the woods were truck-sized concrete pads with a dog house at one end— each boxed completely with six-foot sides and topped with a chain link fence. I used to think they were trying to keep something out until I saw those dogs climb. The kennels once housed some of the finest bird dogs in the nation. Skytop used to host qualifying field trials to narrow the contestants, the best of which would square off every February at the near-by Olympics of quail spotting, the National Championship for Bird Dogs at the Ames Plantation in Grand Junction. Putting either the barn or the pens in order would be low on the priority list for several years.

That was when I met Amos, Andy, and Sapphire. Arthur approached the great bird dog cages, whistling, and out of the doghouse where we used to keep Cleo emerged three skunks single file.

The day after the babies went missing, Arthur had gone back to the ditch and somehow found another one close to its dead mother, a larger juvenile female. When he brought her back to the barn, her brothers appeared one at a time, from below the tack room steps, and soon the three were reunited in the sawdust box made for them. "Sapphire is de boss. Look."

He snatched a great yellow grasshopper resting high on the corner pole and swung open the gate. Sapphire came to us and put a paw on his boot, sniffing the air. "Good girr, Sapphire, good girr." She accepted her treat and munched the squirming bug, loud as a mouthful of Fritos.

"Cain't hole Sapphire. She bites. Other two won't tho. Go ahead." I looked around for a nearby grasshopper. They leaped from tall stalks of wheatgrass all across the field. Two steps in and one landed on my breast. The other skunks sniffed at the air after her, mirroring her every move.

"Which one's Amos?"

Arthur pointed to the next in line, nearest me. Slowly I reached down with the great locust between my fingers. Amos snatched it from my hand and commenced its noisy demise.

36

Amos 'n' Andy

Arthur drove, trading hands for the full turns, somehow shifting with his right, yet hardly disturbing Andy, tucked into the crook of his left arm. We stopped twenty-five yards short of the road where we saw them when we passed and got out cradling our critters. Amos was remarkably calm, but I wasn't. "Arthur!" I whispered, panicky, "This will NEVER work! What are we doing? How are we going to do this?"

"Shhh!" He eased the door closed just short of the latch, and when I did the same mine squeaked loud– *damn*! I knew my side did that! Arthur paid no attention and crossed the road and slipped into the woods. I followed, taking care not to footfall on sticks and dry leaves like we were on a squirrel hunt. We crept that way toward that road... shortly we could see their pickup. When we got to the edge of the canopy we could see them clearly: the man on the passenger side appeared to be staring ahead, and the driver was slumped in his seat, head back, mouth open. Then the passenger rested his arm on the door and his head on his arm, and started snoring. Amos started getting fidgety.

I must say that I have benefited from years of trust in Arthur Campbell. I was petrified, but my doubts that it would work out were falling away. I knew of Arthur's gifts as a chess player (thus, a strategist), and learned by observation that he was usually more than a step ahead of the smartest people, and so miles ahead of the dumbest. Yet, standing at the edge of the woods, holding skunks, with some plan of depositing them into the company of men sleeping in their vehicle... I was terrified. At the moment we were most certainly... the latter.

After the passenger had stopped moving for a minute or more, and seemed to be well under, Arthur emerged from the canopy with a short step, then another. He looked at me and his head (and hat) jerked around: follow me. When I stepped out, my foot skated on a round stick, which cracked with a loud pop, and I juggled Amos, fighting for balance. Being on the verge of panic anyway, he leaped to the ground like a cat and quickly disappeared under the truck.

I froze, certain to be outed and fallen upon as an assailant!

But, no stirring at all from our quarry. Arthur by now had cleared the tailgate and was approaching the driver's open window, all while stroking Andy's thick fur along the full body of his stripes, head to tail. So calm was the skunk, he let himself be gently set into the lap of the driver, Lytle Jenks. Arthur began to slip back, and I came to my senses and did the same, falling back into the canopy, taking extra care near the rolling stick that almost implicated me.

But, Arthur stopped at the tailgate, staring into the bed of the truck. Inspired, he gently lifted out a heavy canvas tarp and began unfolding it, slowly, because of the scraping sound the heavily oiled muslin made against itself. Safely in the shadows, I wasn't budging out of my safe spot to help, but he didn't ask me to. He managed to unfold it quietly to about truck length and began to drape it over the cab, letting the sides cover the windows. He came around to the side against the woods where I stood sweating in the shadows, and started to pull this side even. Amos peered out from under the vehicle and in another inspired move, Arthur scooped him up, and set him behind the curtain onto the sleeping passenger.

Drunk as he was, Jimmer felt two pounds of skunk sink his claws into the side of his face and snapped up hollering.

But Arthur was already retreating like lightning. He got past me and I bolted after him. The odor of two adult skunks letting go beat us to the car. We backed up 100 yards just to the curve in the road where the line of sight could still view the driveway into the road, and a moment later two figures stumbled into the road. Arthur heaved and wracked, laughing a deep smoker's laugh, which quickly devolved into phlegmy coughing.

Hardeman County Sheriff's Deputy Earle Briley had once imagined himself behind the pulpit.

How many Sundays had Pastor Dale Wells so… 'controlled' (was the first word he thought of, though it wasn't quite right… 'inspired', maybe was the better word), the congregation? He was impressive. But, the more Sundays Earle sat in Pastor Dale's pews (skeptically, dragged to church to please his young wife and her parents), the more he was sure there was a pattern to Wells' sermons. The pitch was always the same: bring out a point, relate it to personal experience, then *wham*, hit us over the head with scripture that is close enough to drive the point home. Earle thought it was a bit of a con.

But glancing around, he saw mostly rapturous expressions. This community of farmers joyfully consumes the product— especially the women. They eat it up. Jesus washed the feet of the prostitute, and we fall to our knees. Does that mean we should wait by the well to embrace the next stranger?

It's kind of beautiful… preachers don't necessarily have the answers, but… wouldn't they be out of business if everyone started thinking that? The congregants' eyes moistened with every rise in his voice. What is going on here? Pastor Wells is God's agent of course. Isn't he? Then Earle was struck by the notion that the pastor's job was to be alongside the members of his flock at not only the best, but also the worst of times, and help each decide what paths to travel between them. He experienced a slight shame for doubting the man's motives. And then he got an idea.

Wells immediately discounted Earle's suggestion that he might be able to influence the community to call off the rabid dogs chasing after the Walterlanes' hired man, Arthur. Holy smoke, man, what could he do? But over the next days, the "challenge" deputy Briley presented, that is, "gifted" him with, returned to mind unexpectedly several times.

Then, it was piled upon by an idea of his own (or one from The Inspired Source), not so much a revelation as a conviction suddenly present, where no such notion commanded notice before.

Wells' sermons, always carefully crafted, were sometimes so good in the reading he thought that he could not have devised them, and found after he gave them he was frustrated that their brilliance was dependent on faulty human delivery. He sometimes teared up, re-reading one of his sermons after it got cold, and his mind had long moved on. Such a profound message, unarguable even for the spiritual denier: "A simple word or action, can sometimes re-direct a life for better or worse, the same way a long stoplight might be blamed for a missed train," said one.

Sunday, he laid the groundwork:

"God loved his son David, son of Saul, whose great personal character in youth seemed unassailable. At the hand of God, David's aim was true, and he slew Goliath, the mightiest of the Philistines, with nothing but a rock. After God made him king, David lusted and took Bathsheba, and he killed her husband by sending him into battle. He committed sin upon sin, upon sin. Didn't he?"

"AMEN," said the congregation.

"Yet, God had chosen and continued to love, and support... His son David. The Bible tells us the story and we see it unfold. We judge the sins of David as they pile up, yet we still hope he will make the right decision. But... It can never end any way other than it does. What is God doing? How many times in the Bible does our human logic hit a wall?"

"AMEN," said the congregation.

"What lesson do we take from our God, who supports, and even lifts up the worst of us for redemption?

Our courts recently freed a man about whose guilt we were certain. But the evidence told another story… And now, a member of our community, a member of our family, awaits God's judgment.

Remember Enoch in the Old Testament! The *Book of Genesis* records: Enoch walked with God; then he was no more, because God took him away (Genesis, 5:24). Hebrews Chapter 11, verse 5 elaborates: 'By faith, Enoch was taken up so that he SHOULD NOT SEE DEATH; and he was not found, because God had taken him. Now before he was taken, he was attested as having pleased God.'

It also happened to Elijah as he walked with Elisha: Second Kings says: 'And as they still went on and talked, behold, a chariot of fire and horses of fire separated the two of them. And Elijah went up by a whirlwind into heaven… And he was seen no more.' Can I get an AMEN?"

"AMEN!" said the congregation.

"The tornado that just months ago flattened our community, and killed our beloved Willie Mae Thurmond, took another man up into itself. BUT HE DID NOT DIE! God put him back on the earth because he is NOT finished; GOD HAS PLANS FOR HIM, in the service of our Lord Jesus Christ…"

After that Sunday, there was no more harassment. A week later Charlie Walterlane had a new farm manager, the nephew of forestry consultant Dexter McCullar.

37

The Last Easter

Easter 1953

Billy rode the train from Fort Benning with a buddy from Memphis, Matt Something-or-Other, their first break since basic training. After getting booted from Episcopal and barely scraping by to graduate at Baylor, he flunked his first semester at Virginia and Dad yanked him, saying, "You are wasting your time and my money. You're going into the army." His great gift of self-assurance evolved into relaxed flexibility, which our parents mistook for aimlessness. Billy was never setback by redirection, he cheerfully embraced each closed door, and subsequently, each open one, as his natural path. At one time I too thought this was a shortcoming of intelligence until I had some life experience.

Arthur collected them at the train station in Mother's brand new Chrysler Imperial, a bulbous tank, damn ugly by today's standards, but doggonit, it was the epitome of luxury then, the first car to come out with real power steering. Mother said it was her dream boat, so great was the relief from wrestling a two-and-a-half-ton vehicle around town. Big Charlie joked he gave it to her to give Arthur a break from driving.

I remember the weekend well because I hadn't seen my brother since the day after Christmas when we packed him off to the army on the train. Saturday, we went out to the farm and shot the trap range, and I out-shot my professional soldier brother for the first time. He claimed it was because he let me shoot the Parker.

Easter morning was glorious, cloudless, and warm, azaleas and dogwoods peaking early everywhere, spring bursting with resurrection. The entire family went to church. The Very Reverend Hobson delivered a homily about resolute faith in the Easter Story, and our brief lives being simply preparation, the first step in the Grand Plan for eternity. That may have been the first time I ever really listened to a sermon, I thought about it a lot on the train ride back to Episcopal... the day of the accident.

I can't remember why they missed the 2 o'clock Greyhound. Big Charlie was very angry and said it was purposeful, "Boy, if I haven't made an impression on you in all these years the Army goddamn sure will. They put you in the brig for being AWOL." While he went to call Arthur to race ahead to catch it at Bolivar, Billy said the only way he would make it by 8 am Monday, was to drive. Mother huffed. Big Charlie considered that his oldest son was right, but said he hoped any consequences would build character, and "teach the responsibility you so lack." As the hour ticked by, Dad's resolve weakened. Billy talked Mother into letting him drive the Imperial back to the base, and Big Charlie did not weigh in to forbid it, a decision they would regret for life.

We think Matt was driving when they got past Birmingham at about two in the morning. Just three more hours to Columbus, and another forty-five minutes to the base, depending on traffic. The soggy air finally reached saturation and a drizzle started, and the wipers created a rhythm that put Billy to sleep. For half an hour the Chrysler floated over the beat-up two-lane black top, no other vehicle lights coming or going. They raced into the rain and the blackness... and monotony.

Matt felt his lids getting heavy. Too suddenly, the tail lights of a big vehicle got larger— collision course with the back of a Greyhound bus. Matt hit the brakes pretty hard, but he maintained control. The bus now filled almost the full field of vision, surely a WTF moment, if one is torn from a snooze.

A couple of seconds of recovery, then Matt pulled around the bus, into the path of an oncoming vehicle just yards away. He jerked the wheel hard right, and we think the Imperial's Fluid Control Power Steering greatly magnified his correction. The Georgia State Police report estimated the car's speed was seventy mph or better, stating the Imperial flipped, driver's side first, at least four times.

Billy was killed. Matt walked away with a concussion, broken ribs, and a broken nose.

Monday afternoon, I was in Mr. Tompkins' class at Episcopal, when came a knock on the door. Principal Skinner interrupted and whispered to Tompkins. They both looked at me. "Mr. Walterlane, you are excused."

The last time the principal himself collected someone from class it was Jason Tripp, and we never saw him again. He was expelled for sneaking into another teacher's office to copy a test.

Principal Skinner motioned for me to follow and we walked in silence to his office. He closed the door. The latch snapped loudly.

"Sit, please." No punitive tone was in his voice. Instead, it was grave.

"Mr. Walterlane, I am very sorry to tell you your father has phoned me this afternoon to inform us that your brother Billy was in a fatal automobile accident last evening… well, early this morning while returning to his base at Fort Benning. You are summoned to return immediately to Memphis."

Now, playing this scene later, and over and over in the many years since, I recall exactly what he said. But in that long moment, I did not register anything but "Billy," and "accident." I said, "What hospital is he in? Is he going to be OK?"

I was empty for the first hours of that long ride back to Memphis. The countryside I had passed by 24 hours before was ever so slightly changed: that cow standing in a different spot, a woodpile a bit taller, a field half-cut now completely smooth. Then I thought of things I had not in years, and there were rushes of anguish.

Halfway into my first year at EHS, Dad came and took Billy away, before he could be expelled after receiving so many demerits for skipping out to Alexandria.

We used to ride the *Tennessean* from right behind the Memphis Country Club on Southern Avenue, the so-called Buntin station, all the way to Chattanooga. That early September I was off to start my sophomore year at Episcopal, Billy would be a Senior at Baylor. Because the train would arrive so early in the morning, the cars that carried the Baylor kids were uncoupled and left on a side track, and the train went on north to Knoxville and then Johnson City.

I was tired and said goodbye to my brother that night, not a little angry. We played cards almost all night with the Baylor boys, and he won, and I lost. That December, when I showed Arthur the deck they left in the lounge car, he showed me how it was marked. I tried to remember if Billy ever took a hand when I was still in the game, and I could not remember a time when he did. I don't think I ever asked him if he knew about the deck. But of course, he did. After just a couple of months at the school, he was already a star, leader of the pack— wittiest, funniest, most cunning. I guess if he had let me in on it, it could have blown the cover of assuredness and confidence that was Billy's mantle, but I remember being incredibly disappointed.

In the summers we'd ride the train to Johnson City and get off to go to Linville. Ocie would pick us up in Nonna's 1937 Packard for the two-hour trip from eastern Tennessee to Nonna's retreat in the Blue Ridge mountains of western North Carolina.

Always Billy asked to drive, and always Ocie ignored him. Again and again. Finally, Ocie had to go. He pulled into a gas station that he knew had a colored bathroom. The boys were in the back. Billy asked again, "Ocie, my grandmother lets me drive, and she would be OK with me helping you. You need some rest, I'm sure."

Ocie knew what nonsense this was. He did not respond instantly, but he seemed to sigh. His right arm went to the top of the passenger seat as he twisted around to face the irritant.

"Young man," he said in his most even voice, his jaws partially clenched, his chauffeur's cap centered on his brow. "Mrs. Smith entrusted me with the safety of this automobile and its passengers. I have no intention of releasing it, nor of putting her trust at risk. You will not drive." Nappy gray hairs protruded from his ears and under the cap.

We looked at each other and suppressed giggles.

A colored chauffeur in these parts has few choices. His bladder near bursting, Ocie quickly hefted his long, but slight frame up and out the driver's seat, leaving as always, the key in the ignition.

Precisely 6 minutes later, he walked back out to find the Packard windows rolled up and doors locked, the boys in the front.

"Open the door! What is the meaning of this? Open the doors, young man!"

For the longest moment we could stand, perhaps less than a minute, we ignored him, staring forward, snickering.

Finally, Billy, cracked the window, enough to be heard.

"Ocie," said Billy, looking up into the face of consternation, "in sixty seconds, this car is going Linville. You can ride, or you can walk." Ocie's countenance was unchanged, except he was so close to the window in the cool of the morning, his breath fogged.

"Forty-five seconds, " said Billy. He turned the ignition. We were tigers watching uncertainty turn to fear.

Slowly, Ocie stood up straight. He adjusted his cap, though it sat on his head perfectly centered. He looked again hard at Billy, who pushed the clutch to the floor. Ocie knew by heart the rising whine of his freely disengaged engine in repose. His foot began to come off and the huge car started to roll. Ocie tried the still-locked back door handle. I reached over and unlocked the door. Nonna's chauffeur surprised us with a nimble leap into the back seat.

We rode to Linville with nary another word, which wasn't unusual, anyway. Ocie had never been a barrel of laughs when he was in charge.

My first beer was a Griesedieck.

Honest, that was the name of it. During the war years when all the men were away, Mother would put Billy and me on the Illinois Central, south to spend three weeks with Granddad, Big Charlie's dad, Willie, and his (second) wife Virginia, at their house on Mhoon Lake. It was heaven and mostly another story. Finally, she would send Arthur to come get us. Once, we had worked on a fort for days, on an outcropping of the bank that was like a dock. It was the remaining berm of levee that was knocked down so the lake would flood the cotton field aside, sculpted by the rushing water to slip gradually under the surface, a peninsula of dry land that ran out into the lake twenty yards. We would snatch huge green grasshoppers off the reeds. They were heavy and could be cast way out from there, and would fidget underwater long enough to guarantee a hit. We'd sit in the fort in the shade, while we waited for our painted corks to dive. Arthur showed up in the Woody and was not in very good humor, trying to hurry us.

"I tole your momma we'd be back fuh dinnuh," he said. "So, comeon."

We weren't ten miles out before he pulled into the only gas station in Tunica, but we never said we had to go, and Billy (asking to drive) had already noted the gas gauge said full.

Said Arthur, sensing that his charges were studying him with puzzled looks: "I might have me a greasy dick."

Well, we were too stunned even to laugh as Arthur had never said anything even remotely salacious around either of us.

And then there it was, a big metal sign in the window of the station office, " The Original Griesedieck Bros. Double Mellow Pilsner Beer" of St. Louis, MO.

Billy said, "Well, I'monna have me a greasy dick, too."

To which I said, "if your dick is greasy, so is MINE!"

Well, there was a good bit of this back and forth as you can imagine. Billy said if Arthur was having one he ought to have one too, and of course, so should I. Arthur huffed a bit, but we talked about how it was OK, and Dad would let us do it, and it wasn't our first beer, etc, etc. Arthur knew way, way better than this, but as his Griesedieck might be in danger, and it was kind of a long drive, he brought out three GDs and we went on.

Well, you can try to get right back to a perfect time, and... you just can't. The levee fort stood until late summer, or maybe later... Granddad didn't have any reason to pull it down. But it was just never the same and we only visited it one other time. There were so many spiders, webs, a wasp's nest, and other bugs. We stuck our heads in, and Billy spotted a big rat snake tucked into the branches making up the side, which would have been pretty neat if we could have been out in the open, but neither one of us was too interested in messing with it there.

Arthur and Dad picked me up at the station. Ever stoic, Dad had a tear in his eye and he shook my hand. I hugged Arthur and wept against his chest. Later that day I was sitting at the kitchen table where the servants sat, where Billy and I sat when we were at home, acting older than were, making jokes and saying bad words around the servant women, because though he never did the same, Arthur wouldn't fuss at us.

Cooker's voice was a salve, and when she walked out of the kitchen, I buried my face in my hands and cried, "Goddammit," and was wracked. I started to heave and catch my breath. Arthur was right there, and let me go on like that for a while, saying nothing. Then he left.

After a time I was quiet, and he came and sat down at the table with me.

He asked, "You finished? You finished bein' mad? It ain't gone do no good to be mad... Who you mad at, God? God din drive dat car off'n the road. Eh-body is sad, an das OK. But let me tell you... I bin mad at God too."

Arthur told me about working for months to try and save the people of Greenville, mainly the Tatums and especially Lillibelle. "But that dam bursted, and lots 'o peoples die, and it ain't nobody's fault." He went back to Greenville, and Indianola, and couldn't find Lillibelle or any Tatums—it was like they never existed. Like Pecos Bill on the tornado, Arthur rode a wall of black water for miles, a biblical scene that would put you in a place where you have a direct line to God such as few mortals get. For years he tried to find out what happened to them. He said he asked God, and... nothing.

"I was mad. Mad at God. I was so busy bein' mad at Him, I cu'un hear, and I did not see. Then I had the dream again, and this time I saved some peoples. I road a boat out into the black swirl, and those people came home. Here."

I looked at Arthur Campbell through my tears then and got the message he was trying to tell me. Maybe it's the first time God actually spoke to me or the first time I could hear Him. I had a strong sense like I never had... the duty I have to the living, Mother, Lindsay, Denton, and Mac...

That was Tuesday. Thursday, we buried Billy in Elmwood, and an army Honor Guard raised their rifles and fired three times, and ceremoniously pulled down the flag and folded it into a triangle, a flag with forty-eight stars that I still have. I was very proud of my parents then. Watching their firstborn lowered into the ground, Mother and Dad held their heads high. Standing behind, Arthur bowed his head the whole time. I think he grieved finally.

38

Ethel

September 1953

Arthur was not a talker— you'd get no details from him. I learned never to expect them, having only some idea of those few adventures he chose to share. Then, Arthur was never the subject of the story, but a bit player, bound only to bear faithful witness, a passive observer. Accounts had to be extracted:

'Arthur, you saw Mr. Carlo drop his brother's gun into the water, didn't you?'

'Arthur, tell us the last time you saw Raymond Crick...'

'Arthur, Lindsay told James Anna she spent the night at your house. What is the meaning of this?'

Ethel Kirk had been in the employ of the Beau-Murray family of Birmingham for a generation. She raised the Beau-Murray children as Cooker raised us, and so naturally she was part of the family entourage when their family summered in the Carolinas. We all knew Ethel, as we grew up with the Beau-Murray children, Berry, Lissa, and Nan-Elizabeth.

Mother and Big Charlie returned to Linville the last week of the season— for the climactic Linville Resort Golf Tournament the second week in October. It was a blessed time to be there. Though the flowers were at their last, the hills and Blue Ridge mountains were splashed with magnificent fall color. The late afternoon had a chill that nipped but didn't bite, and the rhododendron and honeysuckle scent still lingered over the lush green course. They had to winterize the house anyway, drain all the pipes and batten down shutters for the long winter.

Doctor and Emmaline Beau-Murry hosted cocktails at their house looking over the 15th green. Emmaline remarked that they had not seen Ethel since shortly after the family returned from summer vacation in late August— she gave notice and disappeared. Of course, as she was part of the family, they had been very concerned... "but you know, now the children are growing up, off to school, and so forth. I wondered if perhaps dear Ethel no longer felt needed or something. It is strange and sad. None of us thought it would be 'goodbye'! Do you think we should be worried, call someone?"

Mother had a passing thought to ask Arthur if he had any knowledge of where Ethel might have gone, remembering the help employed by many of the members often gathered together on their nights off.

Thanksgiving, when this idea revisited her, Arthur was rebuilding the fireplaces with coal (from the storage bin in the old service quarters outside), and Mother was about the house directing servants, planning, and preparing the feast for a full house.

"Arthur, Ethel Kirk has gone missing from the Beau-Murray's house in Birmingham. Would you have any idea what happened to her?"

Arthur stood up straight but looked puzzled. "She has?"

"Well, not just recently, but some months ago, in fact. Not long after the family came back from Linville. I just knew you two—"

"Yes ma'am."

"Yes—?"

"She is my wife."

What?"

"Yessim. We was married in September. Hit isn't a secret."

Personal details of the lives of the help started to fall away even more as Billy and I began to be distracted by our ever-busier adolescence and young adulthood, spending more of the seasons away at school, attending social events, or dating when we were at home.

While I grew up, servants disappeared late, after dinner or parties or what have you, and they reappeared in the morning, and I didn't think too much about it. Arthur seemed to live with the servants in the back house when I went away for my Junior year at Virginia. When I came home for the summer, he lived on Laclede Street, with Ethel.

39

Lindsay

June 1954

Lindsay also had a special relationship with Arthur. He always said Lindsay was hard-headed. Perhaps betraying the incident to our parents, he would have done her a great favor long term. Maybe he kept it close because everybody was still dealing with Billy's passing. Home for the summer, I tuned into an argument coming from the yard: Neal telling Henry of what he had missed of "Miss Lindsay's night on Beale," inserting himself as the hero. Henry, of course, took issue as Neal laid in fantastic details, punctuated with enough logic to sound plausible. Henry knew better, having sat up from his stupor in time to see Arthur deliver the cop car, not twenty feet from the dice game where he had passed out several hours before, after the loss of his week's wages.

I got the real story from Lindsay… eventually. So dramatic a rescue, it was like the bucking pony she was plucked from at age five, just at the most dangerous moment, though that situation was not of her creation. How had she gotten to Beale Street in the first place? Of course, she talked Neal and Henry into taking her.

Fearless as Arthur, but also reckless, Lindsay would push the envelope all her life, which would fascinate some men, and repel others.

People that knew Arthur Campbell for any length of time eventually came to understand that he was a fixer. He slipped the police car Lindsay stole onto March Street, the alley that evacuated and replenished Beale's establishments, and cut the engine, thanking God the street was without grade, rolling it the last half-block, lights off. Its discovery would be interesting—blood in painterly strokes all over the passenger seat and door, and a huge depression in the center of the hood, the spot Arthur had bounced a man before he could throw his bottle at Lindsay through her open window. Detectives would also find a whole clotted thumbnail stuck to the inside of the outside passenger door handle.

Arthur walked back to his house. As it was not more than a mile as the crow flies, the whole trip took no more than an hour...

****

A single bulb illuminated the "stage," highlighting a thickening cloud of tobacco and marijuana floating over the heads of the throng. A powerful female voice blasted out blues of love and loss. When Lindsay got near enough to glimpse through the crowd the origin of that sound, the image was opposite that in her mind's eye. An emaciated, light-skinned colored girl not much older than she was pivoted around a microphone, screaming, taunting... crying. Her hair was short as a pageboy, straight, black, and glistening wet. Neal had tried to put a description of the blues in Lindsay's mind, but he was not a communicator, and his own real experience, if any, was certainly compromised by intoxicants. Not to be outdone, Henry added: "de blues is ever-thing, eh-body got to complain about... wrapped up in a song." Lindsay thought that was far easier to remember, and she decided to keep in mind Henry's definition of the blues. It worked. It was simple. And... here it is.

The singer was surrounded in her tiny space by the musicians. Inches away stood a fat negro man in a zoot suit with a black shirt, white tie, and matching two-toned wingtips, plucking the strings of an upright bass. Behind him was a trumpet player she guessed to be about her age, and a skinny white piano player standing at an upright piano, who pounded the keys so energetically that his thick curly hair, standing up like a rooster's, bobbed in his face. Sometimes he pounded the keys with his feet. Off in the shadows, she could make out the silhouette of a seated drummer, but whatever he contributed was drowned by the others. Dozens of people writhed in the area before her, some of the men in jackets, their armpits stained with sweat.

The sprinkling of young white people present when they arrived had grown to almost outnumber the negroes, most of whom were old enough to be their parents. They danced and mixed like family, appreciative, but not quite matching the uninhibited passion of the others. A thick, ruddy-faced boy attached himself to Lindsay almost the moment she stepped into the club. He shouted again, "Lemme git you a beer," and laid a meaty arm across her shoulder.

No real thought of exit until now. She felt tired suddenly and increasingly, nauseated.

The soaked songstress approached a climactic point and the undulations of the dancers rippled outward, uncomfortably close in an already overcrowded room. What happened next Lindsay likened to the experience of seeing a spider when you happened to be thinking something might be crawling on you. A hand slid up her leg and squeezed her buttock.

She threw up her arms, knocking the boy's bottle into his teeth, and jumped forward into the couple a foot away. When they split apart in surprise, she forced herself between them and knocked over another, but kept going until she was at the door, slipping around the huge bouncer who was the dragon at the outside gate, engaged in spirited debate with a policeman. The policeman turned and tried to grab her, and shouted something she took to be "Hold on, there!" but he missed her arm and was prevented from pursuit by the crowd waiting to get in.

Like a greased pig she spurted out that line to the street, right to his patrol car, idling... faint exhaust puffed from the tailpipe. Looking behind her, she saw that the tumult seemed to be increasing near the club entrance, and she ran around to the driver's side, jumped in, and popped the clutch, squealing tires to dig off west on Beale.

Arthur Campbell, who was home in bed, was as careful with her instruction in driving as he was with his boys. His words were fresh, she was still under his tutelage: "You got to git calm, and stay calm, Miss Linsee, you goin' get yourself in trouble, cause you hard-headed."

By chance, the movie theater across the street was letting out, and the street was starting to flood with patrons behind her, helping to further obscure her escape.

Only one other place seemed alive at the hour, Schwab's Store, but it was closed, and she slowed to pass a couple staggering by the glow of the store light.

She was already taking deep breaths by the time she reached Second, at the west end of Beale Street. The only other place she had been downtown, besides Calvary Church, was Arthur's house on Laclede Street, and with little conscious effort, the car seemed to point in that direction. It would be a few streets to the south, past the dark warehouses and industrial buildings. After a mile, she began to recognize the neighborhood of run-down houses where he and Ethel lived.

Her nervous fingers found a switch under the wheel and flipped it. The beacon on top of the car splashed spinning red on the dark houses. She flipped it off. Back on. Off. She drove a couple of blocks.

Three figures walked the sidewalk ahead on the right, and she flipped it on again when she got alongside. Another switch said "SIREN" and she flipped it. The piercing wail was so loud inside the car she slammed on the brakes, and it bucked to a stop and the siren and engine quit. They broke into a run and split up. One fell on the sidewalk, another ran across the street and disappeared into a side yard. She caught a glimpse of the third toppling over a wooden fence to her right.

This struck Lindsay as so funny, she forgot her nausea and exhaustion and sat there for a moment giggling.

The man on the sidewalk picked himself up and looked at her. She could see by the dimmed headlights his leg was bloody. He studied the scene for a moment, squinting, then took a step in her direction, then another, which brought her around rather quickly.

She turned the key and the engine turned, but the car was in gear, and it bucked a few feet forward, coughed, and died. Jamming down the clutch, she tried the key again. The engine turned over and caught, and the SIREN and rotating red beacon came back on.

Bloody Knee was by this time almost abreast, close enough to see that she was no policeman. He leaped to the passenger door and grabbed the handle at the moment she let out the clutch again, and the car shot forward, yanking him along. With a yell, he turned it loose and hit the pavement hard, tires squealing in his face.

SIREN and rotating red lights in full output, she left him in the darkness, yelling.

She made two more blocks before thinking to quiet the cacophony. In her rearview mirror, she saw house lights coming on, one by one, closer and closer until the waking neighborhood was adjacent and homes lit up past her and on up the street. She turned up another street then another, back in the direction of Beale, she thought, but wasn't sure. Was this Arthur's street? No. Oh... crap. More figures ahead. Lindsay steered the car down more and more side streets, hopelessly lost. What to do... but keep going?

After a while, she found herself in familiar territory, a street lit by front porch lights, and seemingly bustling with activity. There was the fence that...

BAM! Something slammed onto the heavy steel on the hood. The passenger door flew open. Bloody Knee started to jump in beside her, expecting to pull the door behind him, but when it wouldn't close he was jerked back, falling backward off the seat, and just as he looked up to see– *what the hell...* his nose smacked into Arthur Campbell's balled fist.

Arthur tossed him away like a small sandbag, away from the car onto hard pavement, again, his third knock of the night. The other two with malicious intent and the curious fell back into the shadows. Someone said, "ARTHUR CAMPBELL! I see you, Arthur Campbell!"

Arthur had no reason to worry about that. Colored folks were not particularly forthcoming to the po-leece anyway; with certainty, he could count on their reluctance, their lack of initiative to report, unsolicited.

"GO," he said, taking the passenger seat.

They got out of there. What Arthur said to Lindsay exactly, she has never told me, but I have the idea he let her have it. She was put down at his home for the few hours until dawn, probably displacing Ethel's peaceful slumber to a greasy vinyl love seat.

The second week of my third year at Virginia, when my thoughts were only beginning to turn to my studies (being mostly on sultry Sybil, whom I met in Savannah, who kept intruding into my dreams, and sweet Laura Mills, who was far closer to someone I could bring home to Mother), Lindsay wrote to me. She was alarmed at Arthur's cough, and his yellow eyes, and... did I know he had no middle toe on his right foot?

At first read, I thought Lindsay was just going on about being down on Beale and almost getting into trouble, staying at Arthur's, and getting away with it because both Dad and Mother were away. But, I knew something about that, and she knew I knew; you can get just about anything out of Neal, and then test the math with Henry. Of course, this is not verification of truth, nor are either of them known as articulate, thus there is some question regarding actual details.

Not being much of a letter writer, I sent a postcard saying I'd tell her about it (the toe) when she shared the Beale adventure in detail (I was quite curious, having only the servants' perspective). Honesty, sadly, I was so used to his cough, I had thought little of it, and... don't a lot of older colored people have yellow eyes? How many times when I hung my lure in a bush beyond a paddle's reach, had Arthur waded in shoe-less to collect it?

The missing toe was old news.

40

Adjournment

Easter 1957

The azaleas were at their peak. Even in the deep woods the dogwoods speckled still-dark hues with white and pink. The bright lime color that would define the late spring was a very few weeks away. The day after Easter I drove Gail to her parents' home in Athens, and the next day flew out of Atlanta to San Diego, where my orders were to deploy late summer to the Western Pacific aboard the USS WHITFIELD COUNTY. We just learned that she carried our first child, who would arrive in late October. That news made my journey one of anticipation and thoughts of the future, tempered with aching for my beautiful young wife, and the knowledge I would almost certainly be at sea when he/she came. I imagined introducing my baby son, my daughter to the family. I thought... I *can't wait* to tell Arthur.

These last three years, graduating from Virginia, and earning my commission at Norfolk, my returns to Memphis were far fewer than in previous years. When I saw him last Arthur's eyes seemed unnaturally yellow, and he coughed a great deal, though he still seemed strong and vigorous to me.

Ethel found Arthur unconscious on the floor of their home on Laclede Street in a pool of blood. He was taken to E.H. Crump Hospital a few blocks away, and tests confirmed pulmonary tuberculosis. He lost so much blood the doctors said he might not regain consciousness. The transfusion they gave him most likely helped him hang on that week. They were surprised not to find the infection in Ethel and surmised that it had advanced quickly due to his heavy smoking.

By late afternoon his vitals stabilized somewhat, Lindsay and Denton went to see him. No one was allowed close, but they stood for a time at the foot of his bed. He lay comatose, of course, but the expression he wore was peaceful, his violent chest... finally quiet. Arthur was not Arthur without his crumpled fedora or the formal cap of the chauffeur. A hat gave reason for the subtle shadow that divided his face— slightly darker above his nose, just a hue lighter below. This birthmark gave Arthur a powerful look, of intensity just short of consternation. It was sometimes misconstrued as a glare. But now, eyes closed, gray at the temples, and with a slight upturn at the corners of his mouth, Lindsay wondered what was in his mind. She thought of the time at age five or six, when Big Charlie came home from a long trip and enveloped her, and she blurted promises not to kiss Arthur anymore... and she began to cry. Lindsay was the only one who could make Arthur smile, almost every time she tried. Their bond was quite different, but special. What must this man's life have been, she thought, that he so rarely allowed himself to be caught up in laughter?

A nurse came in and Lindsay was returned to the present. Denton squeezed her hand and they stepped to the edge of the room just outside the door. The nurse came back out and pulled the door behind her, but it did not completely close. Through the vertical opening was framed Arthur's face. The sun had come out, just before it would set. Bright sunlight through the window blinds fell in stripes on the white blanket shape of his body– symmetrical as arches, brightening the glow in the room. Lindsay reached into her purse for a handkerchief to dab at her eyes and opened her mouth to speak, but she hesitated. Just inside her ear, there rose a slight buzz— like a makeshift kazoo of wax paper, then clearly, softly from Arthur's room she heard

"*It's OK, Arthur.*"

Denton gasped and his head whipped right to the half-closed door. He heard it too. He reached to push at the door and before he touched it, Arthur said,

"Huck."

"What did he say" whispered Denton, still too shocked to move.

"I think he said, 'Huck'," Lindsay whispered back.

"Huck? Huck? What does *that* mean?"

Arthur slipped away peacefully, sometime during the night. When they related this experience, I was able to offer a theory for the mystery, recalling what Billy told me when we were teenagers trying to clear Arthur. We never told Mother or Big Charlie of the spectral visit, or whatever it was, that the Walterlane children are certain our precious brother was with Arthur at his last, encouraging him to let go, welcoming him into God's peace.

41

Last Call

January 19, 2013

The weather in the last six weeks had been too mild for this time of year, but because it's my birthday, Mac and Denton collected me before dawn and we went to our club near Horseshoe Lake. We're at the eastern edge of the flyway give or take a few miles, so there's always the chance we could pick up a stray mallard, usually a greenhead or gray duck.

It is never quiet. Hundreds, sometimes thousands of geese are constantly overhead, honking, strung out in undulating, geometric Vs a thousand feet up, always southbound. It defies logic, but you can hear them... why if they're so far?

Very few low-flying ducks are in the air, low enough for us to call in, anyway. One group is so high... but Arthur might have called them in. *Arthur!* He comes to mind a lot these days— in stories that I have not thought of in years, thanks to Will. Lately, I have been thinking... if Arthur had not come along how would life be different today? My young brothers' memories of Arthur are foggy. Only Denton can recall specific things, such as Arthur's death, of course, his being on trial, and the big storm out at the farm when he was eight. That is the image of Arthur he keeps, he says: Arthur pulling open the storm shelter, his heroic black silhouette against a fantastic swirling sky.

By 9:30 when we finally gave it up, just two greenheads had dropped in. At least we invited them both to dinner... didn't get snake bit on the last day of my season... did I say it's my birthday?

About 11:30, pulling into the drive I am thinking— I'll back the boat into the garage, store the blocks (net sacks of decoys) and clean my gun... after lunch and my nap. I'm not even beginning to imagine the rest of the day after that, but I do hang my waders up. I walked into the kitchen to find Will sitting at the kitchen table behind ... a chessboard... populated with hand-carved figures- ducks, dogs, paddlers, and hunters. He jumped to his feet.

"Will! Hey, boy! I didn't see your car. What're you doing? I'll be damned. Is that--"

"Hey, Dad! Yes sir! Cooper Permuter had Arthur's chess set, and I talked his son into selling it to me."

"Cooper Permuter? What? *Good Lord!* How did you--?"

"I Google-searched 'Cooper Permuter.' He died in the 1980s, but his name came up on the Facebook page of Jason Permuter, one of his children. Jason lives here. I finally reached him yesterday, and he recognized the name of Arthur Campbell. I told him about you and Arthur, and he was amazed, said his Dad had talked about Arthur all the time. Jason said Mr. Permuter was a borderline Grand Master competitor and considered Arthur one of his greatest pupils."

"I'll be damned."

"Dad, Arthur gave Mr. Permuter this board when he left the club. Jason knew right where it was. In his attic, in a trunk. The figures were wrapped, but every playing piece was there; it's a complete set. The rook paddler you have looks better, maybe it was set aside because he decided not to paint them. And, they don't look like they have been sealed with shellac like that one."

"No—"

"But, look at these. Aren't they great? When I saw this, I felt like I had won the lottery."

Except that they were all ducks, no two pawns: swimming, diving, leaping into the air, were alike. Individually they were faithful to form, well-drafted, and cut, but the scale wasn't exactly uniform, perhaps they were created at different times, wherever Arthur happened to be, without the benefit of reference to the others. One was up off its block by a half inch, flaring, supported by a tip of wing on one side and a splash of water on the other. Most simply floated in circular ripples or swam with a hint of wake. The webbed foot of one pushed out of the back of the vertical wall of its support block, a kick forward. Carved shotgun shells were the rooks. They stood on either end uniformly, and on the brass, each bore the circular legend of a different shell maker: "REMINGTON," "PETERS," "BIZMUTH," "ARROW." The primers were not punched, so these were live, detailed down to the overlapping hexagonal folds, protecting the ordinance, and the tiny star-shaped hole where they meet.

"If this had the weight of a real shell I might try to load it," said Will.

The queens had their chins and eyes to the air, their guns in hand, barrels pointed out, ready to throw to the shoulder: women always got the first shot. One king's fist was closed around the barrel of his gun, the stock resting on his foot, and he looked where his queen looked. The other king's shotgun aimed down relaxed in the crook of his elbow. The kings were confident their queens would not miss.

The four knights were labs, in various positions of readiness, one each set seated, one ready to leap into the water on command. Like all the figures, they were faceted, freed from the wood by single, deliberate, confident strokes, an impressionist's expert technique— which is especially effective in depicting wet fur.

I picked up one of the human figures, dusty, unpainted. A paddler. This one had a slight swell in the breast and fuller hair... a hand with delineated fingers on the top of the paddle. The other hand held a duck by the neck. The other paddlers each stood tall with his paddle in the crook of his arm and wore heavy gloves. All wore hip boots.

"These are the bishops." I stood them side-by-side. The one I picked up first was shorter, slighter, more delicate face... A female paddler? I looked at it carefully, turning it over— "Lillibelle Tatum", was burned into the underside.

"Look, I think this was the woman Arthur left the club for. He never saw her again."

"I thought he couldn't write."

"No, Arthur could write, and read, just not well. This does look like someone with some practiced penmanship wrote it though... son of a gun."

"Happy Birthday, Dad."

Afterward

This story is fiction, but it is inspired by real people and true events.

Arthur Campbell was the last black club keeper, a renowned guide at Beaver Dam Hunting Club, until it closed in 1945. "... and there was never a better man paddling a boat, blowing a duck call and marking down dead birds or watching where singles settled from a covey. He had eyes like an eagle..."

— *Nash Buckingham, Beaver Dam and Other Hunting Tales,* 1993,

by Dr. William "Chubby" Andrews, who was descended from one of the club's founders.

Arthur stepped into the male void in 1946, *after* the men of my father's household were called to and had returned from the war, but during the period the narrator's father was distracted by his cotton business interests until the late 1950s and therefore is much responsible for Carlo's and brother Billy's natural education (perhaps also that of their adolescence), and certainly Carlo's evolution into the world-class outdoor enthusiast, hunter, and fisherman he is today.

My father's Uncle, Ensign Charles **Donovan** Smith, II (Charles Deane Smith in this work) provided a lengthy first-person debriefing (narrative) to the United States Navy on September 18, 1945[1], detailing his experiences aboard the USS HOUSTON until March 1st, 1942, when it was torpedoed and sunk by the Japanese, his escape and eventual capture and incarceration in Japanese prison camps (for 3 years, 5 months) until the war ended in 1945. He was the last person to minister to his dying captain, providing relief with morphine before he dove into his destiny. In the narrative manuscript is a photocopy of a letter personally signed by

[1] Film No. 444 & 444-1

Harry Truman, which reads in part:

> *You have fought valiantly and have suffered greatly. As your Commander in Chief, I take pride in your past achievements and express the thanks of a grateful Nation for your services in combat and your steadfastness while a prisoner of war...*

The framework of this historical novel is accurate, many of the incidents recounted are true. But, far more of the details are imagined, and the names are changed so that the work will not be a historical record, nor in any way be at odds with the memories of the family and people who knew Arthur Campbell and Charles Donovan Smith, II, and their associates.

I hope that the effort to bring to the reader these amazing men and women is honest and engaging so that perhaps they will be remembered as the larger-than-life characters I have come to know.

Will Sonnet

Charles Donovan (CD) Smith II
US Navy Captain, Retired

recognized with the following for
his bravery and sacrifice:

Silver Star Medal
the highest award for combat valor not unique to any specific branch.

Bronze Star Medal with Valor
for acts of valor or meritorious service in combat.

Purple Heart Medal
to service members who suffered wounds as the direct or indirect result of enemy action.

Navy Presidential Unit Citation
for extraordinary heroism in action against an armed enemy on or after 7 December 1941.

Asiatic Pacific Campaign Medal-WWII with Triple Bronze Star
to service members who served in the Asiatic-Pacific Theater from 1941 to 1945. Multiple stars generally indicate the recipient was engaged in multiple campaigns or served a particular length of time for each star.

Knight Grand Cross in the Order of Orange-Nassau
A Dutch order of chivalry awarded to those who helped liberate the former Dutch colonies in the Pacific, The Order of Orange-Nassau is awarded for longstanding meritorious service to society, the State or the Royal House, by the Royal House of the Netherlands.

Phillipine Defense Medal with Bronze Star
awarded to recognize the initial resistance against the Japanese invasion between the dates of 8 December 1941 and 15 June 1942.

American Defense Medal-WWII with Bronze Star
Service members who earned the medal during the first qualifying period, and who again became entitled to the medal, wear a bronze star on the ribbon to denote the second award of the medal.

Victory Medal
was awarded for service between 7 December 1941 and 31 December 1946.

Acknowledgements

Carlo (Charles P. Oates Jr), my Dad, would agree Arthur gets much of the credit for his passion for hunting and fishing to this day. Many of the incredible stories Dad told me about their outdoor adventures are here, punctuated with a lot of imagination.

My cousins Brier Turner, Donovan Smith, and Day Hodges are Ensign Charles Donovan Smith's children. Jane Smart Johnston is their half-sister. Their mother, Jane Cutting Smart Smith, lost her first husband, Lieutenant Junior Grade Felix Garrett Smart on December 18, 1944, when the USS HULL met its fate in what became known as Halsey's Typhoon.

CD's war story is documented and mostly true. I imagine the torpedoing of the USS HOUSTON, the men's brief escape to the safety of Java Island, the incredible suffering between the factual entries in the US Navy brief, and especially CD's connection and appearances with Arthur Campbell.

The photo at left is of Arthur Campbell and George Coors of Memphis, taken at Beaver Dam Hunting Club in 1940. I had the great pleasure of getting to know Doctor Coors in his later years, at an annual dove hunting and fellowship weekend in Mississippi.

Another long-time friend, Lisa Patton, the author of several novels, including *Whistlin' Dixie in a Nor'easter,* provided much of the encouragement I needed to complete this project.

My friend of decades Pete Ceren, photographer, and author of the historical novels, *Waking Remembering,* and *Joseph,* provided invaluable perspective, constant encouragement, and editing advice.

Special thanks to master wood carver Jim Arnold, who worked closely with me to develop Arthur's chess set for the cover shot.

Comments? Visit willsonnet.com.

Printed in the USA
CPSIA information can be obtained
at www.ICGtesting.com
LVHW050822141123
763832LV00016B/38/J